THE DEAD WILL TALK

A DCI GARRICK THRILLER - BOOK 3

M.G. COLE

TANGLEBOX
BOOKS

THE DEAD WILL TALK

A DCI Garrick mystery - Book 3

Copyright © 2021 by Max Cole (M.G.Cole)

All rights reserved. No part of this publication may be reproduced,
distributed, or transmitted in any form or by any means, including
photocopying, recording, or other electronic or mechanical methods,
without the prior written permission of the publisher, except in the case of
brief quotations embodied in critical reviews and certain other non-
commercial uses permitted by copyright law.

Cover art: Shutterstock

READ THE FREE PREQUEL...

SNOWBLIND

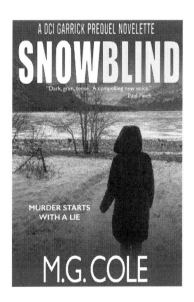

Start the puzzle here...
... and get inside DCI David Garrick's head.

THE DEAD
WILL TALK

1

The rare bit of April sun made Will Sadler feel glad to be alive. Not that he had any reason to complain. At 26, he'd just bought his first house in the Hollywood Hills in a single transaction, bypassing the horrible need for a mortgage such as the one that had weighed his parents down their entire lives. He had his eye on a third Porsche, and his career continued to ascend.

Not bad for a working-class kid from Leicester.

He was now a media darling. A bona fide movie star, all because of a television show that had turned into a phenomenon and spawned the movie he was in. And if life couldn't get any better, women were throwing themselves at him.

A difficult day of work, made worse by the director who had a grudge against him, was looking up when his new leading lady had urgently told him to meet her in the woods. She was drop-dead gorgeous, but for the last few days hadn't responded to any of his advances. He'd assumed she must've been one of these progressive lesbians because his charm was his one asset that allowed him to clamber over the hurdles that others threw in his way. He had reached the top, and always got what he wanted. Such as now, when she'd finally insisted that they meet away from the crew. He knew she would inevitably succumb. They all did.

The woodland was alive with birdsong. Will had spent most of his life in the city, so the sheer range of acoustic warbles, trills, and whistles was a complete novelty. The narrow trail of earth, baked from the last week of unseasonably warm weather, meandered through an ocean of vivid bluebells. It felt as if he were walking through a scene from a fantasy film with the colours turned up to be uncomfortably vivid. He wondered if there was something wrong. He felt peculiar; his senses heightened. He wobbled, struggling to keep his balance. Each step increasingly felt like walking on sponge. Will had experimented with drugs early in his career but had the sense to steer clear after listening to the horror stories that had befallen others. Had somebody slipped him something as a joke?

He ducked under a moss-covered tree trunk that had fallen at a lazy angle over the path. It was then he heard running water. He'd told her to wait at the folly that lay at the crook of the shallow river cutting through the estate. He parted the dangling branches of a willow tree and saw a flash of red ahead.

She was lying there, waiting for him.

She was still wearing the long velvet dress that placed her out of time. Similarly, he was dressed in a figure-hugging Victorian gentleman's riding outfit. Like the bluebells, the dress was almost too intense to look at. His eyes stung as if he were peering into a supernova, forcing him to look away and rub them.

A few steps closer, and he stopped. There was something not quite right with the girl. Increasing foggy thinking hampered him; it was difficult to concentrate. He sucked in a deep breath to clear his mind and took a step closer.

That's when he realised that she was lying face down. The water was only deep enough to come up to her ears, but she wasn't moving.

Will's legs were leaden as he tried to rush forward. He barely had the strength to lift them as he dragged his toes through the broken twigs and leaves at the bank. He kicked pebbles as he splashed into the water and was only vaguely aware of the stinging cold when he dropped to his knees next to the girl and thrust his hands around her waist.

Her alabaster skin was freezing to the touch. She felt incredibly heavy, despite being a slip of a woman. The fabric in her dress was waterlogged and weighed her down. He tried to move her again, but his strength was sapped.

Then his vision tunnelled, giving the distinctly uncomfortable impression he was falling. The world trembled around him, and he slumped forward.

He was unconscious before he landed on top of the dead woman.

2

It had been a long and arduous day for DCI David Garrick. One that he'd been dreading for the last two weeks and had caused many sleepless nights. It was the funeral of Detective Sergeant Eric Wilson in a small church in Orpington, on the warmest day of the year so far. It was a heavily attended service, but Garrick only recognised the few faces from the Kent Police Force. It was a brusque reminder that Garrick had always maintained a division between his work and personal life. Of course, it wasn't intentional; the fact was that his work life had consumed him for far too long and had stripped his social life away. As a result, it was easier to assume his colleagues had the same work/life balance, rather than admit his own life was an empty shell.

Although that was possibly changing. His partner... *girlfriend*... he still found both terms difficult to vocalise, had wanted to come along to support him. In the short time he'd known her, Wendy had been a welcome rock on the shores of his personal turbulence. Yet in a fit of stubbornness and social awkwardness, he had assured her he'd best attend alone.

Garrick expressed his condolences to Wilson's elderly parents, who stood stoically at the church door after the sermon, and then mumbled his regret to his grieving fiancée, who didn't say a word as she gazed at the ground in a state of shock. Only in retrospect did he realise he hadn't introduced himself as Wilson's ex-superior, who had worked with the man on several cases in which they'd brought some real scumbags to justice. To them, Garrick was just one of many other mourners.

Garrick had worked with his DS the previous year, right until his Super had forced him to take leave after his sister, Emilie, was murdered in America. On returning to duty, Garrick had been told they'd seconded his trusty Detective Sergeant to Staffordshire. He had reached out a couple of times but had heard nothing back. Garrick knew that the workload could all too easily swamp any social interactions. There were many people scattered across the force he wished he'd stayed in contact with. Several were still within Kent, but somehow life didn't slow enough to resume once precious acquittances.

The news of Eric Wilson's death had been a shock. Someone had stabbed him repeatedly in the back while on an active investigation. Beyond that, Garrick hadn't been able to find out any more details. The killer was still free, and Garrick's own inquiries to the investigation team had been met with silence.

Despite the spring warmth, Garrick felt a chill run through him as he watched the coffin lowered into the grave. Close friends and family obscured most of the ceremony, which Garrick was thankful for. It hadn't been that long ago he'd been at the funeral of his to-be brother-in-law, who had died with Garrick's sister in America. They still hadn't found her body, so there'd yet to be a funeral for her.

The priest's unusual baritone rendition of Psalm 23:4 carried clearly to those furthest away. But Garrick didn't focus on the words themselves. He'd heard them too many times before. He wasn't a religious man, so they sounded hollow and worthless. Delivered for the sake of convincing the living that life carries on elsewhere. The funeral concluded with people throwing in handfuls of earth into the open grave, another archaic tradition he struggled to see the point of. Then the crowds dispersed to a private wake that they hadn't invited him to.

Walking along the pathway between rows of graves adorned with flowers and ribbons and others left overgrown with nobody left to care for them, Garrick was lost in thought as he headed back to his car. He hadn't even noticed that a man had joined him until he started talking.

"That was quite a moving sermon," said DCI Oliver Kane. The Met Police officer had been the one to break the news of Wilson's death. He walked in lockstep with Garrick, dressed in the same black trench coat he always seemed to wear, and his grey beard was still in need of a trim. Garrick thought the wrinkles and bags under his eyes were deeper than last time, but perhaps he was only searching for flaws in a man he disliked.

"They all start sounding the same," said Garrick, quickening his pace. "Thought I saw you in the church. You didn't know him, did you?"

Kane shook his head. "Not directly, no. But shouldn't we all be sticking together? There are a lot of haters out there."

Garrick hadn't suffered from one of his regular migraines for several days. They had slowly receded since he'd received news about the growth in his head. Admittedly, he hadn't *read* the news, but the less frequent headaches suggested it must be good. By not opening the envelope, he had convinced himself that he could stave off the worst-case scenario. He'd made it through the funeral without incident, but now Kane had turned up it felt as if a needle was being driven through his right temple and pricking just behind his eyeball. The DCI was investigating the death of John Howard, a serial killer – and once friend of Garrick's - who he'd exposed earlier in the year. The mere act of Kane turning up at the funeral filled Garrick with unease, and he was in no mood for politeness.

"What are you really doing here?"

If the question irritated Kane, then he didn't show it. "Just taking stock of who's attending. After all, he was with you when you discovered one of Howard's victims."

"Which has nothing to do with why he was seconded to Staffordshire. As you seem to know all about that, tell me about the case he was working on. Who do they think did this to him?"

"That's still an active investigation," Kane said cagily.

"But not yours. And I'm still a copper, last time I checked."

"It appears Eric was investigating a smuggling ring, which turned violent."

"Smuggling what?" Kane shrugged. Garrick didn't believe him. As they exited through the small wooden gate and stepped onto the pavement, he could tell there was something else on Kane's mind. Cars lined both sides of the road, with mourners slowly flocking back to them. Garrick nodded down the street. "I'm parked this way. Well, I look forward to seeing you spring up again."

"Did John Howard ever tell you about his travels?" Kane's gaze never left the mourners, and he made no motion to head to his own vehicle.

"I didn't see him every day. Sometimes a few months would go by, or if I thought he'd have an interesting insight into a case, then I'd see him a couple of days here and there. As I already told you, it was a cordial, relaxed relationship."

"So he never spoke about travelling?"

Garrick absently massaged his temple as he thought. "I know he travelled all over the country to source new books. Especially when his online sales grew. He developed a reputation for finding exactly what you wanted."

Kane looked at him with a humourless smile. "You mean from fossil cleaning to tomes bound in fresh human skin?"

Howard had used the flayed skin of his young victims to create macabre lamp shades, but had Kane let slip another piece of information?

"Tomes? He used skin on books, too?"

Kane nodded. "It appears Howard may have killed more than the three young girls you discovered."

Garrick's memory had been playing tricks on him since his diagnosis, but he remembered Kane telling him there was a lock-up that Howard owned.

"You found a storage room under Howards' name, didn't you?"

Kane nodded. "He was a busy man." He hesitated and licked his lips before continuing. "And you still have no recollection, or even suspicion, that he may have owned other property?"

Without fail, Kane's questions irritated Garrick. He

always delivered them with a healthy dose of suspicion or disbelief that left him wondering if the detective was trying to implicate him in covering something up.

"No. Or it would've been in my report," Garrick replied testily. "And as I said, he travelled a lot. Most of his trade came through his website, so he could easily afford to close the shop."

"And abroad?"

"Perhaps." Garrick studied the parting mourners. Some had left, others huddled in groups around their cars, catching up after not seeing one another since their last major life event. He heard pockets of laughter. It was a discordant sound at a funeral, Garrick thought, but he knew it was a cathartic response the living needed. "He never spoke about visiting family and he had a very firm belief that holidays were a waste of time."

"He travelled extensively. Europe and America mainly."

"I suppose that's how he sourced stock."

Kane looked at him curiously. "My thoughts exactly. Always expanding his network like any good businessman."

Sensing Kane would happily keep him dancing in conversational circles, Garrick took his phone from the inside pocket of his Barbour and noticed the missed call. He tapped the voicemail icon and waited for it to connect.

Kane hadn't noticed as he continued. "The investigation has become international as we track down some of his more... exotic buyers."

Garrick listened to the brief message. It was from DS Chib Okon. As usual, she was short and to the point. He hung up and noticed that Kane was once again studying the departing mourners. For the first time, Garrick got the feeling that perhaps the DCI hadn't turned up just to hassle him.

"Oh well, duty calls," said Garrick, indicating his phone.

Kane gave a curt nod but said nothing. Garrick hurried back towards his car. Glancing behind, he saw the detective leaning on the wall, watching everybody. Garrick could have sworn the DCI would have followed him, firing off a volley of abstract questions as he'd done in the past. Kane's lack of action filled Garrick with curiosity.

He put that out of his mind. He'd planned to slip home early, but Chib's message informed him he wouldn't be having an early night after all.

One thing that Garrick hadn't been expecting when he turned up at the crime scene was to be thrust back in time. The stately home was a huge Victorian edifice, with one wing clad in dark green ivy to blend it into the sprawling, well-maintained grounds. Three splendid horse-drawn carriages were parked at the front, and several people in top hats and tails were milling around. Their white cardboard coffee cups and mobile phones broke the illusion of timelessness.

Reality was further ground-in when the officers at the scene directed Garrick to park in a large gravel area a hundred yards from the house that was filled with dozens of white trailers labelled 'Star Wagon', that formed the nexus of the film's production offices. Signs hung on the doors, such as wardrobe, make-up, accounts. Towards the gates lay a wide gravel area filled with the crew's cars. A large marquee had been erected at the opposite end to form the canteen. It was filled with bench tables, stainless steel counters, and more crew.

Several parked wagons had their tail shutters open, revealing nests of expensive movie lights on heavy metal stands, some stretching seven feet high. A rat run of cables powered the entire production unit, connected to generators positioned even further away from the mini village.

As ever, Chib was waiting for him when he parked. She seemed to possess a sixth sense and was always fractionally a step ahead of him. It was impressive and unnerving. Despite the naturally grim nature of the crime scene, she couldn't repress a wide grin as Garrick joined her.

"What fresh hell do we have today?" Garrick asked, looking around as a group of teamsters put camera equipment back into the trucks.

"They're filming Broadhaven!" she gestured around, expecting Garrick to respond with equal awe. Instead, he gave a slight shoulder wobble of incomprehension, and Chib's face fell. "As in the TV show? They're shooting the movie now."

"Never heard of it."

"How's that possible, sir?"

"I have a life," lied Garrick.

"It's the biggest British show in the last four years. Victorian romance and drama?" Her excitement faltered under Garrick's obvious lack of knowledge. Gravel crunched underfoot as she led the way through the trailer village and around to the front of the house. "It's an international phenomenon. It's one of the biggest shows in China!"

"I don't get to watch much Chinese television, Chib. So if I can wrench you back to the real world, what've we got?"

"We have one body and one hundred and six suspects on the site."

"They were all present during the time of death?"

"Yes. So that's a lot of statements we're trying to collect. They're mostly cast and crew, but the family who owns the estate live here, too."

Garrick's migraine hadn't eased since leaving the funeral. He hoped work would derail his mind from the thoughts percolating on other crimes John Howard had been involved with. Instead, he now dreaded the imminent lecture on popular culture. He wished Wendy was here. This was the sort of thing that interested her. They walked around the side of the house and joined a narrow trail that crossed the neatly manicured undulating rear garden.

Garrick relented. "Okay, what do I need to know about this show? Just the basics."

"Broadhaven is the Broad family's estate that is always in turmoil."

"Sounds fascinating," said Garrick dryly.

"Lady Edith Broad has been having an affair while her husband was away fighting in the Boar War, but the identity of her lover is a long running secret. Meanwhile, her daughter, Victoria, has fallen for the roguish charms of Stuart Eldritch. His family lost their fortune during a hurricane in the Caribbean, and he's returned to England penniless – although he has told nobody about this. For four seasons–"

Garrick held up his hand to stop her. "I get the idea. And that's going to help me how?"

"It might help you get into the spirit of it all," Chib smirked.

They passed through an archway of trees and down several stone steps that curved through a carpet of bluebells. Chib continued filling him in on the show's international success, and the reasons every star was queuing up to play a role.

They arrived at the narrow river as the forensic team was preparing to lift the body from the water. Garrick and Chib kept to the path so that they didn't disturb the footprints tagged on the muddy bank. From the angle the victim lay, her face wasn't visible. Chib showed him a picture on her phone taken for continuity. With deep brown eyes, dark ringlets, and full lips, she possessed a classic English rose beauty.

"Karen Dalton. She was originally a featured extra, but the director gave her a larger part as Amanda, the movie's teasing distraction for Stuart Eldritch before he proposes to Victoria." She caught Garrick's questioning look. "I skimmed through the screenplay while I was waiting for you."

"She's in costume. What was she doing down here?"

"It appears that she was having a fling with her leading man."

"He was the one who found her?"

They watched as four forensic officers carefully lifted the body from the water and placed her on a stretcher laid on the bank. Even the four of them struggled with the weight of the waterlogged dress.

Chib frowned. "That's where it becomes odd. Will Sadler – that's who plays Eldritch," she quickly clarified when she saw the question forming on Garrick's lips. "They found him on top of her in the river. He was unconscious."

"On top of her? As in, pinning her down?"

"That's difficult to ascertain. It was the Second Unit Director who found them. Gina Brown. She's in shock. She says Will came around right in front of her and became hysterical. He claims that he found the victim like this."

One of the SOCO officers pulled back her white hood and took off her face mask as she watched the body being taken back up the trail. Garrick recognised the woman's auburn hair and distinctive Australian accent, but he couldn't recall her name.

"Oh, hey, Dave," she said, turning to him.

"Hi... er... any thoughts on what happened here?"

"She was face down in the water, so I'm thinking drowning would be high on the list. No obvious signs of struggle, but that sexy fella was on top of her, so that would've kept her under. And that dress weighs a ton."

"Any clue why they were down here? So far from the set?"

Chib couldn't suppress a snort of laughter when the SOCO officer looked disbelievingly between her and Garrick.

"Why d'you think? They were probably gonna shag."

Garrick avoided her gaze and looked at the prints the team had flagged on the bank. "And what was the director doing down here?"

"The Second AD," Chib clarified. "More of a crucial dogsbody role than what you might think. She was looking to get them back to set. Somebody had seen him heading down here. He denies doing anything wrong, of course. He says he found her lying there and tried to lift her up, then he fell unconscious."

"Unconscious? I thought all these actors were fit young things?"

"He's fit alright," the SOCO blurted, wiping the sweat from her brow.

"I was thinking it could be food poisoning," said Chib. "Wilkes and Lord are taking statements, but so far nobody else has complained about the craft services." She caught Garrick's look. "That's what they call catering."

"Why don't they just call it catering?"

Chib shrugged. "We'll need more people or it's going to take all night."

"Then it'll take all night." They both knew Superintendent Margery Drury spent most of her time fighting for their budget, so even suggesting extra resources risked her wrath. It was something to be done only in the most extreme circumstances, and having his team stretched and tired didn't qualify.

"Where's Will now?"

"He's in the house. The producer wanted to keep him away from the others. His lawyer and agent are on their way down from London."

Garrick pointed to the footprints. "This looks like a single set of prints."

The SOCO officer nodded and showed where they originated from the stone steps Garrick and Chib had followed to the river. "She came down here. Then crossed those stepping stones." A series of flat rocks, coated with a fine green moss, stretched across the water several yards away. "Then we think she waited by the tree." A gigantic oak on the opposite bank shaded the entire area.

Garrick squinted and could just make out the remains of a tower concealed by the branches and darkness of the forest beyond. It was three storeys tall, with a pointed roof like a witch's hat. Time had taken many of the slates off, and chunks of brickwork had cascaded into the grass, revealing holes leading into the darkness beyond.

"Did she go into the folly?"

"Oh, that's what you call them," said the SOCO officer in surprise. "I just called it the tower. She approached it but didn't hang around. People have been in there, but not recently, as far as we can tell. She seems to have paced around. Maybe impatient? I'm not sure. Then she wandered into the water. I don't know why she wanted to get wet since she crossed on the stones. We found no blood traces. No signs of anybody else."

She crossed back to the path. "There are several boot prints around here, which are at least a day old." She crouched down next to a deep print. "But these are from Mr Will Sadler. Size nine riding boots made especially for the show. It looks like he came down here and ran straight into the water when he saw her."

"To help her or attack her?" mused Garrick. He knelt and dipped a hand into the water. He quickly retracted it. "It's freezing."

"The weather's only been warm this last week," Chib pointed out. "It'll take a couple of weeks before it was remotely warm enough for a dip."

Garrick nodded. "So why was she standing in it?"

His knee cricked as he stood. He noticed Chib was trying not to react to his struggle. In a pointless display of bravado, Garrick quickly bound across the stepping stones to the other side of the river. He followed the small white plastic markers forensics used to chronicle Karen Dalton's last moments. He scanned the ground for anything amiss, not that he expected the SOCO team to have overlooked any clues. There wasn't a cigarette butt or obvious broken twig to be seen.

A crumbling archway gave access to the folly. It didn't feel welcoming enough to enter, so Garrick activated the torch on his iPhone and waved it inside. There was an accumulation of dirt, and dry leaves covered the floor, but nothing obvious leapt out at him.

He tried to guess what the girl had been thinking, knowing she was going to hook up with some television dreamboat. Was she nervous? Excited? What impulse would lead her to splash into a cold stream?

He looked up to see both the SOCO officer and Chib watching him with a trace of concern.

"Are you alright, sir?" Chib asked.

"Just thinking." From their expressions, Garrick wondered how long he'd been standing there, staring at nothing. His stomach wambled and his mouth was dry, reminding him he hadn't eaten breakfast. He needed a good cup of tea. "I think we should find Mr Sadler and listen to what he has to say for himself."

4

_____

Walking through Laddingford Manor's main entrance was a step back to a time of extravagance and opulence. The lavishly decorated grand hallway was resplendent in red velvet and gold inlay. A sweeping staircase curled along one wall lined with portraits. Four marble columns stretched from the floor to the high ceiling, where a magnificent crystal chandelier hung.

"How the other half live," Garrick muttered to Chib as they entered.

Chib tapped a pillar as they passed. It gave a hollow sound. "If you like fibreglass, it's a real dream home."

Garrick was surprised. "How much of this is fake?"

"Quite a lot, as far as I can tell. The Granger family owns the estate. Sir James Granger. Landed gentry, inherited title, and skint. I spoke to the production manager while I was waiting for you. He said they often hire this place out for film locations and fashion shoots. The family needs all the money they can get just to stay afloat."

Chib guided him across the hallway to a large pair of oak

wooden doors leading to the east wing. He noticed a glow-
ering man with curly grey hair and a grubby-looking tweed
jacket over his jeans. He was watching them from a passage
that led deeper into the house.

"Who's that?"

"That's Sir James."

When Garrick looked again, the man had disappeared. If
it wasn't for Chib's acknowledgement, he might have thought
the figure had been a figment of his imagination. Chib
opened the left-hand door and entered.

Beyond was a room the size of Garrick's house. It formed
the bottom front corner of the east wing. Grand windows
stretched from the floor to ceiling, offering views across the
grounds – or in this case, towards the production company's
unit base. A sprinkling of dead bluebottles littered the base
of the windows.

Two large bookcases dominated the walls, lined with
many precious looking books that Garrick doubted any of the
family had read. A stag's head was mounted pride and place
on a wall. The once noble animal was dusty, forlorn, and
threadbare. One of its antlers had snapped a third of the way
from the tip.

A mahogany cabinet, with grubby glass doors, contained
three hunting shotguns, with a space for a fourth. They had
identically tarnished silverwork around the stock, which he
thought they must be worth a few quid. Several of chipped
and grubby hunting trophies lined the mantle of a grand fireplace that hadn't been lit for years. A full-size snooker table
stood in the centre of the room, with a pair of cues and
several balls still set out.

A woman was leaning against the table with her arms

folded. In her fifties, she had long, frizzy black hair tied back. She was handsome, but the streaks of grey and the lines on her face suggested stress was getting to her. She'd rolled her jogging top sleeves up to the elbows, and her jeans and grubby grey hiking boots told Garrick that she had dressed for purely practical reasons, rather than to impress. A mobile phone was in one hand, and a radio in the other, the volume low as it issued a constant stream of messages from the crew. She recognised Chib, and her eyes narrowed slightly when they fell on Garrick.

"This is Marissa Carlisle, the producer. This is DCI Garrick."

Marissa sagged with relief as she dashed to Garrick and shook his proffered hand. "Oh, thank God," she said in a cut glass English accent. "Somebody who can sort this mess out quickly."

"I'll do my best, Mrs Carlisle."

"Ms. And keep it to Marissa. I like all my staff to be informal."

Garrick bit his lip. Now wasn't the time to point out he didn't work for her. She was obviously somebody who easily took control and was used to getting her way.

"I'll do my best," was all he could manage.

"We're on a tight budget with this movie and we can't afford a shutdown." She dropped her voice. "And neither do we want the publicity, either."

"A young woman is dead, Ms Carlisle," Garrick said firmly. "So that dictates just what happens next."

"Dead. Yes. An accident. Which is a deep shame, but not something they should penalise us for."

Garrick glanced at Chib. She was unreadable, yet he knew she was waiting for him to explode in response to this woman's attitude. He surprised himself by smiling and remaining calm.

"Of course not. If it is an accident, that is purely a matter between you, the actor's union, family, and insurance company. I couldn't arrest you for that now, could I?"

He stepped around Marissa to get a clear look at the figure in the chair. Will Sadler was in jeans and a plain white t-shirt, with a black hoodie. He clutched a silver space blanket over him for warmth. Garrick recognised the face instantly. He'd seen him dozens of times on TV shows and advertisements. With sandy hair, wide blue eyes, and flawless skin, he looked more handsome in the flesh than he did on-screen. Even without opening his mouth, he oozed something that Garrick assumed was the mythical *star quality*. Will clasped his hands over his lap, and he nervously worried his fingers. He glanced at Garrick with a harrowing expression and made no attempt to introduce himself. Garrick assumed he seldom had to.

"I believe they found you at the scene?" Will nodded. He flicked a look at Marissa, and his leg started to nervously jiggle. "On top of the body, in fact."

Will took a halting breath and nodded. "It was horrible," he said in a low voice. "I woke up... on top of her. And, er..." he stared at the floor, eyes darting around the carpet. "When I arrived, she was already in the water. I tried to pull her out. But I felt weak and dizzy. Then I collapsed."

"Why would that happen? Do you have any medical conditions?"

"Must've been something I ate," Will mumbled.

Garrick circled around his chair, peering at the activity through the windows. "Is anybody else not feeling well?"

"Nobody," said Marissa. "We've been using the same craft

services for the last three weeks. I've used them before in the series. There've been no problems."

Garrick took a seat in another green Chesterfield wing-back chair opposite Will. The actor still didn't look up.

"Had you finished work for the day?"

"No. I had a break while they set up the next scene. We'd arranged to meet."

"So, your costume...?" he gestured to Will's clothing.

"SOCO took it," Chib confirmed.

The news the forensic team had his clothing didn't seem to bother Will. Could he be telling the truth? Garrick leaned back in his chair and folded his hands together.

"Why don't you walk me through what happened."

"There's nothing to say," Will muttered. Garrick couldn't recall how the actor sounded on TV, but his mumbled diction wasn't what he expected. "Simon got the take he wanted, and I went for something to eat. Then I was going to head back to my trailer."

Garrick glanced at Marissa. "Simon Wheeler is our director."

"You went back to your trailer after you ate?"

"No. Karen came up to me. Said she wanted to go some-place quiet. I suggested the folly."

"You did?"

He nodded. "She went ahead when Simon came over and started bending my ear about the next scene for about ten minutes. After that, I followed her down."

"Why the secrecy?"

The question surprised Will.

"Because we all try to be discreet on-set," Marissa said. "Christ, in this climate, you've got to be careful who you're seen with. One false allegation can cripple a career."

"In that case, wouldn't it have been safer if everybody knew this was a consensual hook-up?"

"And have my fiancée find out?" said Will with a trace of incredulity.

Garrick caught Chib's smirk, but as she was standing behind the other two, making notes in her pad, it went unnoticed.

"Of course," said Garrick. "That would be terrible. So you followed her. Did you see anybody else?"

"No. I found her, as I said." Will lapsed back into silence and stared at the floor.

"You're a born storyteller," said Garrick, with more sarcasm than he intended.

"He's a bloody actor, not a writer," snapped Marissa.

Garrick sighed. "You said she was in the water already. Was she struggling?"

"She wasn't moving. I thought she must've slipped and banged her head on a rock."

Garrick imagined the scene Will described. "Did you call for help?"

Will shook his head. "I felt really dizzy as I reached her. Tried to lift her, but couldn't. Then I was flat out."

"And you remained unconscious until they found you?"

"I woke up with what's-her-name standing over me."

"Gina, our Second AD," Marissa clarified. "Simon wanted him back on-set. He wasn't in his trailer. Somebody saw him head down to the folly, and she went to check it out."

"How long had elapsed between you leaving Simon, and Gina finding you?"

Will looked at Marissa for guidance.

"About thirty, thirty-five minutes. They were probably

about fifteen minutes away from setting up the lights," she said.

"You were unconscious, on top of Karen's body, for thirty-five minutes?"

Will shivered and pulled the cords on his hoodie top tighter. "Looks like it." The words were barely a whisper.

"As you can see, Detective, poor Will's very shaken. He needs to get back to his hotel and rest."

Garrick ignored her. "When did you first meet Karen?"

"Three days ago, when she arrived."

"She was a late casting choice," Marissa clarified. "Our first choice had scheduling problems, and we thought a new face would suit the role perfectly."

"Had you ever met her before?" he asked Will.

"No."

"What made you think she wanted to have sex?"

Will looked at him incredulously. "It was obvious."

Garrick tapped his top lip in a thoughtful gesture. Even in a daze, Will held a high opinion of himself.

"Detective, Broadhaven is a worldwide phenomenon. There are women on every continent who would do anything to be with a hot Victorian hero." Marissa's eyes narrowed when she saw the look on Garrick's face. "You have never seen an episode of Broadhaven, have you?"

"I missed it when it was on."

Marissa stalked forward, towering over Garrick. "We've just finished series four, with two Christmas specials, and now we're shooting a movie. It's shown all around the world. It's repeated on ITV constantly. And it works because it's all about hot young things seducing one another in forbidden love. Throw in some tragedy, a couple of iconic older characters, and you have a repeatable formula."

"Sounds practically Shakespearian." That seemed to pacify Marissa, and she leaned back against the snooker table. Garrick thought he shouldn't mention the fact the pomp of Shakespeare had never impressed him, either.

Marissa extended her arms. "So that's the whole sorry story. Poor Will stumbled across an unfortunate accident. Of course, our hearts go out to the girl and her family." She ran her fingers through the side of her hair. "Now we have to recast her and have three days of reshoots. Shit. Now do you see why we can't afford to waste time?"

Before Garrick could respond, both double doors opened with so much force they rebounded from the bookshelves on either side of them. A thin man in his sixties, wearing a light grey suit and a bright blue tie, marched in, followed by another suited man, wearing thick-framed glasses, and clutching a bag that swung from his shoulder.

"William!" snapped the older man. "Don't be a prick. You never say a word without your lawyer present!" He jerked a thumb at the man behind. His head twitched between Garrick and Chib like a pigeon trying to work out where the danger lay. "And how dare you interrogate him without his legal counsel present."

"Will was just bringing us up to speed on what had happened," Garrick said casually, although he could feel his cheeks flush with anger.

"I'm his agent, Michael S. Harris, and I decide who he talks to."

The lawyer opened his bag and pulled out a slim folder. From that, he produced a single page letter. "I'm going to have to ask everybody to sign an NDA."

Garrick stood up and took the letter. He gave it a cursory

glance, and then, to the lawyer's shock, he screwed it up and tossed it onto the snooker table.

"That almost sounds as if you're trying to interfere with police business. You are a real lawyer, aren't you? Not an actor?"

"I'm an entertainment layer," stuttered the man.

"I'm still not sure if you answered my question." Garrick saw Marissa had her eyes closed and was pinching the bridge of her nose in despair. Harris already had his arm around Will and was guiding him to his feet.

"Let's get you back to your hotel." He glared at Marissa as he passed. "I'll talk to you later." There was a hint of menace in his words.

Will threw his hood over his head and marched from the room with his agent. The lawyer gave an embarrassed farewell nod and followed.

"You can imagine what it was like negotiating a contract with him," Marissa finally said. "Michael S. Harris, the toughest agent this side of the Atlantic. They say the S stands for Shithead."

"In which case he must have had very prescient parents," Garrick said under his breath.

With Chib in tow, they left Marissa, who was already making a call to the studio to break the bad news about their schedule.

"Will seems a really shallow chap," Garrick confided to Chib as they crossed back through the entrance hall. "A personality vacuum."

"Oh, I don't know. He's pretty shaken up."

Garrick looked sidelong at her. "I didn't have you down as the type to be star-struck, Chib."

"I think he's a good actor..."

"And good looking."

"Detective?" Sir James appeared from the shadows and marched to intercept him, moving with a noticeable limp. He offered a hand to shake and gave a bone crunching grip.

"Sir James. Do I call you 'sir'? Or is it just James?"

"Sir James is the correct title," he said loftily. He glanced around to make sure they couldn't be overheard. "This business with the girl is terrible. What happened? The producer doesn't want to tell me anything."

"All I can say is that she was found dead in the stream."

"Murdered?"

"What makes you say that?"

"The fact nobody is telling me anything and I'm speaking to a police detective."

"Detective Chief Inspector."

"Indeed. We rely on film crews coming here. A story like this might damage us."

He had yet to meet anybody concerned about the deceased. Everybody seemed to have their own agenda, which left no bandwidth for basic human decency.

"Then if this is a murder, I suggest you get the best lawyers you can. Did you or any of your family see anything suspicious?"

"No. My wife and I generally keep to the drawing room, kitchen, and our bedroom when the crew is here. They're not allowed in our private quarters. Freya, that's my daughter, always enjoys hanging around to watch them work."

"They've filmed the show here for several years, I believe?"

"Yes, we know them all. Freya and Will became friends."

Garrick couldn't judge if Sir James approved of that or not.

"And where is Freya now?"

"Out and about somewhere."

Garrick made his excuses to leave and hurried outside with Chib.

"He sounds desperate," he said once they were walking back towards the unit base.

"I told you they rely on money. And this is Broadhaven. The house has become iconic."

"If Freya is friends with our Mr Sadler, then it will be interesting to get her take on him without the filter of fame clouding her judgement."

As usual, Chib was already thinking ahead. "I'll interview her myself."

Back at the production village, Chib left to find Freya while Garrick checked in on DC Harry Lord, who was using a trailer as an interview room. Since being injured in the line of duty, his leg and arm had almost healed, but he still relied on a crutch to get him around. He was taking a statement from an attractive Spanish woman Garrick first assumed was another actress. Liliana Davies turned out to be part of the wardrobe department. In her twenties and, despite her looks, spoke with a slight Newcastle accent. She was bewildered by events. Chloe Aubertel followed her. In her sixties, she was a flamboyant force of nature, with her white hair tied straight up on her head like a palm tree. She was the show's French costume designer with a plethora of awards to her name, including an Oscar. She sobbed her way through the statement. Garrick was unsure what upset her more, the death or her beautiful costume being ruined.

Leaving Harry, Garrick found Gina Brown sat hunched at a table in the catering marquee as DC Fanta Liu took her statement. He ordered a green tea from the craft services staff who were still on hand, then joined them.

Despite the tragic nature of the incident, Fanta couldn't hide her excitement at being behind the scenes on a movie. Garrick felt a twinge of sympathy for the egotistical Will Sadler should he ever find himself interviewed by a star-struck Fanta Liu.

With short ash-blonde hair, a nose stud, and wearing blue dungarees, and Doc Martens, Garrick thought Gina would be at home in a nineties girl band. With wide brown eyes, her steely self-assurance countered her pixie-like appearance. He got the impression that she was more than capable of withstanding the abuse delivered by movie stars, or the pressure foisted on her by a pedantic producer.

"Was Will conscious as you approached?" Fanta asked.

"I didn't see him move," she said with a slight Welsh lilt. "I think when I splashed through the water, the sound woke him. Thinking about it, I shouted his name before that. And he didn't respond."

"But you helped him stand?"

"Yes. He went and sat on the bank, and I turned Karen over." She shifted uncomfortably in her seat as she recalled the moment. "She was obviously dead. Ice cold."

"Then what did you do?"

"I got onto the radio to Marissa. Told her what had happened. Her and Simon came down and took Will away. She told me not to say anything to anybody until the police arrived. I guess she called you lot."

Garrick spoke up. "How did Will seem to you?"

Gina toyed with the empty coffee cup in front of her. She was suddenly guarded. "Out of it. Maybe shocked."

"Shocked. Understandable." He leaned forward slightly

and noticed Fanta, seated next to him, parroted his move. She was new to fieldwork, so he made a mental note to talk to her about it later. "Gina, I understand the need for discretion. And I know people like Will walk around with an army of lawyers and agents dogging their heels, but the smallest details are important. And everything you tell me is confidential."

Gina nodded but said nothing further.

"Was he intoxicated?"

"Drunk?"

"Or high, maybe?"

"I don't... he was shaking. He was wet and cold. His voice... he sounded slurred. If he'd been lying in cold water, then he could've had hypothermia."

"Have you seen him drink or take drugs?"

"Not personally." It was a tactful answer. "Well, not drugs, anyway. He drinks. Every other day I'm delivering a bottle of Jack Daniels to his hotel."

"Have you worked with him before this?"

"Only on series four."

"And how would you describe him as a person?"

The pause she gave spoke volumes. Sadly, it wasn't legally admissible. "Entitled." Garrick gestured for her to elaborate. "There are two types of movie stars I've worked with. Ones who remember your name, have a laugh with you, and know your worth on the set. And the others who don't."

"And what type was Karen Dalton?"

Gina choked on a sob, but quickly pulled herself together. "She wasn't a star yet. But she had it in her. I knew her from the circuit. Commercials, theatre... it's a close-knit industry. She kept on saying that this was going to be her big career break. She was just so happy to be here."

"How would you describe the relationship between her and Will?"

"There wasn't one. She hadn't met him before, but she'd heard the stories."

Garrick frowned. "Stories?"

Gina shifted uneasily in her seat. "Like I said, it's a close-knit industry. People get reputations, right or wrong."

"And what is Will's reputation?"

"Read the gossip sites." She was not any more forthcoming. "But he was on his best behaviour when his fiancée was here."

"His fiancée is here? Now?" said Garrick in surprise.

"She flew home this morning. Back to LA. She's up herself, too." Gina immediately regretted the comment. "Will doesn't enjoy having her around. Says she puts him off his performance."

"Did they argue about that?"

Gina gave a sharp snort of laughter. "They always argued. Every time she was on set, it brought people down."

Garrick thoughtfully sipped his tea. "And how is he with everybody else? The other women in the crew, for example."

Gina fixed her gaze on her cup. "Normal."

"What's normal?"

"Will's Will."

Garrick chuckled and shook his head. "I don't quite know what that means."

Gina drummed her fingers on the table as she searched for an answer. "Like I said. Will's Will. He's a star, and he knows it. Look, Detectives, is that all you need from me? Karen and I might not have been friends, but work colleagues sounds so shit."

It painfully reminded Garrick of his relationship with

Eric Wilson. "I understand. If you remember anything, please let one of us know."

Gina made a swift exit. Garrick finished his tea before suggesting that he and Fanta help DC's Lord and Wilkes take the rest of the crew's statements. A quick glance at his watch showed it was already four-thirty. He'd be surprised if they finished before nine, and since he wouldn't have the pathologist's report until the morning at least. It could all be a waste of time if they reported an accidental death.

Yet something was nagging at Garrick. The atmosphere amongst the crew felt like he was peering into a viper's nest. One where secrets were concealed.

5

It had been close to ten o'clock by the time Garrick headed home. He'd called Wendy and let slip he'd been on the set of Broadhaven. She immediately gushed with fangirl delight, revealing that she'd seen every episode multiple times and was a huge fan of Will Sadler. Garrick felt awkward when the subject of autographs came up. It wasn't something that fit easily into a potential homicide investigation. Before he knew it, he was home with a slight smile on his face when he passed through the front door. Wendy was really having such a positive effect on him that even a quick phone call brightened a tough day at work.

But his dance with joy had other plans in the form of a letter waiting on the coir doormat as he walked in. He suspected what the contents were, so only ripped a corner of the envelope and peered in. The header was the bold logo of Dr Rajasekar's medical consultancy. Garrick considered fully opening the letter and reading it, just to get it out of the way, but instead he tossed it onto a small wrought iron table where he kept his keys.

His consultant had left regular messages for him regarding the results of his last MRI. A recent series of hallucinations had raised the prospect that the tumour had triggered them. Which meant it was growing and putting pressure on his brain. They had been odd, stressful incidents which he'd put down to stress and various head traumas he had sustained during active duty. Fighting a suspect in a burning building, and stopping an aircraft from taking off, were both experiences he had no desire to repeat. As for the hallucinations, he'd decided that was too strong a word. He wasn't sure mental confusion sounded any better, but it didn't come with such negative connotations. Stress related mental confusion sounded even more palatable.

Aside from the migraine rearing up today, everything had settled to just the occasional headache. That had been a surprise, especially after being sent an empty envelope that was sealed with traces of his dead sister's DNA. It was such a twisted, bizarre occurrence that he'd expected severe stress-related after-effects. But none had materialised. He had sent the envelope back across the pond to the investigating team in Illinois, but he'd heard nothing back from them. He knew from experience that the world was filled with people struggling with their mental health, others were born without empathy, and some were just plain sociopaths. It didn't necessarily translate that they posed a physical danger.

With an edge of paranoia, he'd installed a wireless security camera to watch over his front door but had immediately regretted reacting like a victim. It was just somebody playing a sick prank on him. He sat in bed Googling trivia on the Broadhaven series and sped-read gossip sites that broke the story on Will Sadler's sudden engagement to Kelly Rodriguez, a fiery American reality TV star who thrived on

controversy. Aside from looking fabulous together, no colum-
nist could quite work out what the couple had in common
and jokingly lamented that, at 26, Will's famous womanising
days were over.

He learned Will had shot to fame in the first series of
Broadhaven. It had been his first major role after appearing
in several British soaps as minor characters for an episode or
two. But Broadhaven had put him on the map. Leading roles
in two movies had swiftly followed along with a BAFTA and a
Golden Globe nomination. The world was opening for the
young man. He was exactly the type of person Garrick didn't
like, but at least he could acknowledge it was because he was
jealous. David Garrick had to fight for everything positive in
his life, whereas Will sleepwalked from success to success.

A quick check on the BBC website showed nothing had
been reported. Only when he set his phone alarm did he
notice an overlooked message from Molly Meyers, a reporter
who'd recently joined the BBC thanks to Garrick. She'd
caught the scent of the story. He deleted the message.
Without the pathologist's report, there was nothing to tell.

"Drugged?"

Garrick reread the pathologist's email on his desktop
computer screen. He'd arrived at the office early, only to find
the rest of his team were already in, processing the many
statements taken on the set. He'd caught Fanta and Chib
hunched over a desk, engrossed in reading a document. They
were rightfully cagey when Garrick had approached them
from behind and discovered they were reading the screenplay
for the film. Fanta baulked at the accusation that she'd stolen
it as a memento and insisted it was evidence so they could
put things into context should it turn into a criminal case.

For an hour he avoided calls from Molly Meyers, and had very little to do until the toxicology report came in. DC Harry Lord was at his shoulder and leaning on his crutch like a dashing pirate. Despite his injury, he still seemed capable of making endless drinks for the team without being asked. He put a matcha tea next to Garrick's elbow, then tapped a word on the screen.

"*Psilocybin*. That's a psychedelic. So had she taken an E or something while waiting for her Prince Charming?"

Chib looked up from her desk next to them. "It's what's found in magic mushrooms. Laddingford is a big estate. I'd be surprised if there wasn't some knocking around there. It could explain how she drowned in four inches of water."

Garrick leaned thoughtfully back in his chair as he digested the information. "How did our movie star look to you, Chib?"

"Hot."

Garrick sighed. "I meant his behaviour."

Chib looked offended. "As did I. He looked hot and flushed for somebody who had been lying in a freezing river."

"His pupils were dilated." It had been one of the first things Garrick had noticed. Will had constantly looked away to avoid eye contact, so it made it difficult to be sure, but now he was wondering if the young man's body language was induced by drug-fuelled paranoia.

"Do you think he'd taken them, too?" she asked.

"Why would they do that? They were both working. They had to be back on-set after their extracurricular activities, and surely that would plague his performance."

Chib nodded. "And it was her big break. Why would she

risk sabotaging it? Everybody said she was smart and enthusiastic. She didn't need stimulants."

"Let's not overlook the fact they're both young and
stupid," said Harry with some authority. He caught Fanta's
sour expression. "What? I'm just laying down the facts with
you Millennials, or Gen-Xers, or whatever we're up to now.
They just don't think. Present company excepted."

"Offence taken," snapped Fanta.

"He complained about food poisoning," said Garrick.
"Was that just a cover story, or could somebody have slipped
it to him?"

"I'd say the latter is more likely," said Chib. She had the
preliminary pathologist's report on her screen, too. They
were still waiting for a few post-mortem results, but it
contained the crime scene report. She scrolled through it.
"This is interesting. The skin on Karen's knees is bruised,
suggesting she dropped onto the rocks. Her right patella is
fractured from the impact. The thick dress may have saved
her from worse damage."

"Tripping, she stumbled into the stream," mused Harry.
"Toppled on a rock and splashed down. Knocked herself out.
Unconscious, she drowned. An accident."

"But there are no marks or bruises on her hands," Chib
noted. "Raising your hands like this," she stretched her hands
in front of her face to demonstrate, "is an automatic reaction
to protect the head. And there are no marks on her face to
show she'd butted a rock."

"If she was high, maybe she didn't even notice?"
suggested Harry, taking a sip from his own mug of tea.

"Unless she fainted," said Garrick, as he stared thoughtfully at the ceiling tiles, noticing for the first time how they
didn't quite join. It was another sign that the Serious Crimes

Department's new home wasn't fit for purpose. He noticed everybody else looked puzzled. "When you faint, your body slumps straight down. The muscles in your legs go, and gravity does the rest. You only fall forwards in bad movies. If she passed out, then it's likely she would've fallen to her knees, and then keeled over into the water. Maybe it was luck she didn't crack her head open."

"And bad luck she was face down?" Chib wasn't convinced. She scrolled through the report again. She was disappointed. "There are no signs of bruising on the back of her neck. If somebody was pushing her down…"

"If she wasn't struggling, then there would be no need to touch her, other than to angle her face in the water," said Garrick. "And the water was cold. That could slow lividity."

"Will said he woke up on top of her. What if his weight kept her down?"

"An accident?" Garrick mused. However unintentional, that would spell the end of Will Sadler's career.

"My money's on that," said Harry. "You know what these movie stars are like. It was probably part of some weird sex game. Remember that singer, what's his face, Michael Hutchence. Accidentally hung himself just to get his rocks off."

"So it was accidental death," Chib said with a shrug. "That was a short case."

"The fact Will was high bothers me," said Garrick. "Either Harry's right about this being a terrible accident, or somebody spiked their food."

"Wait," said Chib, "to what end? That would mean somebody would've known they were going to sneak off into the woods. Will was heading for his trailer until she said that she wanted to see him, and he suggested the folly.

They'd both be high, but not dead. What purpose does that serve?"

"It would mess up their performances," said Fanta, who was sitting two desks away and had been studying their statements. "The next scene was with them both. A romantic near-miss as she tries to seduce him in order to finagle herself into his fortune, which of course he no longer has, but..." She flushed with embarrassment when she noticed everybody was looking at her.

"If they were both stoned, then that would look bad on them both," agreed Chib.

"The production was already running behind schedule," said Garrick. "He's one of the main stars, so who's going to blame him? She would get the blame."

"Who would have a grudge against her?" asked Chib.

Fanta gave a sarcastic laugh. "How about all the extras? Well, the women, at least. Karen was chosen as an extra before they cast her into the role. Gina told me there was quite a lot of animosity from the others when that happened."

Garrick stood and absently wagged a finger at Chib. "Ask forensics to check Will's costume for any traces of psilocybin. Sean, come with me. Let's have a chat with those extras."

Fanta's hand shot into the air. Garrick rolled his eyes. "I keep telling you, you don't have to do that."

"I think I should come."

"Why?"

"I know what's going on. I'm the only one who has read the script."

The heat from the lights was unbearable. It was like standing next to a small sun. Garrick took several steps to the side to cool down. A small knot of crew was gathered around a bank of monitors with the director, Simon Wheeler, sitting like a fat spider in the middle of them. Gina hovered a few feet away, staring intently at another monitor and scribbling notes on her script.

They were in the lavish ballroom at the back of the house, with views through the windows, across tended lawns, and the forest beyond. Two actors, a middle-aged woman in a long, elegant dress, and a noble craggy-faced man in a long dressing gown, both of whom Garrick vaguely recognised so must have been famous, were the focal point of a cameraman and a woman wielding a microphone on a long pole above their heads. The *boom*, Fanta had confided in him with an excited whisper. Already he was regretting bringing her along.

Marissa stood with Garrick, her eyes on her phone and only straying up to the actors when Simon shouted, "Cut!" with more than a little frustration. Garrick heard somebody shout, "Reset!" before the director stormed across to reprimand the actors on a problem that only he had perceived.

"He's quite demanding," Garrick commented quietly.

Marissa gave a distasteful *mmm*. "He's an arsehole. And he's the main reason we're so far behind schedule. He thinks he's *Coppola*. Always insisting on every little detail being just right." She puffed her cheeks. The stress was showing. "If he doesn't start hurrying things up, I'm going to have to cut scenes or beg the studio for more money."

"If he's so difficult, why did you hire him?"

"I didn't. The studio insisted on using him. I wanted to use one of our series regulars, but they didn't get a look in. That went down badly, let me tell you." She waved a hand around the set. "And now we've got to waste another day getting these small scenes done because Will's feeling 'too delicate' to come to set." She looked disgusted.

"He's supposed to be here today?"

"We had three days to shoot a riding scene through the woods. Do you know how expensive it is to hire horses and stuntmen, and then just keep them standing around, unused? And on top of everything else, the last three days must be reshot because of the accident. And I've got the bond company arriving after lunch to make sure we can carry on shooting."

When they arrived, Garrick had assured her they were still treating it as an accident, but had shared no details of the pathologist's report. A flock of press had gathered at the gates of the stately home but was being kept at bay by security. The production had already issued a press statement regarding the unfortunate death. Because Karen Dalton wasn't famous, they were counting on the publicity to quickly die down.

Garrick detested the way the press valued the worth of the deceased merely on how famous they were. The disparity was one of the many grievances he had between the media and victims. When he'd exposed John Howard as a serial killer, more column inches had been taken up by his life, rather than the young innocent girls whose lives he had cut short.

The change in the shooting schedule had thwarted his original intention to interview the extras. They hadn't been required today, so hadn't turned up. Fanta gave him a surprisingly knowledgeable crash-course on the production flow. The production team issued call sheets each day showing which actors and crew were required, their pickup times from their hotels, times they were needed in make-up, right down to the exact minute they had to be on-set, what scenes were being shot, and all the other details needed to complete the day.

The extras had supplied the investigation team with their details. The twelve women they wanted to talk to all lived within a thirty-mile radius, which stretched into London, Surrey, and East Sussex, so Garrick asked Chib and DC Sean Wilkes to follow up with them all. He assigned Harry Lord to desk duties rather than hobble around the set. Now they were here, it looked as if he and Fanta had little to do.

While watching the next take, which the director halted midway through, complaining that the actor's hand gestures were inauthentic, Garrick received a message from Chib. She had forwarded a report from forensics. They had found traces of psilocybin on Will's costume.

They left the ballroom and stood in the quiet entrance hall.

"It was on his sleeves and trousers," said Garrick. "What does that tell you?"

Fanta thought for a moment. "That he ate it. Or something containing it. Then maybe he wiped his mouth without thinking and wiped his fingers on his trousers." She mimed both motions.

"So the question is, did he know what he was doing, and did he encourage Karen to take it? What's the matter? You look worried?"

"That would make him complicit," she said with disappointment.

"Fame isn't a shield from stupidity. But let's not jump to conclusions. That's the media's job." He looked around thoughtfully. "Have they always shot the series here?"

"Yes. This is Broadhaven. They shoot around the Pennines too, but all the house stuff is here."

"So, how many episodes would that be?"

"Four seasons of six, and two Christmas specials."

"Then it's safe to assume Will knows the grounds pretty well."

"I suppose so."

"And is it always the same cast and crew?"

"The main crew, for sure. Every season they keep throwing on some famous names in the cast to spice things up, but it's mostly the same people."

"I take it nobody suggested Will uses drugs?"

"No. But even if they had taken magic mushrooms, they don't kill people."

Garrick's phone pinged with another message. "No, they don't," he conceded as he read. "But they can leave people in a vulnerable state. And the pathologist's full report has just landed. It looks like somebody murdered Karen Dalton, after all."

6

Freya Granger was the perfect representation of mousey. From her light brown, bobbed hair to the way she looked around the room with large eyes and a timid expression. She was 22 but looked almost half a decade older in a faded dress that Fanta assured him was trendy 'vintage'. She sat upright on the edge of an armchair, with her hands folded in her lap as if posing for an oil painting. Sir James sat on the sofa opposite, watching Garrick and Chib with intense disapproval. Nothing was said as Lady Helen noisily poured tea from a pot, drawing it higher as it reached the rim of the cup with increasing volume. She was a thin woman, dressed in a paint-stained sweater. She'd pulled her white hair into a bun, which seemed to force a permanent smile.

"I always look forward to the filming," she said, adding milk to the drinks. "Usually, of course. When the drama isn't so real."

With gusto, she had invited the detectives into their

private sitting room despite her husband insisting they'd said all they could about the unsavoury incident.

The room was not what Garrick expected of a titled couple. In fact, he'd go as far as to say that it was a dump, with books and magazines piled high on a coffee table and in every corner. A grubby sofa and two armchairs sat in front of a large stone fireplace, decorated with carved rampant lions, blackened and in desperate need of a clean. The scent of burned wood showed the fire was still being used, despite the warm weather outside. A veneer of grime obscured the windows, and a large spread of dead flies covered the sills. The television was at least a decade old, and he couldn't help but noticed a combo DVD-VHS player underneath.

Garrick took the cup of tea. Not to drink it, but to prevent Lady Helen adding anything further as a slice of lemon was dropped into Fanta's cup.

"You must do very well out of it," said Garrick. "Especially considering how popular the show is."

Sir James grunted. "They're a bunch of penny-pinchers, they are. They nailed us down on a fix price for five seasons."

"Can you renegotiate?"

"I think I can now. Their Christmas specials were not part of the contract. Nor was this bloody movie. They owe me!"

"Have you thought about opening up to the public for fans?" asked Fanta.

Sir James pulled a face. Helen chuckled. "James isn't a fan of the public, I'm afraid. And this place needs a lot of TLC to make it safe for paying visitors."

"Surely the production pays enough to cover those costs?" said Garrick.

"An estate this size absorbs money hand over fist," said Sir James. "And that woman won't entertain the conversation."

"Marissa Carlisle?"

"She's a dragon."

Garrick turned his attention to Freya. "You must be used to having the crew here after all these years?"

"Yes. They're like old friends now."

"You never miss a shoot?"

"Not since she quit university," Sir James huffed.

Freya's jaw clenched, but she said nothing.

"I believe you and Will Sadler became friends."

"I knew him before he was famous," she smiled, then blushed.

"Do you see him when he's not filming here?"

"He's invited me to parties in London. And I went to Cannes once when he was there."

Garrick caught Sir James' disapproving look.

"I suppose all the younger cast and crew gravitate together, since you're living in one another's pockets. You must get up to a lot of hijinks." He kicked himself at the use of *hijinks*; he didn't know where that came from.

Freya shifted uncomfortably.

"Detective, what exactly are you driving at?" Sir James asked, rising to his feet and limping to stand protectively behind his daughter.

"Does Will take drugs?"

"Detective–!"

"We're no longer considering it an accidental death. Karen Dalton was murdered." Helen gasped in shock. But Garrick was watching Freya intently. She didn't react. "There are signs of *subgaleal haematoma* on her scalp. That is conducive to hair being pulled, possibly somebody pushing her head into the water to drown her."

"Was she on drugs?" said Sir James. "I don't approve of them on my property, but these creative types won't listen."

"She'd probably ingested magic mushrooms beforehand," Garrick said, without taking his eyes off Freya.

"My daughter doesn't use drugs, Detective, and if this is suddenly a murder case, I presume nobody should be speaking to you without a solicitor present."

"Only if you've got something to hide." Garrick flashed him a warm smile, then turned back to Freya. "And with grounds this big I'm sure mushrooms are easy to find."

Sir James interrupted. "Our gardener is on holiday at the moment."

Garrick's focus remained on Freya. "I mean, technically, they're not illegal. But Karen would've been in a confused state. Possibly unable to fight back if attacked. So if you know Will, or any of the crew, use drugs, however recreational, you need to tell me."

"Will's a nice guy. He doesn't do that sort of stuff."

Garrick nodded amiably. "You're no longer in university–"

"What's that got to do with anything?" snapped Sir James.

"Because university is a real eye opener for the young. People are exposed to all sorts from a wide spectrum of society. Statistically, you probably knew somebody who tried drugs."

"Not at Cambridge," said Sir James snootily.

"Perish the thought. So, what made you leave?"

Freya glanced at her mother before she spoke. "I was reading history, then I realised it wasn't for me. There is no future in history."

"I think she was quite smitten by the entertainment industry," Helen said, but clamped up when Sir James cast her a dark look.

"What did you and Karen discuss?" He had deliberately phrased the question to make Freya think he knew more than he did. The way she shifted position in the chair suggested he'd succeeded.

"Not much. They cast her at the last minute. She'd only arrived a few days ago. She knew Will and I were friends, so asked a lot of questions about him."

"Such as?"

Freya shrugged. "Just the sort of things people ask. What is he really like? That sort of thing."

"Was she too shy to ask him herself?"

Freya pulled a face. "Kelly was here, and she doesn't like *anybody* speaking to Will."

"His fiancée. How would you describe her?"

"A bitch."

"Freya!" snapped her mother.

Freya scowled. "Ask anybody. She always wants to be the centre of attention. She's completely wrong for him."

Garrick gave her time to continue, but she fell silent. "How did the crew behave around Karen?"

"Everybody seemed kind. I heard there were rumours of her character becoming a permanent member of the series."

"Really?" said Fanta. She could barely conceal her joy at discovering a show secret. "So, what will happen between Victoria and Stuart?" Her excitement fizzled under Garrick's stern gaze.

"The actress who plays Will's love interest, Victoria. Is she here?"

Freya shook her head. "Her scenes start next week."

"So she wouldn't have met Karen?"

"I would have thought that was unlikely."

Sir James hadn't moved from behind his daughter. With

his arms folded, he put Garrick in mind of a Victorian guardian.

"I know my DS asked you this yesterday, but just so I can rule you all out, where were you all when Karen was killed?" He directed the question at Lady Helen, assuming she would be the most amiable to talk.

"I spent all day between here and the kitchen. Mostly reading the new Caitlin Moran and watching a little television. I enjoy my quiz shows. I learned long ago that film sets are very boring places to visit once the novelty has worn off. It's all hurry-up and wait."

Garrick looked at Sir James for answers.

"I went into Faversham on some errands. Then spent most of the day trying to get that blasted producer to give me a moment."

"To discuss the fees?"

"She's inapproachable at the best of times. Throughout the day, she kept cutting me short to deal with something or other. Then, when they found those two down by the folly, it was clear my chance had passed."

"And you, Freya?"

"I was mostly in my room."

"Oh? I thought you enjoyed being on set. And with your friends here..."

Freya wrung her hands together before answering. "The day before, I walked into an argument between Will and Kelly in his trailer. She was furious with him. And when I came in, they both had a go at me. Real nasty. Since she's been around, Will's treated me like crap."

"What were they arguing about?"

"I didn't catch that part. I just heard her say his career would be over. That he could f-off and die."

Garrick and Fanta marched across the driveway towards the production offices. They had been trying to hunt Marissa down and had eventually collared a spotty production assistant who had raised her on the radio.

"Thoughts, Fanta?"

"Feels like somebody was jealous about something. Only Kelly had flown home before the murder, so it couldn't be her."

"But somebody could've acted on her behalf. Although why target Karen? She hadn't been here long, and even if she was trying to seduce Mr Sadler, then, according to him, she hadn't managed it just yet. And he doesn't strike me as the type of fellow who would conceal a sexual conquest."

"It suggests the murderer's still on-site."

"Mmm. The plot thins. The next immediate question is what we should do with the crime scene?"

"You can't close the production down!" cried Marissa, thumping the desk for emphasis and sending a pile of invoices to the floor.

"It's standard procedure in a criminal investigation."

"I've done police procedural before," she commented dryly. "Two Miss Marples."

"Then you're a qualified expert."

"The budget for this movie is thirty-five million pounds. That's *million*. Every single person on this shoot has other jobs lined up afterwards. If we stop, it affects their future work, and it doesn't mean we stop spending money."

"I'm so sorry the young woman's death is going to cost you so much."

"Don't play the guilt card on me." She angrily wagged a finger. "I'm deeply saddened that she died, and after the shoot I will grieve properly, but right now I am more pissed off that she's dead. My responsibilities extend to hundreds of other people. Not just those on set today, but at the studio, the post-production, everybody who'll be affected by a shut-down. And what will it serve? The crime scene is about half a mile over there. Not here."

Garrick had been thinking the same thing, but was loath to admit it.

Marissa hadn't finished yet. "And have you thought about the practicalities for your investigation? If you shut us down, where is everybody going to go? I'm not paying for hotels for the next however many weeks it'll take you to crack this case. They'll all have to go home. I think maybe a handful live in Kent. Others in London, Wales, Scotland – and they're just the local ones. The DoP and several of the cast live in Amer-ica. Chloe in France. The director spends most of his time in his villa in Tuscany. Very quickly you're going to have to coor-dinate an international investigation. Good luck with that."

Garrick had already decided there was nothing to be gained by shutting the production down. Letting the cast and crew get on with their work would allow his team to mingle and watch how they interacted. The logistic side to it all hadn't crossed his mind, but now it looked as if he'd caved into the producer's pressure. Perhaps there was some advan-tage in that if she didn't think he was a threat? However, in his mental list of suspects, she was at the bottom of the list. Marissa had everything to lose.

"My team will be here around the clock."

Marissa conceded with a terse nod.

"And I expect fluid cooperation from everybody. I don't want lawyers or agents gumming up the works. I expect you to deal with them and keep them away from the investigation."

Marissa opened her mouth to argue, but thought better of it. Garrick suspected she didn't want to push her apparent victory.

"So let's start with where you were throughout the day."

Marissa sighed and waved a hand in a circle. "I already told your people this yesterday. And it still stands. I don't know. I was practically the first on-set and the last to leave. Check with security at the gate. Everybody coming in has to sign-in. If people said I was somewhere, I probably was." She suddenly corrected herself. "Except anywhere near the folly. I had no reason to be down there. We're using it as a location in about two weeks. Other than maybe somebody from the art department, nobody should've been there."

"I believe Sir James was trying to have a word with you."

Marissa rolled her eyes and slumped into a chair.

"All that prick wants is more money. It's the same old argument every time we film here. Do you know how much we pay him? Ten grand a day, and now he's demanding double."

Fanta gave out a low whistle as she made notes, then realised her boss was giving her yet another dirty look.

Marissa continued. "And every time I point out we have a contract and we're paying a fair price. He can open this place up to tourists and we wouldn't see a dime. But no. That's not good enough for him." She became thoughtful. "Normally he just rants for a while, then shuts up about it. It's our tradition. Except this time, he threatened to shut down the production. He's never gone that far before. Of course, I thought nothing of it."

"How would that help him?"

"We pay the location fee in advance, but any overages are paid on a weekly basis."

"Meaning that any extra days you have to film here, he gets paid?"

Marissa raised a finger. "Bingo. We're three days over now. That's thirty-grand in his grubby hands already."

"But he's still under contract for another series, isn't he? I suppose then you will have to renegotiate."

Marissa looked uncertain. "His lawyers have already been onto the studio saying they consider two Christmas specials, and this movie goes over the contracted terms. I have a horrible feeling they may be right."

"So he has a monopoly on the next series?"

"Which would have to be commissioned before Christmas. It's on a favoured nations basis." She noticed Garrick didn't understand. "In contracts it means people can't get paid way more than their peers. Except stars, of course, and most HODs. I used the term in the location contract so he couldn't double the price when it came to renewal. The estate is Broadhaven. Nobody knows Laddingford Manor really exists. But it would make no sense to the plot if we had to relocate. The house is the star of the show. I think he could drive up a pretty hefty fee and I'm sure the studio will cough up and pay, too. They wouldn't be happy with me, but..." she shrugged; what can she do?

"In your opinion, who would want to harm Karen Dalton or Will Sadler?"

"Will?"

"They found him unconscious on top of her. And there are indications of narcotics being used. The same ones found in Karen's system."

"Shit. What drugs? Tell me it isn't coke."

"Did Will have a problem with that?"

Marissa squirmed uncomfortably. "He's a young actor

thrust into global headlights. A sudden sex symbol everybody wants sleep with. That's a lot of pressure."

Garrick tactfully kept his opinion silent about how terrible it must be to be rich and have every woman wanting to sleep with him.

"I knew he dabbled." She shot Fanta a look. "Don't write that down. I had to sign an NDA with his lawyers, so you're making me break the law." Fanta's pen hovered over her notebook. "And that was pretty early on when fame struck. He did a little rehab and swore to me he was clean. I had my suspicions during the last series, but he's always delivered on camera. The boy can act."

"And Miss Dalton?"

"I guess every actress under her will be envious. All the straight boys fell in love with her. As for whether she used drugs, I can't say."

"She was quite taken by Will when she met him."

"Detective, what do you think happens when you put physically perfect people in a room together and turn up the pressure? It's the privilege of youth. Those bastards," she added under her breath. "But Karen struck me as a sensible girl."

"Why was Will's fiancée on-set?"

Marissa put both elbows on the table. "Because I can't stop her. If she was the one who died, I would be your prime suspect. And boy, she would deserve it. She's bad news for Will. She abuses the crew. Nobody likes her. We're forced to tolerate her."

Garrick took a bathroom break in a row of Portakabins set up at the edge of the set. He'd expected basic conditions, but was surprised to discover it was as if he'd walked into Claridge's. Re-joining Fanta outside, he paused when he noticed she was now wearing a Brookhaven crew cap.

"She said I could have it," she said sheepishly. "I think it'll help me blend in."

It annoyed Garrick that he didn't get one for Wendy.

"I think we need more from Mr Sadler."

"I can–"

Garrick quickly cut her off. "Which I'll do. I want you to hang around and find out everything from the moment Karen Dalton turned up. Also, find out where the gardener is and when he'll be back."

The list of potential suspects was long, but since the crime scene was contained, Garrick had high hopes they would soon get to the bottom of things. He was sure Will Sadler knew more than he was saying. It was time to turn up the pressure on him, and Garrick felt slightly alarmed that he would enjoy doing just that.

7

G arrick didn't know what state he expected to find Will Sadler in, but when the receptionist at the Footman's Hotel guided him through to the spa swimming pool, he hadn't expected to be greeted by a broad smile and a firm handshake.

"DCI Garrick!" exclaimed Will, as if they were old friends. "Can I get you a drink?"

"I'm fine, thank you." Garrick caught the receptionist's lingering look at Will's toned, muscular body. He was dripping wet and wearing only a pair of red swimming shorts. Her smile broadened when Will dismissed her by name.

"Thanks, Sarah."

Will gestured to a pair of loungers at the poolside, and they sat down. To Garrick's relief, Will had the decency to drape a towel over his shoulders. The pool was enormous, with a trickling waterfall on the end wall. Despite its name, the Footman's Hotel was a luxury establishment just outside the village of Leeds.

"First off, I want to apologise for the state I was in yesterday. I was deeply shocked." The smile never left his face. It was as if he hadn't woken up lying on top of a dead girl he'd been planning to sleep with.

Garrick decided to keep on his good side for now. "That's understandable. You seem much better today." Will's diction was now refined, and he maintained eye contact to an alarming degree.

"Sleep and a little exercise can work wonders. So did you find out any more? I have to be careful about how I'm associated with all of this."

"Yes. Quite a bit. Karen Dalton was murdered. Drugged and drowned."

For all his alleged fine acting skills, Will didn't exhibit the deep shock that Garrick had seen on dozens of faces when confronted with such a hideous crime. His smile dropped, and he looked away in an overly theatrical motion.

"Why would anybody do that?"

"That's my job to find out. Tell me about when you first met her."

"She came on the set a few days ago. That's the first time we were introduced. She had a costume fitting in London and had basically rocked up for the shoot. She was staying here, but only checked-in, I think, after her first day. It was all very quick."

"And...?"

"And she was very nice."

"Nice?"

"Obviously she was beautiful, or she wouldn't have been cast, right? She said she was a big fan and, y'know..."

"She flirted?"

Will laughed at the archaic term, and Garrick briefly regretted not bringing Chib or Fanta along to guide the lingo.

Will reached for a glass tumbler on the table. Even from where he was sitting, Garrick could smell the Jack Daniels. He took a sip and swirled the remains of the ice cubes, making them clink melodically against the crystal.

"She gave me a smouldering look and her heart went all aquiver," he said with a grin. "That's the kinda crap they write in the script. But yes, something like that."

His unshakable arrogance was irritating Garrick. The smug smile remained resident, and his entire attitude was firmly self-centred.

"And three days later, you were going to sleep with her."

"That was the first chance we had." He seemed unaware of the inappropriate comment.

"Because Kelly was here?"

Garrick took some satisfaction when his smile vanished. Will swirled his drink with a little more vigour.

"Kelly..." He shook his head. "Now there's a mistake." He looked sharply at Garrick. "Everything I tell you is confidential, isn't it? If the press gets wind of this..."

"It's all confidential and related only to the investigation. If you're asking me to sign another NDA, then I'll shove it up your lawyer's arse, along with the last one."

"Ah, they tried that on you already, did they?"

Garrick returned a thin smile and wondered why Will didn't remember the previous day's incident. How drugged had he been? "So, Kelly..." he prompted.

"We already knew our engagement was a stupid mistake. The question now is how do we break it off without it blowing up Twitter?"

"It's your personal life. What's that got to do with social media?"

"You obviously don't know how the internet works, detective. If they frame the news the wrong way, then it could upset careers. And that costs money. That's why we have publicists."

"But this is an amicable decision?"

"It's more amicable on my side." Will sighed and finished his drink. "She came over to persuade me not to end the engagement."

"Ah."

"Not yet, anyway. She's on the verge of signing a big deal with a cosmetics brand and thinks any negative publicity about us might sink the deal."

"And once she's signed?"

"I can go to hell." He put the glass on the table with a thud. "That confirmed it for me. She was only out to use my name. She didn't care about the real me."

"With all due respect, that must be a pretty common thing in your world."

Will stared glumly at the pool. "I'm still coming to terms with what 'my world' is." He pulled himself together, and his cocksure smile reappeared. "But I am a survivor."

"Unlike poor Miss Dalton."

Unease crossed Will's face. He glanced around to ensure they were alone and dropped his voice.

"I'm very sorry for what happened to her. It's horrible. She seemed like a nice girl. But beyond sex, there was nothing between us." He hesitated. "To be honest, when she said she wanted to see me alone, I was surprised. She'd been cold towards me."

"She was just another girl on your scorecard."

"You get it." He stared at the water, once again failing to recognise how inappropriate his words were. "I thought we'd been discreet. I don't know how anybody could've known we were meeting."

"Did Kelly meet her?"

"Of course. She vets every woman in a hundred-mile radius. She hated her."

"And what about Freya Granger?"

Will looked straight at Garrick. His face was now unreadable. "What about Freya?"

"You've been friends for a long time. Had they met before?"

"A couple of times. She doesn't regard Freya as a threat."

"You mean she's not good looking enough?"

Will shrugged non-committally. "She didn't like her hanging around."

"Was Freya aware you two argued?"

"She knows. She's been caught in the crossfire more than a few times."

"Did she know you wanted to end the engagement?"

"I probably mentioned it. These days we text more than speak. She's been to LA and Cannes, and we hung out. And when I'm in London, we try to make time. It's only when I'm at her house, do we really see one another?"

"So you wouldn't categorize her as a *close* friend?"

"I'd say she used to be a good friend. But lately she's been a pain. Always asking for favours."

They lapsed into silence. Will gazed back at the pool, lost in thought. Garrick was struggling on how to frame his next question, so he opted for bluntness.

"We found traces of psilocybin on your costume."

"I don't know what that is."

"You told me you were feeling unwell yesterday. You

suspected food poisoning." Will nodded. "Could it be because of the magic mushrooms you ate?"

Will spluttered with laughter. "Shrooms? I've never taken shrooms!"

"Psilocybin is the compound that causes people to hallucinate when they take them."

Will frowned; the first genuine emotion Garrick had seen him perform.

"I was feeling out of it. Somebody must have slipped them to me."

"Possibly. But who and why? It can't kill you. At least not in the doses either of you ingested. There was more in her system. It could have left her confused and unable to fend off her attacker. Did you share any food? Any drinks?"

"I don't think so." his frown deepened. "Trying to recall anything from yesterday is a little foggy." He tapped the side of his head.

"We could take a blood test to see if there are traces still in your system."

"No," Will retorted quickly. "No needles. No."

"And you're not taking any other... medication. To help with the stress?"

Will locked eyes with Garrick and gave a firm, "No!" Then he put his head in his hands and all pretence of being in control wavered. "Now what? Is somebody trying to kill me? Set me up?"

"You seem to think this is all about you."

Will looked sharply at him. "Of course it is. Who else?"

Garrick was fuming as he drove to the station. He didn't trust himself to answer a call from Wendy, and three from Molly Meyers. Will Sadler's arrogance had repeatedly irked him. The man was a borderline sociopath. At least that would give him something to discuss with his therapist tomorrow.

Dr Amy Harman had been appointed to him as a condition for returning to work after the mental trauma of his sister's death. Despite his initial reluctance, he'd found her sessions to be useful and calming. After spending forty minutes with the self-centred actor, Garrick was tense, and his migraine had returned with fury.

It didn't help his mood when his aging Land Rover stalled twice at traffic lights. It had struggled to start when he left the hotel, and he suspected the vehicle would face a post-mortem of its own soon.

It was after four when he arrived at the incident room. Chib was setting up the evidence wall. DC Wilkes was still out interviewing the extras, and Fanta was staying on the set until they wrapped. DC Harry Lord didn't hold back his annoyance at being left to run the office.

"The first time we get a glamourous case and I'm stuck in here!"

"Best place for you, mate. They'd be sure to recognize your handsome mug and try to lure you off the force."

"It wouldn't take much luring, let me tell you."

Chib placed a beguiling photo of Karen in the centre of the evidence wall. It was the headshot she'd used on her acting résumé. A similar one of Will was to the side.

"If we put everybody up here, we're going to run out of space very quickly," said Chib as she stepped back.

Garrick filled them in on his conversations, and pictures of Kelly Rodriguez, Marissa Carlisle, Simon Wheeler, and Sir James and Freya Granger went up, too.

"Currently, the only people with direct connections to

Karen Dalton are the producer, director, and Will Sadler. Kelly didn't like her, but she was out of the country."

"I can confirm that," said Harry. "She was on a Virgin Atlantic flight the time Karen was murdered. It's a pretty solid alibi."

"We should talk to somebody at the LAPD about getting a statement from her," suggested Chib.

Garrick nodded. After liaising with the Americans over his sister, he had no desire to offer to do so again.

Harry sighed. "Well, I guess that'll be me then."

"So where are we on motives?" Chib asked as she studied the wall.

"Thin on the ground," said Garrick. Other than somebody trying to get at Will, I can't see why she was killed.

"You wouldn't spike them both with psilocybin unless you were trying to ruin the scene."

"Then the spotlight falls on who has to gain from that," said Garrick. "Which is Sir James. Every day the shoot goes over schedule is money in his pocket."

"It looks like he's the only one who stands to benefit," said Harry.

Garrick wasn't so sure. "I asked Will for a blood sample. He flatly refused."

"Do you think he's still taking drugs?" asked Chib.

"I think it's highly likely, even if it's only a little."

"He was already going to score with her," Harry pointed out. "So he wouldn't need to drug her, would he?"

"Something doesn't stack up with any of this." Garrick rubbed his throbbing temple. All hope of a swiftly resolved case was vanishing under a mountain of mismatched motives and evidence.

"There must be somebody else who stands to benefit,"

said Chib. "Marissa Carlisle would lose her job and her franchise if the show got cancelled. The studio would lose a lot of money. All the cast and crew would be out of a job. And Sir James would lose a lucrative deal. And without a show on telly, he couldn't afford to open his house up to the public."

Garrick nodded. "So if there's no financial motivation, then it's one of the heart."

"His fiancée was out of the country," Chib pointed out.

"We're looking at this down the wrong lens." It disappointed Garrick they didn't pick up on his film pun. "We're assuming it's all about him. What do we know about Karen Dalton?"

Chib checked her laptop. "She lives in a house share in Croydon. Worked part time in the theatre there at the front of house and did plenty of extra work. She started to get more commercial work. Lately she'd been in a NatWest advert and one for a yogurt."

"Partner? Parents?"

"We don't know."

"Send Wilkes to find out everything we can about her. Chib, tomorrow I want you on the set with Fanta. Make sure she doesn't get distracted. Sean can join you when he's finished. All our eggs are in that basket."

"And what about me?" said Harry.

Garrick smiled and gestured around the room. "You can keep this place tidy. And get the kettle on when we all get back."

8

Criminal investigation work was a relentless race to catch up with facts, draw together intelligence, and combine it with hunches. An elaborate concoction designed to push towards an inevitable conviction of the guilty party. Garrick mused that the work itself took up about ten per cent of the time. The investigation into Karen Dalton was currently lounging in the ninety per cent 'sit and wait' zone. In all his experience, the longer this continued, the more the investigation relied on the guilty party making a mistake, or some piece of overlooked evidence to be revealed. Even with the most diligent policing, this was the perilous time when all the culprit had to do was go to ground in order to get away with murder.

DC Sean Wilkes had spoken with Karen Dalton's house-mates and family, but found out nothing useful. She was well-liked and had dreamt of being an actress since she was six. She paid her rent on time; had a group of close friends from several theatre productions she'd been in for the

London Fringe scene; and she'd a string of brief relationships that had never been very serious. Her career was the driving force in her life. Every winter she would help at a homeless shelter, dishing out warm free meals, and she'd occasionally go to church despite telling people she was on the fence about religion.

Nobody could draw up a list of disgruntled lovers or rivals able to sneak past on-set security and kill her. It furthered the investigation's core assumption that the killer was still on the grounds, although they could not draw any motive. Garrick had reminded his team that some crimes didn't need a motive. They were often the more chilling and dangerous ones.

The press had finally reported the story, but it had fallen under the headline of *Fatal Accident at Broadhaven*. Karen was mentioned once, and the thrust of the story centred around how Will Sadler was distraught but had been rallying the cast and crew to complete the film in her honour. The actor's publicity team had done an exemplary job in portraying him as the hero of the hour who had found the body. With him as the focus, the sketchy details passed without scrutiny.

DS Okon and DC Liu spent the day on the set when Will Sadler returned. Garrick tried not to think about Fanta geeking out around the actor and reminded himself that she was a competent detective when she wanted to be. Garrick had spent most of the day with DC Harry Lord, combing through Sir James' public accounts and the history of the estate.

Laddingford Manor had been in the Granger family since 1582, with the title handed down between generations. Sir James had been working in a pub when his estranged father passed away and he'd automatically inherited both the title and a house that was badly in need of repair. From all accounts, the estate was a money pit. It had sucked every penny into maintaining the basic levels of functionality. While there were assets, such as paintings, furniture, and gilt mirrors that could raise a princely sum at auction, it would only fend off insolvency for so long, and Sir James had steadfastly refused to sell any family heirlooms which he valued more than the house itself.

The grounds had been opened for game drives, but that had barely lifted the flagging coffers. Their principal source of income came from being a location for film, tv, commercials and fashion shoots. It had been quite lucrative, culminating in becoming the internationally recognised setting for Broadhaven. That had been both a blessing and a curse. As the series rose in popularity, the estate's demand as a location dwindled. Nobody else wanted to use such a recognisable house for their own projects.

That had led the family to suffer severe cash shortfalls, and Garrick appreciated why Sir James was demanding a rise in the location fee. He had applied for a licence to become a wedding venue, but that was still pending until they made some major improvements in the property itself.

Garrick's assumption was that being *to the manor born* was a life of unearned privilege. So far, he was struggling to see any benefits. And the Granger family was not without its tragedies. Sir James had high hopes for his son, Daniel, to inherit the estate, but he had died nine years ago in a traffic accident while his father was driving. He was fourteen. It had left Sir James with a limp, and he'd suffered deep depression ever since.

Lady Helen was more of an enigma. They'd been married for thirty-one years, and she'd come from a middle class family with Scottish roots. Harry had found several photographs of Freya online, taken with Will at parties and premieres. They always referred to her as a friend, and they were always in the company of others. There was no suggestion of any romantic involvement.

Freya's lack of presence on social media had surprised Harry. She was their key demographic, and until two years ago she'd been active on Twitter, Facebook, and Instagram. Her sudden abandonment of the platforms coincided with her leaving university, which ran parallel with more pictures of her and Will appearing online.

Harry had taken great delight in researching Kelly Rodriguez. Every few minutes he would exclaim, *"what a babe,"* or something coarser as he fell on a photograph of her in a swimsuit or dress that barely covered any skin. She had shot to fame in the US reality show *Jungle Warrior* – a cross between *Love Island* and *I'm a Celebrity, Get Me Out of Here.* A squad of young, good-looking city slickers were thrown into the jungle to fend for themselves as they solved problems and teamed up to find the million-dollar prize. Only one couple could win, and Kelly seized the public's imagination by being a girl with zero inhibitions. She had a ruthless tactic of switching partners at the last second to get what she wanted. Many considered her a tough *go-getter*, while others thought she was a ruthless bitch. Either way, she became something of a feminist role model. Garrick could imagine her and Will in a room together. She would tear him limb-from-limb. They shared little in common, and it was clearly a relationship designed to feed the publicity machine. The reaction online to their engagement had been enormous. It baffled Garrick why people didn't put that amount of energy into scrutinising their own lives instead of pandering to celebrities who they had nothing in common with, yet they somehow admired more than their own grandparents.

An entire day of research left him just as clueless why Karen Dalton had been murdered. He felt a growing pang of disassociation with a world that was getting younger while he was getting older. A torrent of spam emails promoting life insurance and retirement plans compounded that feeling. He was wondering if the universe was trying to send him a message. Although, at 41, he knew he shouldn't be feeling over the hill just yet.

A quiet lecture from Superintendent Margery Drury punctuated an ostensibly fruitless day. She was delighted to have Garrick and Lord – the two older hands on the team – alone. She'd spent her day fielding calls from lawyers representing the studio, the production company, and Will Sadler. They were followed by calls from publicity representatives from the same three entities, and finally Will's agent, who had infuriated her so much that she warned him never to call again.

It emphasised that the investigation had the potential of turning into a media circus, and after Garrick's last case had seized the headlines, the Kent Constabulary didn't really need the attention again. Garrick wasn't sure if he was being oversensitive or not, but he suspected Drury wasn't pleased that he was leading another high-profile case.

It gave him a lot to pack into his sessions with Dr Harman. His Super had assigned the therapist to him, to ease him back to work after the traumatic aftershock of his sister's death. He wasn't sure if it was a good or bad sign that her services had been extended for a couple more months. Garrick was both pleased to use her for self-reflection but concerned that somebody somewhere thought he needed monitoring and wasn't fit for active duty.

During his darker moments, he thought that, too.

The evening light filtered through the window, warming his face as he sat back in the armchair with his hands clasped over his chest. If he closed his eyes, he could easily fall asleep. His headache had surfaced a few times during the day, but other than that, he was feeling more like his old self. The last few therapy sessions had focused on the empty envelope from the States that his dead sister had apparently sealed. Or more specifically, it had contained traces of her DNA. It was unnerving. They'd spent a session discussing countless examples of people's erratic behaviour. Garrick knew from experience that some killers like to taunt their victim's families. It gave them a twisted sense of fulfilment they hadn't received by carrying out the murder itself. He'd consoled himself that if it was serious, then the Flora Police Department, who were investigating the case, would have contacted him.

Just by talking through it with Dr Harman, it felt as if a weight had lifted from his shoulders.

He'd wanted to tell her the details of his case, but couldn't. He missed having somebody he could toss details around with; it helped find new angles on the most difficult subjects. Instead, she probed around his physical health. He'd eventually told her about the tumour, but every time she raised it, he assured her in subsequent sessions that it was no longer an issue. Whether or not she believed his dismissiveness, Dr Harman learned to circle around the subject.

"And you've been sleeping well?"

"Better than ever. I'm still taking the sleeping tablets, but only a few times each week."

"And no auditory or visual side effects?"

Garrick smiled. "You mean, have I been seeing things? No. Nothing." He was relieved when she returned the smile. Her eyes sparkled behind her jazzy, red-framed glasses and today she wore her wavy shoulder-length blonde hair down. She always dressed smartly but projected an image of somebody who didn't have to try in order to be eye-catching. He suspected she dressed down to avoid such clichés. As ever, Garrick felt guilty for even the slightest attraction towards her. But he was only human, after all.

Her pen rhythmically tapped her notepad. "I have to say, David, you are a remarkable person. What you've gone through, what you do... trust me, there are few people who can hold it together as well as you do. And certainly not under the pressure of your job."

"Do I sense a '*but*' coming?"

"That depends on your point of view. I've been here holding your hand while you've been cycling along, but I don't think you need me. You're pedalling hard all by your-self. And popping wheelies," she added with a gentle giggle.

Garrick chuckled. He loved her terrible analogies.

"I don't think I can be of any more use to you." She put the pen and pad onto a side table in a wholly symbolic gesture, but Garrick felt it was a powerful one. She mistook his disappointment for hesitation. "Honestly, you don't need me. By the sound of it, you have a healthy relationship growing with Wendy. Since returning to work, you've excelled in two very high-profile cases, and from what I read in the news, complicated ones, too." She let him absorb the rare compliment. "You know I have to submit a report to your HR department. I'm afraid I'm going to have to do so with a glowing recommendation."

Garrick looked out of the window at the sun's fading rays. The nights were drawing out, and as they did, so his mood improved. Time with Dr Harman had turned from a chore to something he looked forward to. Taking it away felt like a step backwards. Or was he addicted to having an attractive woman listen to him moan about his life for an hour a week? He could hardly disagree with her, especially as a bad report would easily see him out of a job. He forced a smile, even though he didn't feel it.

"So this is *au revoir*?"

"No. This is a firm goodbye." Her nose wrinkled as her eyes narrowed. "I know this is more difficult for me." Her voice dropped. "I'm the one losing money. But don't be sad for me." She chuckled.

Garrick stood and awkwardly shook her hand.

"Thanks for everything, doctor. It's been very helpful. And I mean that. I didn't want to be here in the first place and now..."

And now he was finding it difficult to go. The Force was paying for her time, not him, so he had associated the time with her more as a friendship than a medical necessity. And he was very short on friends.

"I have a feeling you'll go from strength-to-strength, David."

It felt odd to leave Dr Harman's practice after months of relying on her wisdom. He had told her things he'd never had the guts to impart to anybody else, not even Wendy.

Garrick glanced at his watch and considered calling her so they could pop out for a drink. He hadn't seen her for a few days and was missing her company.

That was another first for him.

He hesitated as he decided whether to answer it. Instead, he let it ring out and headed to home for an early night instead. They were seeing one another tomorrow, and as he was going to be on-set asking a few more questions, perhaps he could snag a souvenir for her. He was sure she'd appreciate it.

His car refused to start for several minutes. At first he thought the new battery had died on him. Only by accidentally closing the central locking while inside, then unlocking it, did it turn over. He had vague recollections of a friend having similar troubles with his car's disabler. Yet another problem to throw on the list.

It was a dusky twilight by the time Garrick returned home. The sky was clear, and birds were singing an inspiring melodic opus that put him in mind of a midsummer evening.

It was spoiled by his front door standing wide open.

Garrick skidded to an abrupt stop in his drive and gripped the wheel as a pang of fear struck him.

This had happened before. Unlike the last time, his first instinct was not that he was the victim of theft. It was something worse. Had he left it open? Was his memory failing him? A burglary would be the happier outcome.

He took his phone from the inside pocket of his comfortable, worn, dark green Barbour and selected Chib's number. His thumb hovered over the call button as he climbed from his car. A quick glance at the newly installed security camera assured him it was still pointing in the right direction.

As stealthily as possible, he approached the front door and strained to listen for any sound that was out of place.

Nothing stirred.

He crept straight into his living room, which appeared undisturbed. The TV, Blu-ray player, and laptop were still there. He was about to tiptoe into the kitchen when he heard a noise from upstairs.

His blood froze.

It had been the delicate sound of something being accidentally knocked - followed by utter silence.

Garrick considered shouting out, but any intruder would have heard the car pulling up, so he'd already lost the element of surprise.

With his phone clutched tightly in hand and his finger fractionally above the screen, he ascended the stairs. Garrick knew his house well enough to know where the squeaky floorboards were. He kept his weight to the edge of those steps and stayed as close to the wall as possible. It would give him some limited support should an attacker spring for him.

He was near the top when he regretted not taking a knife from the kitchen. He was completely defenceless.

On the landing, he stopped and held his breath.

He could only hear the blood pumping in his ears.

Then the faintest of sounds from his bedroom. Somebody was in there.

The door was partially open, but he'd have to shove it wider to get inside. He took a breath – then shouldered the door open.

"POLICE!" he bellowed.

There was a terrified yowl – and a large ginger cat sprang off his bed and bolted between his legs. By the time Garrick had gathered his wits and retrieved his phone from the floor, the feline had already bounded down the stairs and out of the front door.

He was about to swear loudly when he noticed he'd dialled Chib. He quickly hung up before she could answer. Knowing she'd call him straight back and to avoid any immediately embarrassing questions, he put it on airplane mode. He sat on the edge of his bed and waited for his heart rate to drop back to normal.

This had been the second time he'd left his front door open. Not just unlocked, but open. And that worried him. He realised he was touching the side of his head where the tumour lay. He snapped his hand away.

He always parked in the driveway facing the house, so how hadn't he noticed it was open when he'd left in the morning? His mind drifted to the empty letter sent from the States... it was absurd, of course...

He still checked the security camera app on his phone. Sure enough, it showed the view outside, complete with the neighbour's ginger moggy now sat at the end of his drive, calmly preening itself. He rewound the footage, watching him stalk from the house to his car – then leave.

It only recorded video when there was movement, so the next clip was of the cat snooping around and entering the house. He checked further back. There was nothing. Not even him leaving the house. That was odd.

He tapped through the camera settings to check if it had stored any images on the onboard memory card. Nothing. It was as if it had stopped working the night before. He had been the one to install it; the one to set it up. Had he messed that up, too?

Dr Harman may have signed him off, but he hadn't been completely honest with her. Was that a mistake? He remembered the letter from his medical consultant. It was still unread on the table downstairs. Perhaps he should read it.

Not tonight, of course.

But soon.

When he had time.

9

When arriving on the Broadhaven set, DC Fanta Liu's initial excitement on learning that they were shooting an action scene involving horse-riding through the forest, was tempered when the process took hours to set up for the few seconds worth of film that would finally appear on screen. She was further disappointed, as a stunt double would mostly play Will Sadler's role. While the search for Karen Dalton's replacement had started immediately, her stunt double would have to do the shoot while the new actress was being cast.

The out-of-sequence structure of film-making was something Garrick appreciated. It wasn't entirely dissimilar to putting together the chronology of an investigation, and the long bouts of waiting around on the set for something to happen paralleled most cases. With the wider interviews concluded, Garrick assembled his team at the estate; all except Harry Lord, who remained behind to run the incident room.

Garrick was still shaken from the previous night's incident and had spent breakfast staring at his consultant's still-sealed letter. There was something comforting about not knowing answers. Something that went against the grain of being a police detective. His personal anxieties vanished when he turned up at the stately home. His first port of call was to have another word with Sir James, but DC Fanta Liu told him he'd left early for business. She was still proudly wearing the crew cap and now had snagged a Broadhaven branded dark-green body warmer. Garrick decided not to press the matter as they walked through the production trailer park. There was a lot of hubbub caused by the camera department hauling cases and heavy pieces of equipment. The wardrobe department was a flurry of activity moving back and forth with costumes for the extras – thirty of them all wearing Victorian riding outfits and sporting perfectly coiffured hair.

Amongst the crew he recognised Liliana Davies pushing a rail packed with costumes. Fanta gave a smile of acknowledgement. Chloe Aubertel marched past and gave a terse "*bonjour*," without breaking her stride, as if pausing for a few seconds would throw the entire production into turmoil.

"Any idea when Sir James'll be back?"

Fanta shook her head. "I was talking to a runner this morning who heard shouting from the Grangers' private quarters. She started with the company during the last series and says they're a weird family. Nobody seems to like Freya. She was even warned to stay away from her."

He couldn't tell if Fanta was pleased to report on her intelligence gathering or simply sharing gossip. "Why?"

"After she got kicked out of uni, she'd got it into her head to become an actor. Trouble is, she's rubbish."

"She got kicked out of university? She said she'd left because she didn't like studying history."

"I don't know if it's true." She glanced around to make sure nobody overheard. The nearest extras were far too busy with their phones; probably trying to line up their next gig.

"Look into it. But I don't understand why people would stay away from her just because she wanted to be an actor."

"She annoyed everybody. From the casting director, to the producer, to the rest of the cast. They think she's one of those privileged toffs who thinks they should always get her own way."

"But she's friends with Will."

"That's why people avoid her. They're worried if they upset her, then he'll throw a tantrum."

Garrick smiled. "Tantrum? He strikes me as the type," he said with heavy irony.

Fanta's sunny disposition clouded. "Yeah. I've heard stories. But everybody is too afraid to talk."

"What stories?"

"Refusing to come on set because the director had annoyed him. Or he didn't like lunch. There's plenty about him sleeping with the crew. One time he trashed a dinner buffet—"

"Drugs?"

"Nobody is saying." Fanta gave a disappointed sigh. "He sounds a bit of a... prick." She brightened a little. "But apparently he helped her get a couple of theatre roles. So maybe he's not all that bad."

"He sounds like a regular Prince Charming." Garrick reached for his phone as it rang. "You know what they say: never meet your heroes." It wasn't his phone ringing. For a second, Garrick shuddered. Was he hallucinating again? The ringing continued right next to him, but Fanta hadn't reacted. He looked around.

"Are you okay, sir?"

"The phone...?"

Fanta looked puzzled, then jerked a thumb to the trailer behind them. "It's coming from in there. It's not mine."

"It's loud..."

He looked at the large white trailer. It was a posh version of the sort of caravan he'd stayed in with his parents and sister when they were younger, often enduring the elements of a British summer while holidaying in North Wales. While a family of four had to share one large caravan, this trailer was exclusively for Will Sadler's use.

"I thought you said he wasn't on-set today?"

"Not according to the call sheet."

Garrick knocked on the door. There was no answer. He tentatively tried the handle – and the door opened. He raised his eyebrows at Fanta.

"Look at that."

"Is this legal?" She looked around uneasily.

"The door is open," Garrick said as he slipped inside.

The trailer was furnished with a white leather sofa, a drinks cabinet, and a small bespoke kitchenette. He presumed the door beyond lead to a bathroom and bedroom. It was utter luxury by any glamping standard. A couple of gossip magazines were on the table next to a bowl of fruit. The ringing continued from the direction the couch. Garrick edged closer and just caught the glow of a screen from between the leather cushions before it fell silent. He retrieved an iPhone from the crack.

"Looks like Mr Sadler left his mobile in a hurry."

He tapped the screen and brought it to life to reveal the

missed call number. But that wasn't what made him suck a breath in surprise; that had been the picture on the screen. It wasn't Will's phone. It was Karen Dalton's.

The police Portakabin was from another era when compared with the stars' luxury trailers. An old, wonky, metal-legged square table filled most of the room, with four uncomfortable plastic chairs positioned around it. An electric kettle, a jar of coffee, and several chipped mugs sat on the floor next to a four-pack of bottled water. It was the team's own space a dozen yards away from the other trailers, and it would have been laughable if David Garrick had been in a humorous mood.

"How the hell did we overlook her phone?" he barked at the others seated around the table. When he paced side-to-side, the entire cabin trembled on its uneven foundations.

"She went to the mortuary still in her costume," said Chib. "SOCO took her actual clothes from the wardrobe department, and that included her purse and handbag. It was all catalogued and put into evidence." She waved a hand. "As there was no mobile in it, nobody thought to check if she had one."

"And not everybody has a mobile," said DC Wilkes defensively. He looked away, under Garrick's hawk-like gaze.

Garrick was annoyed he'd failed to notice such an obvious piece of modern life missing from the evidence. With his team stretched while gathering over a hundred witness statements, it was something that was so easily overlooked. SOCO teams focused on what evidence there was, not what was missing.

"The phone's locked, but we hope facial ID will unlock it. Otherwise, it's going to be difficult to crack. The question is, what was it doing in Will Sadler's trailer?"

Wilkes looked through the collected statements on his computer tablet. It wasn't the most responsive hardware to use for investigations, but it was the one the force had purchased, so he didn't have a choice. At least he could access the HOLMES system to keep track of the investigation.

"He definitely said they'd only spoke to her between takes on set. There's no mention of them getting together in his trailer."

Fanta pulled a face. "Why would he lie? He's not like that."

"I think you're conflating his character with the real him," Garrick cautioned. "Remember, he's an actor. A professional liar." Something occurred to him. "Do they have the same people doing their hair and makeup every day?" Chib nodded. "I want to speak with them. Do we have a timeline on Karen's last movements?"

Chib checked her notes. "She was driven in at 6 am and had twenty minutes for breakfast. She sat on her own, but several people took time to say hello. Then she went to the wardrobe for her costume, hair, and make-up. Then the second AD came for her and took her to set. Everything they shot that day was outside at the front of the house."

"And she was with Will in all of those scenes?"

"Yes."

"Was there any time she was alone?"

"No. After her last scene, she went for a drink and a snack. People saw her speaking with Will, then she left to hook-up at the folly. That's when the director collared him."

"And that's the last time she was seen alive," muttered Garrick. "She was murdered in those few moments Simon Wheeler was speaking to Will." He wondered if she would still be alive if the director hadn't stalled him.

"So the window for her to take any magic mushrooms was between those takes."

Chib checked her neatly written notes as she spoke. "It takes psilocybin thirty minutes to take effect. But combined with a hot drink, it could be as quick as five or ten minutes. And she had a coffee handy while shooting her last scene."

Garrick shaped the timeline in his head. "Were there many people in the canteen?"

"No, but people come in and out regularly. It's seldom empty, apparently. Lunch was over and they'd set it up for snacks while they prepared food for the early evening. It was a long shooting day. So the team was setting up a new shot. The lighting, camera, and electrical teams were busy, so unlikely to be there. Office staff go in when the crews tend not to be there, so Marissa was there at the time. The wardrobe department was preparing fresh costumes." She noticed Garrick's look. "They have multiple costumes in case they get dirty. And make-up would've had a few minutes' downtime too."

Garrick popped his lips. "Wonderful, so one half of suspects had time to spike their drinks and food while they were shooting. The others had the perfect window while they were not shooting."

"But the time it takes for the drugs to kick in gives us either the people specifically around the camera during the shoot, or those immediately in the tent during the set-up."

Garrick nodded. "Okay. Work with that and whittle names down."

"And how was Will's day?"

Fanta chimed in. "I tracked his timeline."

"Stalked, you mean," muttered Sean Wilkes under his breath.

Garrick caught a flash of irritation in Fanta's eyes. She and Sean had been covertly dating, or at least they thought it was covert. The cute looks and edgy body language spoke volumes. Garrick had turned a blind eye to it. It wasn't something he'd any interest in knowing more about. However, it was also prone to frosty moments, like now.

She sat stiffly upright and purposefully blanked Sean as she flicked a finger through the notes on her phone.

"He was driven here thirty minutes after Karen. He had breakfast in his hotel room and when he arrived, he went straight into make-up and wardrobe. Will stayed there until they took him to set. In between takes, he was in his trailer and stayed there, having lunch alone. The only time anybody saw him in craft services was at that moment Karen spoke to him. The director had been giving him a hard time for the last few days, so I think he was avoiding him."

"Why?"

"Simon didn't think Will was performing well enough. Everybody says he's picky."

"He was the one who stalled Will." Garrick tried to guess at any motives the director might have for knowingly letting Karen walk into the arms of a killer. He drew a blank. "We have been looking at this too closely. At a micro-level about what they were all doing here." He pointed to the ground. "This isn't some *Poirot* locked house mystery. Where are Simon and Marissa staying?"

Chib looked through her notes and shook her head.

Fanta raised her hand to the heavens, seeing the obvious for the first time. "At the same hotel as Will and Karen. The rest of the cast have different accommodation. According to Gina, most of them wanted to avoid staying with Will."

"So, the four of them could see a lot more of each other than we first supposed."

Chib wasn't so sure. "If Will and Karen were at the same hotel and so desperate to sleep with one another, why try to sneak away between takes?"

Garrick felt as if he was clutching at straws to find a likely motive. He hadn't discounted the idea Karen Dalton's murder may have been opportunistic, but a faint voice was telling him he wasn't looking in the right place.

10

"Do you have any idea how hard we work?" The pretence of civility was cast aside the moment Garrick entered Will Sadler's suite at the Footman's Hotel.

"I'm sure it's very demanding work," Garrick lied convincingly.

Will poured a healthy measure of Jack Daniels into a crystal tumbler and slammed the bottle down against the table to emphasise his point.

"Up before dawn, then to bed late. Six-day weeks. The constant pressure to perfectly perform each time. And now this whole fiasco is exasperating the shoot. They're already talking an extra week for reshoots!"

"By fiasco I take it you mean the murder? Yes, I can see how irresponsible it was of her to die like that."

Will snorted as he paced the room, taking swigs from his drink with such careless abandonment the liquid splashed from the glass and onto his hand and the pale carpet. He didn't seem to notice.

"Don't try to get in my head!" he snapped. "Don't paint me as the bad guy in this. Me and Karen didn't go beyond a quick hook up – and that didn't even happen."

Garrick was trying to work out if Will's erratic behaviour was because he was drunk, high, or both. He recalled how the actor had suddenly become paranoid when he thought somebody might be out to get him.

"Let me play devil's advocate," Garrick said in a measure tone. "You claim somebody must have slipped the psilocybin in your food or drink?"

"I don't do shrooms. I told you this. Could you imagine trying to act while being off your tits on a psychedelic?"

"I imagine it would cripple your performance."

"Damn right."

"So, who would do that to you? What purpose would be served poisoning the star of the show?"

"Isn't it your job to find out?"

"My job is to bring the murderer of Karen Dalton to justice. Not save your career." Garrick took some pleasure when Will's lip curled. "But if the two causes intersect, then it's certainly in your favour."

Will stopped pacing and sat on the edge of the bed, nursing the glass with both hands. His head gently rocked; convincing   Garrick   the   young   man   had taken *something* illegal.

"We discovered Karen Dalton's phone in your trailer today."

Will's head snapped up in alarm. "You were in my trailer?"

"It was open, and the phone was ringing. I assumed you wouldn't mind."

"Of course not," he mumbled with little conviction.

"Which raises the question: when did she leave it there?"

"Karen had never been in my trailer."

"Yet her phone…"

"I don't know how it got there. Maybe she went in when I wasn't there. Like you did." Will looked away, his eyes following the wet blotches on the carpet. He was distracted. No, he was agitated.

"You spent most of the day cooped up in your trailer. Why?"

"Simon was giving me a hard time. Marissa's a pain. And I'd just had several days splitting up with Kelly. The moment she left that morning felt like a weight off my neck."

"So you saw nobody in your trailer that day?"

Will's head bobbed to the side as he thought. "Tons of people. Gina was in and out, but that's her job. Same with people from wardrobe. I just wanted to be left alone." He rolled the tumbler across his forehead.

"Who would want to sabotage your performance? Even if it was a joke done in bad taste?" If Garrick widened the list to people who thought Will Sadler was an annoying dick, then he'd have to put his own name on it.

"When you get to the top," Will said, barely above a whisper. "A lot of people want to knock you off your perch." Garrick resisted the urge to press him further. He let the silence play out. Will was in no hurry. After another sip of JD, he said, "Wheeler."

"Simon Wheeler? Your director? I don't understand. If, God forbid, something happened to you," Garrick hoped he'd sounded convincing enough, "the shoot would be shutdown, and he'd be out of a job."

"He doesn't care about that. This industry is small. Every-body knows somebody who works with somebody else." He made a rolling motion with his hands. "The six degrees of Kevin Bacon thing is really much smaller. Three degrees, maybe. Marissa didn't want Wheeler on this job. And Wheeler has always hated me."

"For what reason?"

Will held up a finger. "First, he and Marissa used to date. I don't know the details, but it was very messy when they split. I heard there was physical abuse, but I stayed clear. Just after that, Wheeler had a movie of his own set up. He had finance, distribution, the whole caboodle. It was his dream project he wrote years ago. Thought it would define his career."

"What happened?"

Will smirked and watched the alcohol in his glass swirl around. "The one caveat the financiers and distribution had was that I starred in it." He took a sip and looked smugly at Garrick. "So naturally I turned it down. After what he did to Marissa, he didn't deserve success. I really tore the project apart at my agency. Word spreads. Suddenly nobody wanted to do it."

"It's a very fickle business."

Will drained his glass and laughed. "Tell me about it. He never got over it."

"And being a contained industry, he learned it was you?" Will shrugged. He clearly didn't care. "I'm confused. If neither you or Marissa like him, why is he directing this film?"

"Because his last movie made a shitload of money. The studio had a three-picture deal with him, and he pleaded to be a part of it." Will laughed at the surprise on Garrick's face. "The things people will do out of spite. Marissa might be the producer, but that doesn't mean she has all the power." He waved his hand around the room. "There's always a bigger fish."

Garrick digested the information as Will walked to the cabinet and poured himself another generous measure of Jack Daniels. It was apparent the window for coherent conversation was rapidly closing.

"Just a couple of last things. Were you attracted to Karen?"

"She was smoking hot. Sure. She hadn't been cast because of her witty repartee."

"And you were both staying here. So...?"

Will smirked and wagged a finger at Garrick. "With my fiancée here, yes?"

That hadn't occurred to Garrick. "Of course. But she left the day Karen died. So that evening, or any evening for the rest of the shoot, you'd have ample opportunity."

Will gave him a strange look. "You must have a really boring sex life, Detective."

Garrick couldn't refute that. He pulled a face to encourage Will to continue.

"Where would the risk be? That's what makes it fun. Who wants a vanilla life?"

"You mean the thrill of getting caught?"

Will shot him a mischievous look.

"No, Detective. The thrill of getting away with it."

Waves rumbled against the shore, then gave a pleasant gurgling hiss as they receded through the shingles. It was a sound nature had devised to soothe life's stresses away. David Garrick and Wendy walked along Laysdown Beach as the sun sank on the horizon.

To the left stood a mud and clay cliff, while opposite, half in the water, were enormous concrete World War Two pill boxes and gun bunkers that had once been atop the cliff, but decades of erosion had toppled them onto the shore where the sea was slowly consuming them. It was such an incongruous thing to find on the beach that Garrick had always thought it would make a good film set. Just not for a Victorian period drama. It was also one of his favourite spots to unwind and stumble across the occasional fossil.

After leaving the hotel, Garrick hadn't the taste to return to the incident room. Throughout the day, he'd suffered an intermittent headache and imagined he could feel the tumour throbbing out of his skull like some alien growth. Talking with the actor had reinforced his dislike for the arrogant man, but it still had shed no light on Karen Dalton's murder. He made a note to talk to Simon Wheeler first thing in the morning. He just didn't have the energy for it right now. A walk on the beach with Wendy had been an impulsive idea. He wasn't really the type to be spontaneous, but there was no doubt it had been a terrific suggestion.

This was the first time since the case started that he'd had a chance to see her, and she'd been more than happy to join him, despite the rather long drive to get here. He hoped that her enthusiasm was about seeing him, but he couldn't ignore the fact that she was a huge Broadhaven fan, and that had been one of the first things out of her mouth.

"I'm not too sure how easy it will be to ask a person of interest for his autograph," he said, sidestepping the question.

"Any of the cast will do!"

"More arrive next week. And now they have to replace the actress, that could be pushed back a few days." She almost hid her disappointment, so he made a mental note to get the autograph by other means. DC Fanta Liu being his obvious woman on the inside.

"Can you drop some plot details?"

"I haven't read the script."

"Oh, David! It's the biggest show on telly! Surely you're curious?"

"I've never followed it," he said defensively. "And I can't really discuss details of the case."

"Right. This weekend you and I are going to binge watch season one."

Garrick groaned. He couldn't think of a worse hell. Wendy increased her grip on his arm to signal he couldn't get away. "That's six episodes."

"That's six hours of my life I won't get back!"

"We'll do it at my place. I'll cook us something nice. Buy some wine..."

"I'm going to have to be hammered if you want me to enjoy that."

"Several bottles of wine, then. And you can maybe stay over so you don't have to worry about driving home."

Garrick couldn't believe he hadn't seen what she had been gearing towards. A miraculous offer to stay the night. It had come out of nowhere and broadsided him. Not in a bad way, just one that left him groping for a suitable response.

They had been dating for three months and only seen each other during the occasional week-night or weekend, but each time the kiss goodnight had grown more passionate. Phone calls had become more frequent and longer. It was a situation Garrick was wholly out of his depth, and he had nobody to discuss it with. The physical attraction had always been there, but Wendy had stated from the very beginning she wanted to take things slowly. Garrick had nodded and asserted how he respected her wishes. In reality, he was relieved. While he'd love nothing more than a night of unrestrained animalistic passion, it wasn't really his style. He'd had a handful of one-night stands, which made him feel awkward the following morning. He could hear the lecture he'd get from Harry Lord if he ever found out, telling him to lie down and give it like a man. But then again, Harry took pride in being a stereotype.

He knew that he may have paused too long before answering. How long had it been? Seconds? It felt more like minutes.

"I would really like that." He smiled and gave her a quick kiss. "It might even make Broadhaven interesting."

There was a wicked twinkle in her eye. "I guarantee it will."

Something on the ground caught her attention. She stooped to pick it up. "That's an unusual pebble."

She handed it to Garrick. He angled it in the fading light. There was a definite curved shape raised on the surface.

"Y'know, I come down here a lot and look around. If I'm lucky, really lucky, I might find a fragment of a fossilised tree. My last big find was an ammonite." Which he had accidentally destroyed while cleaning.

"So, I've found a twig?"

Garrick held it up so they could both see. "You may have found an oddly shaped stone. Or you may have found a tooth."

Wendy was delighted. "A tooth?"

"Maybe." He pointed out to the sea. "Once there would have been sharks out there the size of a bus feeding on whatever they could."

She held him tighter as they looked out across the

uninviting brown water. Garrick felt an unfamiliar feeling. It was contentment.

Then he remembered what Will had said.

There was always a bigger fish.

There was something about that which struck a chord, and he felt certain that tomorrow he'd find out why.

11

Ignoring their grumbling, Garrick had sent DC's Liu and Wilkes to the hotel to interview staff, hoping to flesh out Karen Dalton's timeline away from the set. Meanwhile, Chib had gone to London to talk with Will Sadler's agent, and finally arranged a Zoom call to talk to Kelly Rodriguez in Los Angeles. With such a wide canvas of potential witnesses, Garrick was only just now feeling they were close to locking a timeline of everybody's movements, although they were no closer to an actual suspect.

Digital forensics had come back with Karen Dalton's phone after they'd unlocked it. She'd taken dozens of selfies in the three days on-set. There were calls with her agent, the casting director, and Marissa, which all seemed worked related, and a handful to her parents. The number that had called her phone and attracted Garrick's attention was unlisted in her contacts. It was from the provider EE and unregistered. An unsolicited sales call, or phone scam, it was impossible to tell.

Garrick scrolled through the stored photos. On each,

Karen was beaming widely. The light in her eyes was one of innocence and unadulterated joy. She had achieved her dream, and it showed in every wide-eyed twinkle.

Garrick felt hollow. Every good detective had to get into the mind of the guilty party; inhabiting their world was critical to understanding their darker motivations. When it came to the victims, their world had to be explored with equal veracity, which brought with it the sickening confirmation that a life had been extinguished; dreams shattered; hopes taken. All that would remain was a legacy of sadness and heartache.

Every aspect of her life on the set was recorded. Her hair, make-up, and wardrobe crew crushed around her, all mugging for the photo. Karen was in front of the shoot's main camera, with her arms draped around the grinning Director of Photography as she posed like a 1940s femme fatale. Several with Will Sadler, who, for once, looked as if he was having as much fun as her. The only picture that stood out from the pack was with the director. With a dog-eared script in his hand, unkept hair, large round black glasses, and wearing scruffy shorts to just below his knees, Simon Wheeler hadn't even cracked a smile.

Garrick's attempts to have a word with him resulted in several terse remarks about how busy he was. A constant stream of questions was thrown at him from various members of the crew, and when Will Sadler turned up, Simon's mood darkened. It was approaching lunchtime when Garrick's patience finally snapped.

"We can talk now, or I'll formally invite you to the station, and we can spend a couple of hours chatting there."

It was enough of a threat for Simon to call an early lunch and guide Garrick across to a huge marquee in a field beyond the house, far enough from the production unit to feel like a fresh location. It was dripping with bunting, fake flowers, and unlit flame pits, all artfully combined to exude Victorian extravagance.

Inside, huge movie lights, teetering on sturdy metal poles set on large flat plastic flooring slabs, were positioned around long tables filled with fake food – fruit, meats, fish, and an enormous roast hog – all artfully arranged on tables and tiered display stands. Garrick still hadn't read the script, but the set was giving out a strong wedding vibe. Thick power cables laced the floor in a disorganised spaghetti snarl. With several expletives, Simon dismissed the technicians prepping the set. His attitude was already enough for Garrick to get a measure of the man, and Simon must have sensed it as he raised an apologetic hand.

"I know you think I'm a complete asshole, but I'm under a lot of pressure." Simon's British accent was infused with a nasal Californian whine.

"Marissa said the production is now behind schedule."

"Christ, yes. I've had to leave the second unit picking up the rest of the riding scene, while we get the close-ups of Will. And we're still waiting for the girl playing Amanda to sign the bloody contract."

"How difficult could it be to find a willing actress?"

Simon snorted derisively. "That part's a doddle. Her agent knows we're desperate, so she's screwing us for every dime. We're going to go over by a week, at least."

Garrick added another seventy grand into Sir James's purse. "Tell me about Karen Dalton."

"I gave my statement on that day. Nothing's changed. I fought to get her cast when our first choice dropped out. An unknown face gave the role more innocence. Her reel was good, but the reviews of her theatre work were outstanding. She's just what this movie needed. We auditioned her three times, and each time she knocked it out of the park. Marissa was dragging her heels, so I made sure a couple of execs from the studio were at the last reading. She got the job before she reached the Tube station to go home. To be honest, if they hadn't cast her in this, I had her lined up for my next project." He looked around the set, searching for what else he could add. "She was nervous but turned in steady takes. It doesn't help when you're acting with a smug little twat like Will, but she held her own." He folded his arms tightly and shoved his glasses further up the bridge of his nose.

"Did you get an impression about what the rest of the crew thought of her?"

"They're always happy to meet new people. Karen made an effort with everybody. She was a real spark of joy. So happy to be here. She was close with the wardrobe and make-up departments. They're mostly young women, and they're the ones who make the actors look good for the cameras, so talent always treats them nice. And the DoP too. The rest of us come second."

He angled his body one way then the other, as if wrestling indecisive thoughts. "I feel awful about what happened, Detective. I know you might not think it, but I have a responsibility to everybody out there." He pointed towards the tent's entrance. "I'm captain of the ship. I can't afford to go to pieces when the shit hits the fan. They look at me to keep us on track."

"That's what Marissa says, too."

"She pays them, I lead them. I know people like you think this is just a film, so what's the point? Entertainment gets people through the darkest times of their lives. We may not be doctors or soldiers, but we're not irrelevant. And for every single person out there, this is their livelihood. It's what pays the bills."

"I understand. You said your contact with Karen was minimal—"

Simon raised a finger. "The night she arrived, I'd arranged dinner at the hotel for Will, his harpy fiancée, Marissa, and Karen. A *getting to know you* deal."

"And how was that?"

Simon pulled a face. "Will and Kelly spoiled everything, as usual. They constantly fought and brought the tone down. Kelly was very hostile towards her. I don't think she's mature enough to separate Karen and Victoria as characters. One seduces her fiancé, the other is an actress playing a role."

"So they argued?"

"Oh, no. Kelly is the bitch-queen of passive aggression. I think Karen handled it really well. It left a nasty taste in my mouth. And Freya turned up, complaining about some shit. Her and Will have history. Unsurprisingly, Kelly hates her, too, and she seems to think she's part of the production."

"What about Marissa?"

Simon considered his words before answering. "We're mature enough to get on at a professional level. It's not a secret that she's no fan of mine."

"Which makes me curious why you took this job. As I understand it, you and Will are hardly friends, either."

Simon gave a dark chuckle. "All water under the bridge. It wouldn't be show business without the deceit and back-stabbing."

"So you forgave Will for sinking your passion project?"

Simon's eyebrows raised. "Is that what you've been told?"

"Your financiers and distribution wanted him onboard. So when he refused, they pulled out."

Simon shook his head in bewilderment. "That would've been a more honourable reality than him sleeping with Marissa." Garrick's surprise made him laugh. "Don't be a prude, Detective. A hot young star sleeping with a producer to get a part? It's not all lecherous Harvey Weinstein's seducing young girls. It works the other way around, too."

"Is that why you and Marissa split up?"

"Of course!"

"Will said he'd heard stories of abuse…"

Simon laughed humourlessly. "You've met her, right? She'd hand me my balls in a napkin."

Garrick wondered who was lying — Will or Simon. And why would they? He had to remind himself that image was everything in this business.

"The kid has his beefs. Especially when he's threatened to be written out of the series," Simon added with a smile.

"Who, Will?"

"His agent has been playing hardball and giving the studio a headache. Plus, there's a new kid on the scene. Duncan Reynolds. He took the last series by storm and is featuring at the end of the movie." Simon lowered his voice and glanced around. "Only a few people know about this. But we're killing Will off at the end of the film. Well, it's going to be ambiguous. We're shooting two endings. But it'll leave the studio open to terminate him. You're supposed to sign an NDA before you know about that. So I didn't tell you."

It surprised Garrick that Fanta hadn't mentioned such a pivotal plot point when she read the script. Simon was already a step ahead.

"It's not in the script, if you read it. The crew has an alternate ending that we'll shoot. Then a scaled down unit will shoot the other finale. The one I intend to use."

"I imagine Will isn't happy about that."

"He swore he'd close the production down. But there's little he can do about it."

Simon's situation suddenly became clear. "You wanted to direct this just to kill Will off?"

The smile on Simon's face broadened. "Sweet revenge. And I get paid by Marissa to do it. And by directing it, I get a steer on how the script should play out. Anything I can do to make that little punk suffer."

"And Marissa?"

"Like I said. Water under the bridge. She's pissed off I'm here, but she's stuck with it."

"How does she feel about axing Will's character?"

"She thinks it will kill the show. She's dead against it."

Garrick weighed up the additional information. "Who do you think killed Karen?"

Simon didn't even hesitate. "The only one crazy and jealous enough, in my opinion, is Freya Granger."

12

G arrick was halfway to the manor and lining up questions to pose to Freya Granger when DS Chibarameze Okon phoned him. He stood quietly to the side of the grand house to take the call, watching the ebb and flow of crew members moving from the woods to the production village. It put him in mind of a military campaign.

"Hi Chib, what've you got?"

"I'm heading back after speaking with Michael Harris."

"Ah, the battle-ready agent."

"He wasn't so tough today. He actually came across as quite nice. But I think that's because he's worried about his client."

"Well, they're planning on writing him out of the series."

Chib gasped. "Really?"

Garrick had forgotten she was a fan of the show and regretted letting it slip so soon.

"Keep a lid on it for now," he cautioned.

"Mr Harris is concerned about Will's safety. It seems Will

has received a few death threats recently. That's nothing new for the famous, apparently, but the timing worries him."

"Does he have the letters? We should run them past forensics."

"Letters?" Chib chuckled. "It's all done via email these days, sir."

Garrick inwardly groaned. He didn't feel old, but every day there were subtle reminders.

"And he says they're sent from different email addresses, which are easy enough to set up. So he's assigning a body-guard for Will in the next few days. The agent's opinion is that it might be some nutcase fan who isn't happy about Will's engagement to Kelly Rodriguez, and maybe was jealous of Karen being cast in such an intimate role with him."

Before they parted, Simon Wheeler had warned Garrick that tomorrow there would be a hundred extras on set for the wedding scene in the marquee. It was to be a visually impres-sive set piece for the middle of the movie. He wondered just how coincidental the agent's timing was when over two-hundred potential threats surrounded his star client.

"He was reluctant to tell me something else about Will. He's been suffering from depression for the last six months. A doctor in LA diagnosed him as bipolar. To be honest, I think that concerns his agent more than the death threats."

"Fair enough, Chib. But this is all very Sadler focused." He couldn't help but feel that the movie star's gravity was distorting the investigation. "What about the victim?"

"Still drawing a blank, I'm afraid. However, there was something Fanta flagged up. She was looking into why Freya quit university. She didn't. They kicked her out for threat-ening another student. Some girl who claimed Freya was stalking her. Things got heated and police involvement was threatened. Then Sir James charges in with his cheque book to calm everybody down. They pressed no charges on condition Freya left."

"Did it get physical?"

"I don't know. I was going to track the girl down and talk to her."

Garrick looked at the house he'd been about to enter. The family's private quarters were at the back, including Freya's room. She hadn't been on-set all day, which Gina Brown had commented was unusual. He wondered if she was watching events from one of the many windows on the first floor, putting him in mind of Norman Bates's mother in *Psycho*. Then he decided he was being too melodramatic.

"Send Liu. I'd like you to be here tomorrow. What was Freya's defence for stalking the girl?"

"She claims she was being bullied because of her friendship with Will. They'd been in some photos together at the time and suddenly her friends were accusing her of being upherself."

Jealousy is a powerful emotion that leads people to commit the most baffling crimes. He'd postpone talking to Freya until Fanta had dug into the facts. Then another thought struck him. For a moment, he wondered if he'd imagined it and was almost hesitant to bring it up.

"Didn't Fanta say Freya did some theatre work?"

"I'll check. I'm talking to Kelly in three hours' time."

"Good. Ask Wilkes to dig deeper into the Granger family, too."

He finished the call and assessed the growing leads that were pulling the investigation in different directions. With scant resources, he would have to narrow the focus to the

Grangers and the feud between the director and his star. The most irritating dead end was how Karen Dalton's phone had got into Will's trailer. What was the actor hiding?

As he was pondering this, his phone rang again. He answered it without thinking, but immediately recognised the voice on the other end. And it sent a chill down his spine.

Staplehurst was an average village south of Maidstone, with the charm sucked out as modern orange brick semi-detached houses had consumed it. It now conveyed the air as the sort of place people were happy to leave. Garrick supposed that was a fair description of any commuter town. He followed the directions on his sat nav as he passed south bound through the town and turned left onto Frittenden Road. The narrow B-road passed the cricket club and several nice-looking houses hidden behind fences and gates. At the behest of his sat nav, he slowed and turned into a driveway. The gate was open, and just beyond, Garrick recognised the parked black Hyundai i40 Saloon. He stopped alongside and took in the small yard. It was an outbuilding of the farm beyond. He listened but could hear nothing aside from the occasional bleating sheep in the adjacent field.

"Thanks for coming, David."

Garrick jumped and whirled around. DCI Oliver Kane stepped from the building's entrance. From the moment he had called, Garrick had been on edge.

"Oliver." As they were apparently now on a first name basis, Garrick wouldn't let him have the upper hand.

"I know you have your hands full at Laddingford Manor, so I wasn't sure you'd have time."

"I was intrigued, and you were as vague as usual."

Kane had made a point of constantly turning up when Garrick wasn't expecting him, so a phone call requesting they meet was something new. The mere mention of Garrick's case was probably just a polite comment, but he couldn't shake the paranoia he experienced every time the DCI was around. He was convinced that the Met detective had been following him on several occasions, and this had made him even more curious about meeting and discovering just what Kane was playing at.

Kane gestured around. "Have you been here before?"

"No. But I'm guessing John Howard owned this?"

"He had a long-term lease from the farm. Come inside."

Garrick followed and braced himself for what he might find. He hadn't been expecting an unremarkable empty room. It was a single rectangular space, with whitewashed walls and power sockets halfway up the same long wall. Sunk into the floor were a pair of drainage grids, covered in metal grates. He suspected the shed had once kept sheep or cattle. A pair of naked bulbs hung from the ceiling.

"You've dragged me away from my investigation to show me an empty room?" Garrick shook his head in disbelief. "I've seen plenty of empty rooms. D'you know it's an offence to waste police time? And you've done it to the both of us."

Kane gave a smile that didn't quite reach his eyes. "Your friend, John Howard, used this as a storage space. We lost more or less everything else when his house in Wye burned down."

Garrick knew this all too well. He had been fighting for his life with John Howard as the flames spread.

Kane continued. "We tracked this down via a standing order on his bank statement. When we arrived, this was all filled with boxes."

He took out his phone and showed Garrick pictures taken with plain-clothed officers entering the building. A huge sturdy wooden table took centre stage. Large brown archive boxes were stacked against one wall, and three large rolls of plastic stood in the corner. Garrick had an idea where this was going, but let Kane continue.

"There were various items in the boxes. Mostly metal parts. There was a blowtorch too, so it seems as if those lamps he sold were made here."

John Howard had killed three women, and used their skins to create macabre lampshades, a remnant of a hideous practise some Nazis performed during the war. He sold them to online buyers using sites on the dark web. Once Garrick had cracked the case, he had been quickly ushered off it. John Howard had died in the fire at his home, with Garrick as the only witness. Understandably, he couldn't take part in the wider investigation.

The fire had destroyed the skins, leaving only scorched metal frames. However, the shed at the back of his property was unscathed, and the police found flayed human skins drying inside.

"But we also found two books here, bound in skin. DNA matched it to one victim, Galina."

Garrick was hardened to the most gruesome crimes, but the image of the young woman dying at Howard's hands filled him with anger. With a sudden wave of dizziness, his migraine made an unwelcome return. He steadied himself against the wall, but Kane hadn't noticed. He selected another picture to show Garrick. A close-up of the table. Now he could see it was constructed from thick rail sleepers, set on a steel frame. There were deep grooves etched on the surface. He zoomed in on the photo when he noticed dark stains on the wood.

"Blood," Kane confirmed.

"John skinned his victims at the crime scene."

"And the blood doesn't match them." Kane spread both hands to where the table had been. "These were different victims. And they were carved up right here."

"Christ. How many?"

"Six different people. None of which we have yet identified."

Garrick slowly turned, taking the room in. "What did he do with the bodies?"

Kane pulled a face. "That we don't know either."

"That's nine victims in all."

"And we're talking about a relatively short period. We have estimated the earliest blood here dropped in the summer of last year. To put that in perspective, the Yorkshire Ripper murdered thirteen women over a five-year period."

"He's been busy..."

"We have reason to believe he leased other properties. The rental of this place only goes back to May last year."

Garrick put his hand across his mouth as the implications sank in.

"You think there will be more?"

Kane hesitated for a moment. He flicked through several photos, but then put his phone away.

"We can theorise about that, and there's no evidence at the moment. So you might see, with an operation this large, why I'm curious how people didn't notice even the slightest unusual behaviour from him."

"You have all my statements on that."

Kane nodded and held up an apologetic hand. "Don't misunderstand me. I don't think he did this alone."

Garrick didn't know how to react and just let out a confused "*Huh?*"

"For a start, we know he had a network of people who placed orders for his, uh, unusual art. But on those dark web sites, we also discovered people making requests."

"Requests?"

Kane nodded. "I can't go into that right now. We are coordinating with police forces from all around the world, but it's difficult, maybe impossible, to trace the buyers. As I told you, Europe and America were his favoured destinations. I think it was to meet some of his clients in person. Do you know he was charging upwards of thirty-grand for a single lamp? And people paid that."

"There's a hell of a lot of depravity out there."

"For sure. But I don't think he was just meeting buyers."

Garrick held up his hand to stop him. With the other, he pinched the bridge of his nose as his head pounded.

"Oliver, I know there are things you can and cannot say about the case. I appreciate that. And I am extremely interested in what the bastard was doing, but I can't cope with your passive-aggressive line of questioning. I don't know what you expect me to say about any of this. I just wish you'd get to the bloody point!"

After a deep sigh, Kane's right hand flexed into a fist as he searched for his words.

"He had partners all around the world. Not just buyers. I believe he had some affiliation with other killers."

Garrick couldn't stop his disbelieving snort. "What? Like a club? A killing club?"

He expected Kane to correct him. Instead, the DCI nodded.

"Exactly like that."

"Holy shit."

"My sentiments exactly. This isn't just some hypothetical.

We've found messages. People sharing stories, and even techniques."

"That is beyond sick."

"My investigation is just scratching the surface. But there is a... a coincidence that I need some clarity on."

"I'm not a big believer in coincidences."

Kane nodded. "That's something we shared then." He licked his lips before continuing. "Did you know the last time he'd travelled abroad was in November?"

Garrick tried to think back that far. "I've told you that I didn't see him regularly, and October, November, I hadn't seen him much. So I don't recall him telling me about that."

"He went to America."

"That doesn't ring any bells."

"He flew to New York. Then on to Chicago."

Garrick felt his blood grow cold.

"He flew back to the UK the day after Thanksgiving."

The room was spinning so badly that Garrick pushed himself against the wall for support and closed his eyes.

John Howard was in the same State, at the same time his sister had been murdered.

13

G arrick had to stop during the drive home. It was dark and the crisp white beam of his headlights cutting through the inky black country lane seared his retina. He pulled in at a gate leading into a field and rubbed his eyes. He had to get a grip.

He'd been numb when he left DCI Kane. Garrick had a deep mistrust for coincidences and believed there was something larger at play. It had been a staple instinct during his police career. Yet now, he was facing one that tested the very limits of acceptance: a serial killer and his sister in the same state at the same time.

A coincidence.

It had to be. Illinois was the size of England and Wales combined. His sister had been on a road trip across several states with her fiancé and even they didn't know where they were. He hadn't seen John Howard to tell him she was there, so there was absolutely no way he would have known.

His head throbbed, and he wished he'd brought some ibuprofen with him. From now on, he'd keep some in the car.

He had to pull himself together and calm down, so he shifted his attention to Wendy. It was almost miraculous that he felt the tension in his shoulders suddenly melt, and his grip on the steering wheel slacken.

He reminded himself about the date they'd set for the weekend. One filled with the potential of passion. One that would elevate their relationship to the next level. A level he hadn't been certain he was ready for, yet now he was craving.

Without trying, Wendy had become the cornerstone of everything positive in his life.

Then, without warning, he felt the fingers of doubt claw at his stomach.

Wendy who?

He opened his eyes and blinked in confusion. What was her surname? Surely he knew? But for the life of him, he couldn't remember. He pulled his mobile phone out and unlocked it. There was a text message waiting for him, but he ignored it and skimmed through the apps he'd downloaded, searching for the *HeartFelt* dating app on which they'd met.

It wasn't there.

His stomach knotted, and he trembled. Was she real? Had he imagined the relationship? What the hell was going on?

A distant part of him recognised he was in the grip of a panic attack. He'd never experience one before. He'd never been an especially anxious person, but in a single night, a lifetime of anxiety was suddenly descending on him.

He gripped the hard steering wheel tightly. The firmness was reassuring. He forced himself to take long breaths. He listened to the rise and fall of his idling engine. The rev counter occasionally dipped, threatening to stall, but the elderly Land Rover then coughed enough to keep running.

Of course, the app wasn't there. He'd deleted it after the first month of seeing Wendy...

... Sinclair.

The name slapped him in the face. Wendy Sinclair. Of course, he knew it. With a shaking hand, he checked his phone's call log. There were plenty of calls to and from Wendy. He laughed at the absurd notion that she'd been a figment of his imagination. His levity was quickly squashed by the knowledge that his anxiety had been, at the very least, aided and abetted by the tumour in his head. He was deluding himself by not getting it treated, and it was deluding him.

His finger hovered over Wendy's number. He could really do with speaking to her right now, but he was in such a state she may discover just how fragile and broken he was.

Pull yourself together, David.

He wouldn't call her. There was no way he could fake being cheerful, and she would lace the conversation with questions about Broadhaven that he was in no mood to answer. After five minutes, the pain had subsided, and he felt he could continue driving. Heading home and sinking into a warm bath, followed by an early night, would do wonders for him.

Before he put his phone back in his pocket, he checked the text message, in case it was from Wendy. It was an unknown number; probably trying to phish his bank details or something. He tapped it to read.

Meet me in the marquee. 6 am. Have something important.

Garrick frowned. His initial assumption was a wrong number. But the mention of the *marquee* was too *coincidental*. But who had this number? He'd given it to Simon Wheeler,

Will, Marissa, and Sir James. Why the theatrics? If it was important, why not just phone him now?

The phone number was oddly familiar. He racked his memory, trying to recall who had given him a number recently. Then he remembered.

It was the same one that had called Karen Dalton's mobile phone when he'd found it in Will's trailer.

He'd taken the bait. After a restless night, David Garrick wasn't feeling in optimum condition, and the vague message had confirmed his suspicion that somebody in the production team was playing games. To what end, he didn't know. Anybody with evidence could have gone straight to the police, but this had all the hallmarks of somebody he'd spoken to. At least that narrowed his list of suspects down.

The security guard at the gate waved him through. The press had quickly tired of the story when it was mooted as nothing more than an unfortunate accident. Once again, Garrick lamented it was a grim society that was no longer interested in a young woman's death just because she wasn't famous.

There were already a few vehicles in the carpark as the wardrobe department and office bound members of the team were the first to arrive. Everybody's first port of call was the craft services where breakfast was just being served.

A mist rose from the surrounding fields as the sun gently broke through the light cloud cover. There was a slight chill to the air, so Garrick thrust his hands into his Barbour's pockets as he quickly followed the path through a copse of trees and out to the field where the marquee stood. The pleasant scent of petrichor flared his nostrils as morning dew sank into the parched soil. He stepped over several bright yellow pedestrian cable covers, neatly bridging the power cables stretching from the marquee to a generator on the other side of the estate, well out of range to spoil the sound recording. A soft glow from the lights within the marquee lent an ethereal sense to the scene.

In just a few hours' time, the field would be under siege from a hundred extras and about the same complement of crew. All for a few minutes of screen time in a film. Right now, there was nobody around.

He was forty yards away when a loud crash came from inside and shadows shifted across the translucent walls. The sound of shattering glass almost masked a squeal of pain. Garrick sprinted forward, casting the entrance flap aside as he entered. Three of the six large film lights were switched on, positioned to cast shadows at the far end of the marquee where Garrick glimpsed movement - but his attention was drawn to the fallen light in front of him. It had crushed somebody underneath. The thick glass covering lens had shattered on impact, and one of the four metal barn doors – used to control the amount of light shining through – had sliced through their thin blue jacket and into the person's left shoulder blade. Blood pooled out across the smooth plastic floor panels that carried the weight of the equipment.

"Give me a hand!" he yelled to whoever it was at the far end of the marquee. He knelt next to the body and was struck by the pungent smell of burning flesh, not too dissimilar from a barbeque. With the glass broken, the powerful tungsten bulb was searing into the person's face. Garrick touched the side of the light – but immediately pulled away as the hot metal burned his palm.

"Dammit!"

He shifted position to plant his feet under the body of the lamp and pushed. It was heavier than he thought, and his knee cricked in complaint, but the light rolled just enough for the barn door to slide out of the shoulder like a knife from a wound. Blood sprayed from the gash, but at least he had stopped the bulb from burning flesh.

In the heavily shadowed illumination, he could now see it was Gina Brown, the production's Second Assistant Director. The light had partly crushed her skull and her short, blonde hair was matted with blood. The left side of her face was barely recognisable from the raw red flesh that ran from the centre of her forehead, across her left eye, and turned her cheek into a red-raw pulp.

Her blood covered Garrick. A gasp escaped her mouth, more blood bubbling on her lips. Her hands twitched. She was still alive.

"I need help!" Garrick bellowed as he pulled off his Barbour and used it to stem the blood flowing from her shoulder wound. He looked around for the other person he'd swore had been present. There was nobody. He was too far from base camp for anybody to hear him, and the set was filled with fakery, offering nothing useful to soothe a burn.

Recalling the dozens of first aid kits he'd seen in the production trailers and knowing there was a unit doctor – if they'd arrived yet – Garrick had little choice but to pull his coat tighter over the wound and scoop Gina up in his arms. He slipped in the pooling blood, but kept his balance as he ran for the exit. He left a streak of crimson across the tent flap as he pushed through and out into the misty field.

14

P eople flocked to help as soon as Garrick had stumbled into the nest of production offices. First aiders rushed to do what they could to stop the bleeding. After thirty-minutes, a Leonardo AW169 helicopter came soaring to the scene, sporting Kent Air Ambulance's distinctive black, white, and turquoise livery. They airlifted Gina Brown to the trauma unit at Tunbridge Wells Hospital.

Garrick made use of the shower facilities at base camp, but his jacket, shirt, and trousers were soaked with blood. He was still trembling from the incident when he returned to the marquee. DS Okon had just turned up and was keeping everybody at bay until the forensic team arrived.

Garrick joined her, wearing a flouncy white shirt and a tight pair of Victorian period riding trousers that Chloe Aubertel had found for him. Despite the gravity of the situation, Chib struggled to keep a straight face.

"How're you feeling, sir?" she asked, turning her head away so he couldn't see she was biting her lip.

"Bloody awful," he replied, taking in the broken light and

the congealed blood spread across the white flooring. It was hot inside the tent, and the temperature was steadily rising.

Chib circled around the light. "As far as I can tell, the legs look intact. Somebody must've pushed it over."

"It was a bloody good shot to smack her right in the face. She must've been on the floor already."

"Did you know she was the one who contacted you?"

"No. And I don't know what she wanted to talk about. She texted me from the same number that rang Karen's phone when I found it. It's not the same number she uses for the production."

"She has everybody's number as part of her job. But since she knew Karen was dead, why would she call her phone?"

"I thought it was a loud ring tone." He saw Chib frown as she thought back to when he'd found the mobile. He laughed at his own naivety. "It's as if somebody wanted me to find it." He didn't blame her for looking doubtful. "Gina called me from the same number. Was it a coincidence, or did she want me to find it in Will's trailer?"

"In order to set him up?"

"Or she knew it was there and was too afraid to come forward."

They walked around the marquee, taking care not to disturb anything before the SOCO team arrived.

"Why are only some of the lights on?" Chib asked. "That's what's making it so hot in here. Did Gina put them on, or her attacker?"

They reached the opposite end of the tent. There were another two exits to the left and right.

"I definitely saw somebody else in here." Garrick looked at the flap nearest to him, the same one the shadowy figure must have bolted through. He didn't dare follow. The culprit would now be long gone, and he didn't want to disturb any potential tracks. His mind was racing in overdrive, vanquishing all feelings of fatigue. "Security should've a list of everybody who was here. I don't think the attacker is stupid enough to have checked-in, so look for disparities. People who were seen, but had checked in later, that sort of thing."

He noticed Chib contemplating the fallen light.

"What's on your mind?"

"You're working on the assumption that Gina arranged to meet you here. Why would she do that? This is far enough from the unit base to be private, but she wouldn't run any risk of being caught if she'd taken the meeting *anywhere* else but here."

"If she didn't call me, who did? And why bring both of us here if she was the intended victim?"

Chib shook her head in bewilderment. "I can't think of any connections between Gina and Karen." She was suddenly reflective. "Kelly Rodriguez had a lot to say about Will."

"Nothing about Karen?"

"Oh, she didn't like Karen at all, but she saw her as just another of Will's sexual conquests. The reason she says they're separating is that he sleeps with everybody. She claims he's hit on every girl on set."

That didn't surprise Garrick, but it clearly concerned Chib.

"And she doesn't think they're all willing. She claims that he's a sexual predator."

"Ah..."

"And that throughout the last series, she'd heard rumours of him groping extras, and making them feel uncomfortable."

"Were any complaints made?"

"None that I've heard of."

"I'll ask Marissa."

Chib sucked her teeth. "I was thinking it would be better if I did that."

Garrick gave a gentle chuckle. "It's okay, Chib. You're not offending me. The middle-aged male wallowing in to talk about sexual misconduct probably isn't the best approach. Although, tread carefully. They'd slept together, too."

He quickly filled her in on the Simon Wheeler angle.

"Where's Fanta today?" he asked.

"You sent her to Cambridge to dig around Freya Granger's story, remember?"

Garrick considered ordering her back after this morning's incident. She'd be good at nosing around the crew to sniff out any hints of misconduct, but they also needed to eliminate Freya as a suspect.

"Okay, here's a hypothetical." He indicated the fallen light. "Gina was a whistle-blower on a certain person's misconduct. Maybe Karen put up too much of a struggle or threatened him when he hit on her? We only have his word that she was the one who wanted to speak to him. What if *he'd* lured her to the folly?"

Chib pulled a face. "That is going out on a limb."

"He was literally found on top of Karen's body."

"He'd taken a hallucinogenic, and aren't we working on the assumption someone had slipped it to them both?"

"And her phone was in his trailer."

"But you just thought it was planted."

They looked at one another in silence. He eventually broke it. "Okay. I admit it's thin."

DC Sean Wilkes noisily entered the marquee and took

everything in with a quick glance. "Morning, sir, Chib. I came down as soon as they told me..." he trailed off as he did a double take at Garrick, dressed in figure hugging jodhpurs and a billowy shirt. He burst into laughter. "Bloody hell, sir. What happened to you?"

Garrick scowled. "I'll tell you what's bloody happening. I'm going home to get changed while you knuckle down and start getting me statements."

With his dignity shredded, Garrick stormed from the marquee, ignoring the giggling pair behind him.

By the time he'd returned home and dressed more casually than he preferred in jeans and a navy-blue shirt, as he'd nothing else clean, he received a message from Chib stating that Gina had suffered such terrible head injuries and burns to her face that they'd put her into an induced coma. The light had cracked her skull open, so they feared severe head trauma. Her windpipe was partially crushed, and the doctor saw signs of strangulation. She'd lost a lot of blood after severing the cephalic vein and was in a critical condition. The medical team was doing everything they could for her.

He arrived back at Laddingford Manor and was barely out of his car when Marissa Carlisle ambushed him.

"You can't close down my shoot!"

Garrick noticed Chib had been taking the brunt of her wrath until that point. Simon Wheeler was leaning against a parked Range Rover, but he said nothing.

"We've just had an attempted murder. And by the way, your Second AD is in a coma and fighting for her life."

Simon hung his head in shock. The news took the fight out of Marissa, but only for a few seconds.

"I have two coachloads of extras waiting to go on-set–"

"It's a crime scene!" snapped Garrick. "Right now, I don't

care if you film something inside the house or up a damned tree. It helps to keep you lot where I can keep my eye on you. But the marquee is out of action."

"For how long?"

"For as long as it takes!"

Marissa snarled, spun on her heels, and marched towards the row of trailers. "Let's see what the studio says about that!"

"Who cares?" Garrick muttered. He saw Simon throw him an apologetic look before wordlessly following her.

"She can't take no for an answer," said Chib. "Sean is taking statements from the crew that were here at the time. There were sixteen of them. Nineteen, including catering."

"And the family?"

"The Grangers were all home too, although Sir James has since left for an appointment in London. Will came down for breakfast at his hotel. And Simon and Marissa arrived about fifteen minutes after you left. SOCO is on site now." Chib led the way to the crime scene. "Oh, and it's Zoe and her team."

"Zoe?"

"The Australian whose name you never remember."

"Is it that obvious?"

"Embarrassingly so, sir."

He heard Zoe's bellowing voice before they entered the tent. As soon as they did, the Australian held up a blue-gloved hand to stop them.

"Don't trail your dirty hooves in here, Dave!"

Garrick stopped in his tracks. Six white-suited forensic officers were checking the light and surrounding area. Another pair dusted the tent flap the figure had escaped through. Zoe walked up to the detectives.

"Your DS told me your muddy trotters were all over my crime scene. You know how to make life difficult for me."

"I'll try to find a tidier crime scene for you in the future," grumbled Garrick. The adrenaline that had been pumping through his system earlier that morning had gone. Heavy limbs, weariness, and impatience replaced it.

"Lights are full of prints, but that ain't surprising because the crew move them all the time. And there are hair fibres everywhere, which I think will be useless. Same for the exit over there. So, if your suspect is amongst the crew, then I don't know how you're gonna eliminate prints. So far, our best evidence are the footprints outside where they did a runner. As far as we can tell at this stage, they circled around towards the house."

Garrick said nothing, but he was certain the fleeing person would've masked their identity. So far, they had sown confusion and misdirection, so he was sure they wouldn't have overlooked something so obvious as leaving easily identifiable footprints.

Zoe pointed to the floor around the light. There were muddy scuff marks amongst the blood. "This looks to me like a struggle. But not a very long one."

"So she was taken by surprise or by somebody much stronger than her?"

"I guess so. Once we isolate your paw marks and hers, we'll have a better idea, but I don't think we're gonna get much outta this scene. DNA, prints, hair, whatever, most of it will match almost all the crew, I reckon."

"Let's draw up a list of people *least* likely to have come into contact with any of this," he said to Chib. "Like Freya, for example."

"I have some good news," said Zoe with a half-smile. She crossed over to a blue sheet on the ground. They had laid a single plastic evidence bag on it. She handed it to Garrick.

Inside was a mobile phone. "I found it over here." She pointed under a nearby table. "It's unlocked and according to the photos on it, it's hers."

Garrick didn't need to open the bag to wake the iPhone up. He went into the pictures and saw hundreds taken of various sets and actors.

"They'll be for continuity," said Chib, who had made a valiant effort to find out what each person's role was amongst the crew.

A quick scroll through the emails showed they were all related to the shoot. His next stop was the messaging app. There were dozens that appeared to be related to the film. One name caught his eye. She showed Chib: *Karen D*.

Tapping on it revealed there was no message. Just a recorded voice memo. He played it and a woman's voice, which he assumed was Karen's, spoke in an agitated tone.

"*I told you I didn't want to do this! I don't feel right doing it, so leave me alone or I swear you're finished!*"

Garrick's eyes went wide. "We better take a deep dive into how Gina and Karen knew each other. I think we've overlooked something quite big here."

15

I n the incident room, DC Harry Lord had completely rearranged the evidence wall. With the actors' head-shots, it was looking more like a spread from Cosmo. Karen Dalton took centre place with Gina Brown's crew ID photo just to the right.

Pictures of Sir James, Freya, and Will Sadler were in the row beneath. Marissa, Simon, and Kelly Rodriguez took up the bottom row. Along the top ran a timeline of Karen's movements.

The team had assembled, with Fanta only returning from Cambridge in the last fifteen minutes. Garrick brought everybody up to speed with recent events. He was knackered as the previous night caught up with him. DCI Kane's revelations had plagued him every moment his mind had drifted away from the case. Thinking about his sister led him down paths he'd rather not venture.

"Gina Brown remains in a critical condition." Images of her burned face haunted him every time he closed his eyes. It was a savage attack. "The doctors confirmed someone had strangled her. Possibly from behind. She'd fallen, and then the light had been deliberately toppled on top of her."

"Then we're looking at somebody physically stronger," said Harry thoughtfully.

"She was a slip of a girl," said Garrick. "So that's just about everybody."

"There are easier ways of killing somebody." Everybody looked at DCI Fanta Liu. From her tone, she was still taken by the excitement of the movie shoot. For Garrick, Chib, and Wilkes, the novelty had worn off, and Harry had never cared. "What I mean is, strangulation seems a spur-of-the-moment thing to do after an argument. The magic mushrooms took some forethought, and if I wanted to silence somebody, why not use a knife and stab her in the back?"

"A good point, gruesomely made," said Garrick. "Her phone number is the same one that dialled Karen's, leading us to discover it in Will's trailer. Will denied Karen had been there, and we have no witnesses placing her there either. However, Gina was in and out of everywhere. Will confirmed she'd been in his trailer dozens of times."

Harry absently played with his crutch, batting it from one hand to the other. "The only reason Gina would call it was so that you'd find it. Did she plant it, or had Karen Dalton been in there and dropped it?"

"Which would mean Will is lying," Chib pointed out.

Garrick sat back in his seat and slowly half-rotated as he thought through the timeline. "If Gina had planted it, then what reason did she have to call me?"

"If she *didn't* put it there, it suggests she somehow knew the phone was missing, and she was trying to find it," said Wilkes. "How would she know it was missing?"

Fanta snapped her fingers. "I was told the director went

nuts at everybody because actors had their phones just visible in pockets during scenes, and some had even forgotten to take their watches off." She caught Sean's look and explained. "An iPhone looks bad in a period film, which is why wardrobe or make-up usually keep that sort of thing. They have a safe in the trailer."

"Gina had received a voice memo from Karen," said Garrick. "There was only one, but I suppose she could've deleted the others. We still need to check Karen's phone to confirm she sent it." He played a copy of the message stored in the virtual evidence folder. Karen sounded stressed.

"*I told you I didn't want to do this! I don't feel right doing it, so leave me alone or I swear you're finished!*"

"Any theories about what's playing out here?" he looked at his team in turn.

Harry spoke first. "On the surface it sounds as if Gina has been coercing her to do something, and now Karen is threatening her back. Sounds like a reason Gina would want to find the phone before us."

"Which would imply that Gina, a lowly Second AD, had some power over the new starlet," said Chib doubtfully. "That doesn't seem right. People said they got on fine. That voice message could've been forwarded to her by Karen."

"Why?" mused Garrick.

Chib pursed her lips. "For safety, maybe? If the original recipient was somebody else, then perhaps she sent a copy of the message to Gina for safe keeping? Just in case something happened to her. It may also explain why Gina was so keen on finding the phone and reached out to you."

From the nods around the room, Garrick had to agree the theory had merit. "But of course, that leads us no closer to the context of the message. Presumably it was intended for the killer." He fell silent for several moments, then added. "Everybody seems to have a motive."

"We have a limited number of people who were on set that early." Wilkes consulted his notes. "Several security guys, craft services, a few of the electric and camera crew, wardrobe, and some from the production offices. Marissa, Will, and Simon arrived later with separate drivers. And the Grangers were all home at the time. They're my prime suspects."

Garrick counted the family members off on his fingers. "Sir James is demanding more money for the use of the estate, and every delayed day is an extra ten-grand in his pocket. Freya was friends with Will, but that has gone stale since she said that she wanted to be an actress. And Lady Helen... I have nothing on her."

All eyes turned to Fanta. It took her a moment to take the cue.

"Cambridge! Yes!" she peeled back the pages of her note-book. "Freya was reading history at St Johns the year before last. Michaelmas term was bumpy." She glanced at the others. "That's Cambridge-speak for the first term." She continued reading. "She didn't make friends easily and behaved as if she was above the other students. Which, believe me, is difficult to do in Cambridge. She had real prob-lems with a classmate, Emma Rowan, from Bristol. Emma claims that Freya was obsessed with her. Stalking her, wanting to be her friend, and generally acting creepy. I asked others about this, and opinions vary. Some people think Emma teased her over her friendship with Will Sadler because she was jealous. It's a little murky. In October they appeared to be friendly, but it broke down quickly after that. Just before Christmas. Emma accused Freya of breaking into her room and destroying a pile of textbooks. The College became involved, but it didn't go to the police. Freya denied it, and there was no evidence that it was her. Before the end of term, Emma claims Freya threatened to kill her. Several students confirmed it, but again without evidence. The College cautioned Freya."

Fanta turned the pages in her notes. "Fast forward to Lent term. There was an altercation in February that left Freya with a black eye. Emma punched her, but Freya didn't report it, and Emma denied it to me. Others saw it happen. Then something occurred on March 6th. In a bar, Freya struck her with a bottle. Luckily it didn't break, but Emma dropped to the floor where Freya then tried to choke her."

Garrick leaned forward in his seat. "This had been reported?"

"The whole bar saw it, but nobody knew what the altercation was about. College security became involved, and Emma had to have stitches. Old man Sir James hurried down to smooth over the situation. According to Emma, he offered her money not to go to the police, and she accepted the cash." Fanta chuckled at Garrick's disapproving expression. "She's a student. She needed the cash more than justice, and she got into Cambridge on her own merits, not family connections. Sir James made her sign an NDA. There were heated words with the College, and Freya left."

"Expelled?"

"They say it's a private matter. So unless we want to make an official request, they're being discreet. But, asking around, everybody thinks they expelled her. They think that Freya was obsessed with Will. She was always dropping hints they had a secret relationship. Others say Emma was a fan of Will's. I mean, who isn't?"

Sean gave a disapproving harrumph. Fanta shot him a dirty look before she continued.

"Emma and Freya may have had a brief relationship, or a fling at least, in October when they were getting on. Emma is now nearing the end of her second year and says she's not had any contact with Freya since."

Chib put her hands on her hips and nodded knowingly. "I think Freya is a definite person of interest. If she's really obsessed with Will, it's reasonable to think she may have a grudge against Karen Dalton."

Harry nodded. "Don't underestimate the rage of a failed actress." Chib looked quizzical. "My Claire's a failed actress because of me. She had to quit the dream to raise the kids. And she is amazing at that," he added defensively. "I just don't think she quite forgave me."

"Should we bring Freya in for questioning? It might unnerve her enough to let something slip?" Chib suggested.

Garrick gazed long and hard at the evidence wall. He couldn't deny that Freya made a perfect suspect, and he was certain she hadn't been completely forthright with them. But something was still niggling him.

"Karen Dalton was asked to do something. Was it by Freya? They had only met three days before she died. That message suggests it was somebody who had a secret she thought might derail her career just as it was starting."

"And let's not forget the sex pest rumours," Sean Wilkes said with a little more glee than he should. "What if she sent that to Will?"

"You mean Will lied to us about the reason they were meeting?" said Garrick. "I want you down there tomorrow asking questions," he said to Fanta and Sean. "We're hearing second and third-hand rumours, but nobody wants to say anything because they're worried about their career. Start getting people to open up."

"Why me?" said Fanta, folding her arms in a huff.

"I thought you wanted to be at the forefront of the investigation?"

"Yeah, but..." she couldn't think of an excuse to refuse.

"And keep an open mind."

She nodded, but didn't look happy about it.

Garrick glanced at his watch. It was almost six, and he was feeling wasted. He also wanted to make an important call, which he was afraid he'd now left too late.

"Can somebody take Karen's phone out of evidence and comb through it for any voice messages, texts, anything that she sent to Gina, Freya, or Will."

Sean raised a finger. "I'll do it."

"Good. Chib, wheel Freya in for tomorrow afternoon." Chib nodded and said something in reply. Garrick wasn't listening as a thought occurred to him. "Before you do, didn't Will get her a few theatre jobs? Did we find out what they were?"

"Not yet."

"There are two ways to fail at being an actor. One is to marry Harry; the other is to get a couple of roles to fail in. Find out who was in those productions and cross-check them with everybody on the production team." He stood up and took the thin, dark green rain jacket from the back of his chair. His Barbour was still in with forensics, and even when he got it back, he doubted the blood would wash out.

"If you can just hold on a minute, sir," said Chib, looking at her laptop screen. "The forensic report has just come in."

While he waited for Chib to skim through the summary, he saw Superintendent Drury at the office doorway, beckoning to him. He sighed. He would never get out of here at this rate.

Chib summarised. "All the prints they found matched the registered crew. No surprises there. Although smudge marks on the lighting stand and the power switch to turn them on, indicate they were last touched by a gloved hand. The footprints match a man's size nine shoe. Specifically, the soles are the same as the riding boots from the costume department that were made especially for the shoot. And they made sixty pairs for the film, with nearly all of them in allocated and in the wardrobe truck."

Garrick threw his hands in the air. "Great!"

Chib raised a finger to stop him. "Although the impressions were not even…" she reread, but still didn't understand. "The weight wasn't distributed evenly in each step." She looked at the others for clarification. "Somebody with a limp?" She continued reading. "The assailant ran around the house and towards the east side of the estate. They couldn't find any further signs."

"What's on the east side?" Garrick asked.

"More woods and a field. Then the old gatehouse, which isn't used anymore."

"Is it a way out of the estate?"

"It's a padlocked gate but, yes."

Nobody needed to vocalise how that could further complicate matters. They had whittled down a list of people who had been on site, but if there was another way of entering, then they could be back to square one.

Exhaling loudly, Garrick put his coat on and yawned. His mind was elsewhere when he gave a curt goodnight and joined Margery Drury in the corridor, and they strolled to the car park.

"You heard all that, ma'am?"

"Enough of it. I believe you're allowing them to continue filming?"

"Without the coachloads of extras, yes. The moment I close the production, people will leave. We can't force any of them to stay. Every suspect will be scattered around the South East. Some out of the country."

"I think that's a sound decision." Garrick had been expecting a flea in his ear, so felt relieved. "I had the head of the studio call me directly to thank me, which was nice. They want this wrapped up as quickly as possible."

"Do they think I'm enjoying it?"

Drury was uncharacteristically hesitant. "There is a certain amount of pressure, David. I also had the Culture Secretary call me."

Garrick was surprised. "Are you telling me a government cabinet Minister is a fan of the show?"

"He is. He also pointed out that film services are a premium industry in the UK. Worth three point four billion pounds. Obviously, having anything upset that will ruffle government feathers." She sighed. "And I believe the Prime Minister is a huge Broadhaven fan too."

"Wonderful…"

"Your Molly Meyers called me. Several times."

"You've had a busy day."

"Apparently, you're not returning her calls. She is reporting about Gina Brown's accident on the Six O'clock News. Of course, that's two *accidents*… so questions are being asked."

Garrick didn't trust himself to say anything. If the press could mess things up, they would. They stopped at the door leading to the rear car park. Drury was clearly not going any further. She checked they were alone.

"I know DCI Kane told you a little about his investigation."

The word *little* made Garrick wonder just how far out of the loop he was. He nodded.

Drury squeezed his shoulder. It was a firm, friendly gesture, but had it been the other way around, Garrick thought somebody would shout '*harassment*'. Still, that was Drury. She didn't care, and she hadn't reached such a senior position without being a force of nature. What worried Garrick was just how quiet and composed she was being.

"Don't let it impede the investigation," she said. It sounded friendly enough, but Garrick's paranoia infused the words with a deeper warning. "And I received the report from Dr Harman."

Garrick instinctively glanced at his watch. That was who he had wanted to call.

"She said she was done with me."

"Yes, she is. I'm relieved. It turns out you're not a detective on the verge of a nervous meltdown. It would have been a shame to lose you. Goodnight, David."

Garrick reeled. In Drury's lexicon, that was a tremendous compliment.

"Night, ma'am."

He quickly left the building and couldn't shake the feeling that Drury had been behaving out of character. Had she? Or was it him? Was he seeing yet more things that were not there? After last night's anxiety attack, he felt he needed Dr Harman more than ever. He worried he wasn't on the verge of a breakdown; but he had stepped over the edge of one. The merest hint that his old friend, John Howard, had killed his sister was just beyond reason. Even though the man was a murderer, he just couldn't stretch reality *that* far.

By the time he reached his Land Rover, he'd called Dr Harman's practice and got the answerphone. He left a message to call him back. Even while standing, when he closed his eyes, he could feel sleep embrace him. Yet he knew the moment he got into bed he'd be wide awake with either Kane's speech or the case playing through his mind. He'd head home and double up on the sleeping tablets.

He was pretty sure that the case was now on the right track as they targeted Freya, but something told him that Will Sadler wasn't completely out of the picture yet. He was confident the dominos would start toppling tomorrow as layers of the case revealed themselves.

He just didn't know how hard things were about to fall.

16

Knowing the film makers left for set quite early, Garrick ambled into the Footman's Hotel at a more respectable breakfast time. It was after nine and the dining room was empty, save for two bored teenage waiting staff. They informed Garrick that the Broadhaven team had left early as usual, and the only other guests were German tourists who'd checked in yesterday and had already breakfasted.

Garrick sought the manager, an officious man who introduced himself as Mr Dillinger. He'd been schooled in the obsequious levels of customer service the rich demanded, and everybody else found irritating. He even wrung his hands with theatrical concern when Garrick asked about any complaints from the staff regarding the production team's behaviour. Dillinger was dismissive and filled with praise about them, so naturally, Garrick didn't believe him. It took several attempts, and the threat of asking each staff member to come to the station for a formal statement, before Dillinger agreed to let Garrick speak to them himself.

They tracked the housekeeping manager to a top floor corridor where she was overseeing a cleaner changing the bedsheets in the rooms.

"Mrs Smith, this is *Detective* Garrick."

Mrs Smith spoke in a soft Scottish accent and had obviously attended the same customer service course Dillinger had.

"How may I help, Detective?"

Her delivery was smooth and relaxed, but Garrick caught the fleeting glance towards her boss when he'd introduced him. Garrick turned to Dillinger and positioned himself between the manager and the housekeeper.

"Thank you, Mr Dillinger. I'll take it from here."

Dillinger made no motion to leave. "It's no problem at all. I'm quite happy to assist."

"And your help isn't needed," said Garrick firmly. He took some gratitude from the manager's nervous twitch. Unable to see Mrs Smith, he bobbed and weaved slightly, but Garrick didn't move. Eventually, he excused himself and scurried back down the corridor.

"I can't imagine working with a man like that." Mrs Smith's smile didn't falter, but her polite chuckle was confirmation that she agreed. "I wanted to ask you about the film crew staying here."

"I thought you would."

"Oh?"

"I've seen the news." Garrick had avoided it. "And I'm sure Mr Dillinger has said all he can."

"I wasn't asking him. I was asking you. I imagine Mr Dillinger spends a lot of time in his office or prowling around the reception or dining room. Why come all the way up here and mingle with the proles?"

Mrs Smith's smile tightened. "I couldn't say."

"I didn't imagine you would." Garrick's smile broadened. The polite reply would have been to deny his accusation. Now he had a firmer understanding of the boss/worker relationship. "And I imagine in a quality establishment like this, discretion is absolute priority. Especially when it comes to famous people staying."

"As they say, discretion is our watchword."

Garrick kept checking over Smith's shoulder. The cleaner in the room had dramatically slowed her pace as she eavesdropped.

"Did you or anybody else hear any commotion when Kelly Rodriguez was staying here?"

Smith's smile tightened. "They were a boisterous couple."

"Boisterous in a good way?"

"In a loud way. One could almost think they enjoyed arguing, but I know Mr Sadler is an excellent actor."

"Did this increase when Karen Dalton arrived?"

"It's difficult to judge. Mr Sadler is fond of arguing with many people."

Garrick watched the cleaner plump the same pillows for the third time as he tried to unravel Smith's meaning.

"So he's always shouting at somebody?"

"Boisterous," she quickly corrected him. "I suppose that's his manner, and after a good few snifters. I don't think he and Ms Dalton had any vigorous discussions, though, if that's what you're asking. Sadly, she wasn't with us long enough."

"What did he argue with others about?"

"Sir, it wouldn't be prudent to listen in." Her placid exterior was cracking. She glanced into the room and noticed the cleaner's half-hearted work. Garrick expected a stern reprimand, but Mrs Smith just sighed. "One could guess it was about the film. I heard the term 'written out' being bandied quite a lot. Of course, not being part of the business, I assumed it's a technical term." She added the last statement with no conviction at all. Garrick was beginning to understand the cast of Broadhaven were not the only people in the hotel with acting skills.

"And how would you describe Will Sadler's attitude to your staff?"

Mrs Smith's glacial pause was all too telling. "He is very generous with gratuities. Then again, I suppose it's not his money."

"But there is no suggestion of anything... inappropriate?"

Mrs Smith raised an eyebrow. "Good Lord, Detective. I cannot recall the last time somebody was inappropriate to me. Not even my husband. Perhaps you are barking up the wrong tree?" This time there was no mistaking her glance towards the cleaner. "Mia used to tend Mr Sadler's room."

"Used to?"

Mrs Smith stepped into the room, and Garrick followed. Even with her back to them, Mia tensed.

"Mia has been with us for two years, and in my view, she is exemplary. Aren't you Mia?"

Mia turned to face them. She was a young, petite Filipino woman, who Garrick considered quite beautiful. She stared at the ground, refusing to meet his eye.

"She is quite shy. Not prone to talking tattletale. And as she's on a visa from the Philippines, she is very circumspect."

"Hello, Mia." She still didn't look at him. "Mrs Smith tells me you used to clean Will Sadler's room. Is there a reason you stopped?"

She looked uneasily at Smith, but said nothing.

"As I have repeated *many times* to Mr Dillinger, Mia is one of the hotel's finest employees." She looked pointedly at the girl. "And is not in any trouble of any kind. No matter what she thinks."

Mia picked up the hint and hung her head. She spoke with a soft accent.

"I don't like Mr Sadler."

"That makes two of us," said Garrick with a lazy smile. "I don't like his television show."

She smiled back and looked at him for the first time.

At six feet, Garrick towered over her. He sat on the end of the bed to appear less intimidating.

"Aside from his acting, why didn't you like him?" Mia looked at Mrs Smith. "Mia, this is just a conversation between me and you." He held up his hands. "I'm not recording anything or making any notes, and you don't have to talk to me if you don't want to. It's just a friendly chat, so you can educate me."

From the corner of his eye, he saw Smith give her a slight nod of encouragement.

"He kept touching me." She was hesitant. "He would call room service and I would come." She faltered and looked deeply embarrassed.

"It's okay, Mia. Tell him what you told me. You've done nothing wrong. Mr Dillinger is in his office."

Mia took a deep breath. "When I came into the room, he'd hold the door open just wide enough that I would have to rub past him. If I was carrying something, he would touch me." She blushed as she indicated her breasts. "One time he asked for fresh towels. I came up, and he was in the bathroom with a towel around his waist. He told me to take it off to change it." The silence drew out as she recalled the incident. "I put the new towel down and ran out."

"Did he ever say anything overtly sexual to you?" She shook her head. "And did you complain about him?"

"I told Mr Dillinger."

"And what did he do?"

Mai looked at the floor, prompting Mrs Smith to take over.

"He told her not to be silly. When I found out, I immediately put her on different duties, and Dean took over room service. Apparently, Mr Sadler wasn't happy and complained to Mr Dillinger, so Mia was put back on his floor."

"That was the end of it?"

Mia shook her head and looked forlorn. She gathered her courage.

"I was turning down his bed when he arrived back early. He was in a foul mood."

"When was this?"

"It was the night before his fiancée arrived," Smith said.

"He pushed me face down on the bed. I tried to get up but couldn't. His hand went up..." She was mortified as she tugged at her short black dress. "He said that I had teased him for too long. That he would have me deported if I didn't..." she gave a shuddering breath.

"He raped her, Mr Garrick. There is no other word for it. And no ambiguity."

Garrick's old school reaction was to ask if she was sure, but he knew that was a pathetic question. Like every other officer, he had to attend courses on how to deal with sexual harassment and to believe the victim first and foremost. He felt awkward and wished Chib was here with him.

"There are people you can talk to–"

Mia shook her head and wiped a tear away with the back

of her hand, and with it cleared any impression of vulnerability away. She stood defiantly.

"What did Mr Dillinger say to that?"

Mrs Smith stood with Mia and placed a hand on her arm. "I think you should pop along and have a break for ten minutes." She gave a maternal smile. Mia nodded and hastily left the room. When she was out of earshot, Smith continued.

"I gave him hell, Detective. I threatened to call the police there and then. Needless to say, he had his opinions about that. Saying it was her word against his. She's on a work visa. He's a millionaire who can afford an army of lawyers. The matter was dropped, and I put Mia on different duties. After that, Mr Sadler didn't complain about having Dean attend to his needs."

Garrick felt his shoulders tense, and the urge to dole out a little GBH to the self-important actor and the manager gripped him. Unfortunately, that wasn't his style, although he could imagine DC Harry Lord crossing the line of justice.

"This is a serious allegation."

"And one I don't think Mia will pursue. She's too afraid of what will happen to her. I gave her the number for Beach House in Maidstone."

Garrick was aware of the sexual assault centre and their sterling work in a difficult and demanding area. At least they would be a protective space for her. "Have there been any other incidents?"

"I made discreet enquires. Some of the girls are in love with him, others think he's a creep, but nobody has come forward. Only Mr Dillinger and I know about Mia. It wouldn't do her any good if the others found out. I knew his reputation as a Lothario from day one."

"What do you mean?"

"There's always a steady flow of girls from the set coming and going in the evenings."

Garrick wondered just how many of the crew had slept with Will. He took out his phone and showed her a picture of Gina Brown.

"Does she look familiar?"

She gave it a quick look and nodded. "She was here regularly. Overworked, in my opinion."

"And what about Karen Dalton? Did she ever go into his room, or vice versa?"

"I couldn't say."

He switched to a picture of Freya. "And her?"

"Mmm. I have seen her around," she said disapprovingly.

Something occurred to Garrick. "Mia has been with you for two years? So didn't she see Will the other times he stayed here, when he was filming the TV series?"

"Oh no. This is the first time he has stayed with us. The producer and executives from the studio regularly stay, along with actors who are only filming for a few days. I believe the *stars,*" she dripped sarcasm, "usually have their own apartments for the duration."

Garrick stood up and scratched his chin. To his surprise, he felt a couple of day's stubble growth. When was the last time he looked in the mirror?

"I'd like to take a look in Will's room."

"Don't you need a search warrant for that?"

"Well, technically, it's not his home. But I suppose..."

"Or would an access card do?" said Smith with the ghost of a smile as she offered her universal key card.

Will's suite was pristine since Garrick was last here. They had replenished the Jack Daniels; the bed was made, carpet cleaned, and a fresh fruit basket sat on the coffee table amongst a few personal possessions. Mrs Smith stayed at the door as Garrick walked to the bed. He felt a flush of anger over what he had done to Mia. He opened the bedside table. Inside was a Kindle and a packet of tissues. He tapped the Kindle's power and saw he was halfway through a screenplay. It appeared to be a science fiction movie.

The shirts, jeans, and two pairs of beige combat trousers in the wardrobe were hung neatly. Will had obsessively folded three jumpers and several polo tops on a shelf. It looked more like a display in a clothing shop. Garrick picked up a pair of tan loafers and checked the size. Size nine.

The bathroom was filled with skin care products, a range of Cowshed shower gels and shampoos, and a Braun electric razor. A small white box caught his attention. The pharmacy label read: *lamotrigine.*

A quick Google on his phone revealed it was a mood stabilizer given to bipolar patients. He took a photo of it and returned to the room. There was nothing out of place. Nothing incriminating. He was about to leave when he noticed something on the coffee table. A keyless fob for a car. He pointed to it.

"Whose keys are these?"

Smith shrugged. "I assume they're Mr Sadler's."

"But he has a driver."

"He also has a car."

Garrick blinked in surprise.

Mrs Smith led him to a red Audi Q5 in the staff car park. Garrick thumbed the key fob, and the central locking clicked open. He noticed the Hertz hire sticker on the licence plate.

"That young woman from your photograph dropped it off the day he arrived. He uses it to run around when he's not on set."

Garrick mentally kicked himself. All this time, they had assumed he was reliant on his driver when Will could go where he wanted. Of course, he had filmed in Kent so often he knew the area well.

He circled around the car. It was dusty because of the lack of rain. He opened the driver's door. There was an empty McDonald's cup in the holder, and a screwed-up brown bag in the passenger footwell. Garrick leaned across and opened it. Inside was a crushed burger container and a cardboard fries holder. Drawing back, he noticed dried pale dirt on the pedals.

"Can you fetch a sandwich bag or something from the kitchen?"

Mrs Smith returned a few minutes later with one. Garrick used his own car key to scrape some of the dirt into a bag. He sealed and pocketed it. He checked the front of the hotel.

"I take it you have security cameras?"

"Of course."

A message on Garrick's phone told him that Freya Granger was on her way to the station. He took a deep breath as he tried to marshal his own thoughts into something more coherent than speculation.

17

"I hadn't expected to see you," said Garrick as he dragged his chair nearer to the desk in the interview room.

Wearing his threadbare tweed jacket, Sir James sat rigid and stern, giving nothing away. He refused a drink, but Freya nursed a cardboard coffee cup in both hands. She wore a red checked shirt underneath an over-sized Aran jumper, with skinny blue jeans, and gave the impression that she was bored.

"This is an informal interview, is it not?" said Sir James. Garrick nodded. "And I used to be a barrister, so I'm taking the opportunity to find out what's going on."

Chib entered the room carrying a mug of matcha tea for Garrick and a coffee for herself. She sat and smiled pleasantly.

"Thank you for both coming in," she said, taking out her notepad. "And you have saved us a little more time by coming along, Sir James. I wanted to talk to you, too."

There was a hint of a scowl; he hadn't planned to be of help. Chib pressed on.

"As you know, we have to eliminate everybody from our enquires. Freya, how long have you known Gina Brown?"

"How is she?" Freya asked with concern.

"Still in critical condition. It was a brutal attack." Freya nodded, but said nothing. "So, how long have you known her?" Chib prompted.

"Since she came onto the last season of Broadhaven. She was the Second AD for that, too."

"And you had no contact with her beforehand?"

"I think she has made that clear," Sir James interjected.

Garrick sat back and folded his arms. His lordship had jumped straight to aggressive defence, which in Garrick's experience often indicated something was being hidden.

As ever, Chib was unruffled. "I shall take that as a no, then. And would you say you were friends?"

Freya shrugged. "Not particularly. Acquaintances, maybe."

"Oh." Chib checked her notes. "But I see you regularly stayed in touch between the filming of the series and the start of the movie. Her phone records show you both talking every month. I don't see some of my closest friends that often."

"I don't see what your personal life has to do with it," snapped Sir James.

"It helps provide a mutual understanding of degrees of friendship. And since Gina's in a position to know about upcoming productions," she looked knowingly at Freya, "and you're a budding actress."

"I *am* an actress," came Freya's tart reply.

"Of course. Your theatre work." Chib riffled noisily through her notes. It intrigued Garrick. His DS was exceptionally well organised, and would have all the facts lined up, yet she deliberately took her time. He noticed Freya's composure was breaking as she gently tapped a finger against the side of her cup. "Ah, here. You had several auditions in London for theatre shows. And I see you'd been cast twice last year. Once in *Mood Music*, at the Other Palace, for a four-week run, and the other for a new production at the Troubadour in Wembley. *The Sins of Agatha*, but they recast you."

Freya's eyes narrowed. "They were terrible people. Impossible to work with."

"I spoke with the director. He claimed you didn't get on with the rest of the cast."

"They were a bunch of amateurs."

"I really don't see what the ebb and flow of my daughter's *hobby* has to do with anything."

Like a disgruntled child, Freya huffed and sat back in her seat with folded arms. She gave her father a dirty look but said nothing.

"My point is that Will Sadler pulled some strings to get you both roles." Freya shrugged. "Rightly or wrongly, you were given short shrift in *Mood Music*."

"The director was a complete dickhead," Freya snapped.

"I saw the reviews," Chib said with cruel good humour. She was enjoying needling Freya. "But back to *Agatha*. The bickering amongst the cast was centred around you. There were accusations of bullying. Some of the other women in the cast said they felt you were stalking them."

Garrick shifted in his chair. He wasn't up to date on Chib's line of enquiries, and he was curious to where she was heading.

Freya gave a laugh that sounded forced. "The entertainment world is full of frail egos and prima donnas."

"And which are you?"

Garrick inwardly cheered Chib's rapier response. She was bloody good. He made a note never to get into an argument with her. He could feel the frost emanating from Freya.

"I let it wash over me."

"Good for you," Chib said jauntily. "Although you haven't been in anything since. Is Will no longer pulling you any favours?"

Freya looked hurt and remained silent.

Sir James put his palms on the table and leaned forward. "Once again, I don't see the relevance. My daughter came to talk about the terrible incident with Brown, not seek career advice from the police."

Garrick disliked Sir James with each passing moment and had to reign in his compulsion to interrupt. It wasn't as if Chib needed help, and the gnawing throb of a migraine was beginning again. His thoughts drifted to the letter on his kitchen table. He needed to open it, and he needed to come clean about his condition to Wendy. It was unfair to continue a relationship that might have a very terminal future.

Garrick was so astonished by his own morbid line of thought that he'd missed what Chib had asked, but it provoked a lively response from Freya, who was waving a hand dismissively.

"I don't need him to help my career! He told me about auditions, but I got the parts on my own merits."

"I'm sure your talents played a key factor... only the director for *Agatha* said Will had *considerably* pressured him to cast you."

"He's lying!"

"I feel you're wasting our time," said Sir James.

"I'm sorry about that. I only raise it because Gina Brown

was a production assistant for *Mood Music*, so you got to work with her for the entire run."

Freya shrugged. "You asked if we knew each other *before* she came on season four. Mood Music was just after. And you asked if we were friends, not if we'd worked together."

Chib nodded. "Forgive me. I will be more precise with my questions. Karen Dalton was working part-time at the Troubadour at the front of house."

Freya became agitated. "We were in rehearsals. We didn't fraternise with the theatre staff. They're just there to tidy up from the previous production."

"Would it surprise you to learn they cast Karen in your role after you were fired?"

"I wasn't fired," Freya snapped indignantly. "I quit."

"I'm only going off what the director and producer told me."

"And I didn't know nor care who replaced me. After I left, I had no interest in the production at all. Why would I? I certainly didn't meet my replacement, if that's what you're insinuating."

"I'm not insinuating anything. I'm merely establishing facts and pointing out coincidences. When was the last time you saw Will before he arrived to do the film?"

Freya gave it a little thought. "It was the last season of Broadhaven. After that he did a film that will be out in September, I think. He's been busy. No, we met in London at Soho House, four months ago."

"Is it fair to say that you haven't spoken to him as much as you used to?"

"Like I said, he's busy."

"So you must've been looking forward to seeing him again?"

"Of course."

"I suppose when his fiancée arrived, and he had to get to know his new leading lady…"

"We're all professionals," Freya sniffed, then snatched her cup from the desk and sipped.

"Kelly doesn't appear to like you."

"She doesn't like anybody. Ask the crew. Nobody likes her either. She's only a reality TV star," she added disparagingly.

"How would you define Kelly's attitude towards Karen Dalton and Gina Brown?"

"From what I hear she loathed Karen, and I don't think she was aware Gina existed – even if Gina stood in front of her, waving her arms."

Chib tapped her pen on her pad, and Garrick recognised that an awkward question was coming.

"How would you characterise your relationship with Will?"

"We're good friends."

"Is it a sexual one?"

Sir James slammed his palm on the table. His face was livid. "How dare you ask such questions! If you have brought us here to insult us—"

"Not at all," said Garrick calmly. "We could have done that anywhere. As DS Okon told you at the start, this is to eliminate you *both* from our investigation."

"None of these questions are related to the two women!"

Chib drew herself upright in her chair and gave a hawkish smile. "Then I shall get to the point. Where were you both when Gina Brown was attacked?"

"In bed," said Freya. "My own bed," she added pointedly.

Sir James "I was in the kitchen. I rarely sleep when we're being invaded by a production. And as you know, I had an early appointment in London."

"And who can verify this?"

"My wife can. And Freya came down when the helicopter made all that racket as it landed."

"So the three of you can verify each other's movements?" said Garrick.

Sir James nodded. "Yes."

"And you were all in the house when Karen Dalton was murdered. And again, you can verify this?"

Sir James's eyes narrowed as he nodded again.

"But other than the three of you, nobody else can confirm where you were?"

Sir James leaned forward and treated Garrick with a predatory look. "Allow me to put it this way, Detective. Is there a single person who is claiming otherwise?"

Garrick answered with a smile, then addressed Freya. "Are you aware of any allegations towards Will from the crew?" When she didn't react, he added, "Specifically sexual allegations."

"There are a lot of women who get weird around him. It comes with the job."

"Shall I take that as a yes?"

Freya shrugged. "Nothing specific. But people often take things the wrong way. Everybody is a snowflake these days."

Chib opened a laptop and accessed the audio files stored on HOLMES. She played the message from Gina's phone. Garrick studied Freya's face carefully.

"Can you shed light on it?" Chib asked.

"I've never heard it before. I don't know what she's referring to."

"We also retrieved Karen Dalton's phone. It wasn't with her personal effects when she died."

That got a reaction from Freya.

Garrick indicated the laptop. "That message sounds a little like blackmail, wouldn't you agree?"

"If she's threatening to finish somebody, it sounds as if she is the one doing the blackmailing," said Sir James.

"Any idea who that may be?" Chib asked.

Freya slouched in the chair and shrugged. "I do not know. And I think you don't either."

So far, the entire day had done nothing for Garrick's spirits. Back in the evidence room, he told Chib and Harry Lord what he'd learned at the hotel about Will forcing herself on Mia.

"What an utter scumbag," Harry growled vehemently.

"She isn't reporting it at the moment," Garrick pointed out. "But I would be shocked if she's the first." He soaked in the evidence wall as Will added Mia's name and underlined the word 'raped'.

"The problem right now is a sudden abundance of motivation," said Chib as she paced the room. "Freya Granger knew Gina Brown from both Broadhaven and the theatre. She also worked in the same theatre as Karen Dalton, but denies they ever met."

"And Karen then gets Freya's role when she's fired," said Garrick. "A role it seems Will Sadler pulled some favours to get her."

"Freya has a history of violent and antisocial behaviour at Cambridge," Chib added. "And she was at the location for both incidents."

"To be fair, only because she lives there," Harry pointed out.

"Which brings me on to Gina's assailant," said Garrick. "We've been working on the assumption it has to be someone amongst the crew who was already on-set, or living in the house," he added darkly. "Placing Simon Wheeler, Marissa Carlisle, and our favourite heart-throb, still at the hotel. Now it turns out Will has a car. As part of his contractual rider, he got one so that he's not confined to the hotel when he has time off. He had plenty of time to go to the house and get back before his driver was scheduled to collect him. And the shoe size SOCO found fleeing the marquee are the same as his."

"But it's all circumstantial," Chib said, busying herself with her phone. She had found something that interested her. "I thought so! Will's agent said he was bipolar, and you found the tablets that confirm he's getting treated for it. Do you know what else is supposed to help combat it? Psilocybin. Magic mushrooms."

Silence fell as they pondered the various scenarios. Finally, Chib spoke up.

"What if Gina knew about Will's behaviour and was blackmailing him? Maybe using Karen as the new girl to set him up? She's been a Second AD for a while and hasn't been promoted."

Garrick rubbed his unshaven cheek thoughtfully. "Then why drag Karen into it?"

"If things have gone too far, maybe she was calling you to blow the lid off everything?"

Garrick shook his head. "It's too cloak and dagger. She could've phoned me instead of texting and ended it there and then."

Chib's phone rang. She glanced at it. "It's Fanta." She walked to the corner of the room to take it.

Harry Lord flexed his injured arm. "Who has anything to gain from setting things up, so you and Gina are there at the same time? That doesn't make sense. No. She wanted to see you there for a specific reason."

Chib hung up and returned to the conversation.

"Fanta and Sean have been nosing around all day. The atmosphere is gloomy. Nobody is openly talking, but she gets the vibe that Will is a bit of a sex pest. Nobody enjoys being left alone with him, although there are also stories some girls are happy to sleep with him."

"But nobody will risk their careers on speaking out," said Garrick. He stood up and approached the evidence wall to study the faces in the hope they would spill some secrets.

"I think Sir James has a lot riding on this," Chib said. "He's protecting his daughter from something. What about the other voice messages on Karen's phone?"

"There were none," said Harry. "So she either deleted any she made, or there is just that single one on Gina's phone."

Garrick tapped Simon Wheeler's photo. "Simon has the most to gain from all of this."

Harry snorted. "By sabotaging his own film? Wouldn't that tarnish his career, too?"

"If it's spiralled out of control, like it seems to have done, yes. He's aware of Will's reputation. What if he's the one trying to expose it?"

"How does killing Karen Dalton factor into that?"

Garrick wagged his finger. "I'm not saying Wheeler killed anybody. But it feels as if there is somebody pulling the strings. And let's face it, as a director, he's the most qualified to do so."

18

For another two days he left Fanta and Wilkes to pry information from the crew about Will Sadler's behaviour, but it was increasingly apparent the culture of secrecy was so tight that an outsider couldn't penetrate it.

Chib spoke to the staff at the hotel, but there were no more tales of assault from the other women there. She obtained the CCTV recordings from the morning Gina had been attacked. Somebody had used Will's car at 5 am that morning and returned thirty minutes before the driver arrived to pick Will up. Unfortunately, the security camera had a fine spider web nestled across the lens, rendering the image blurry. It could have been anybody taking the car.

He regularly checked in on Gina's condition. She was still frail and kept in the induced coma. There was no chance of her talking any time soon.

It was now the weekend. His much-anticipated evening with Wendy had arrived. He'd spent half the day contemplating cleaning up the fossil she'd found, but instead had tried to tackle his idling Land Rover engine. He was no mechanic, and after watching several troubleshooting videos on YouTube, he'd concluded his car had simply reached the end of its life and he'd have to bite the bullet and buy a new one.

He tried not to think about the fact everything he was doing was a displacement activity to stop him from thinking about John Howard. When his sister had gone missing, he'd received regular updates from the American police force dealing with the crime. As time dragged on, the calls became less frequent. Her body still hadn't been found, but he'd been kept in the loop with the latest developments, such as fibres and blood discovered in an abandoned car. The theory was that she'd been abducted before being killed. After that, he'd heard nothing further. He had disliked the constant updates but found the prolonged silences more disturbing. Deep down, he doubted they would find her body. Too much time had passed, and unlike the UK, America still had plenty of space to bury secrets.

He'd also avoided opening the letter from his doctor, which still lay on the kitchen table. The intensity of his migraines had eased, and a part of him was once more feeling optimistic that it was a sign the tumour hadn't grown at all. Denial was a seductive comfort blanket. He noticed that his own inner monologue had increased, and he wished Amy Harman would return his call. Even if it was just a few sessions paid out of his own pocket. But she hadn't, and he wondered if there was some ethical code he was violating, just as she'd signed him off as a patient.

The media interest in the Broadhaven incidents had died down, and Garrick imagined that Molly Meyers was being wooed by the studio to keep the narrative favourable.

He bounced a few text messages back and forth with Wendy, who was preparing an Italian meal. Something safe and simple, she'd warned him. He'd eaten little all day, so he was hungry enough to eat anything – no matter how bad it was. As the evening drew near, Garrick was surprised by how anxious he was feeling. He ran a bath and prepared for a long soak, but after twenty minutes bathing in hot sudsy water, he was uncomfortable and eager to get out.

He took time to shave and sighed at the dark circles under his eyes. There were more wrinkles than he remembered last week, and his hair was getting more salt 'n' pepper by the day. As he rubbed in some hair gel, he regretted not getting it cut. Age was wearing him like a crumpled sack. He'd even put on a stone or two, which he felt around his waistline and lower back. He couldn't fathom what Wendy saw in him. Then again, he'd always expressed surprise when any woman shown an interest. They accused him of being modest and thought he qualified as a dashing figure. Compared to somebody like Will Sadler, he felt like an abomination.

It just goes to show, whatever a person looks like on the outside, nobody can see the rot within, he mused darkly.

He put on his favourite white Ralph Lauren shirt and a pair of tan trousers that were tight at the waist, before swapping the shirt for a black one when he remembered Italian food was on the menu. A squirt of Polo eau de toilette from a bottle that was so old it made him wonder if it still smelled as it should, or did it now really smell like toilet water? He couldn't tell.

Then he was ready to go.

After another ten minutes of swearing at his car as it failed to turn over, Garrick called for a taxi. He finally turned up at Wendy Sinclair's house thirty-five minutes late.

It was the first time he'd stepped inside Wendy's modest terrace house. For most of their dates, they'd parted at one or the other's car. A few of times he'd taken her home, dropping her off outside and watching as she made it safely through the door.

Now, at 41, his heart was hammering as he nervously sat on a sofa that had seen better decades and was held together by a fluffy scarlet blanket. Embarrassed, she explained most of the furniture were hand-me-downs from her parents. A low coffee table sat before a modest TV hung on the wall. Three Ikea bookshelves covered most of the walls of the small living room, all crammed with books. Garrick nosed through the titles to discover she was into her classics, with several well-thumbed Dickens and Bronte volumes. Any spare wall space had photos of Wendy with her parents, and another woman he discovered was her older sister.

Garrick had always steered the conversation away from family. She'd picked up the hint and never pressed the issue. Confronted by pictures of her family, he now found it awkward not to ask questions.

Wendy's parents were still alive and living in Rochester. Her mother had worked as a school receptionist, and her father in insurance. Her sister, Paula, was married and had a two-year-old. Being a full-time mum had freed her from a series of mundane office jobs.

A radio channel played through the TV, providing forgettable background music as they chatted. Wendy poured them both a sparkling white wine, which tasted perfectly fine to Garrick's primitive pallet, and she asked the inevitable question about his own family.

"I'm originally from Liverpool."

Wendy laughed. "That's what it is! Your accent occasionally pops back, subtle, but I couldn't place it. I had you pegged as a Northerner."

"It only comes back when I'm tired, which is most of the time lately. I left there as soon as I could and joined the police. My parents both passed away not so long ago." He wasn't in the mood to elaborate. "And I had a sister."

Wendy nodded, but the use of the past tense wasn't lost on her. Garrick sipped his wine and felt the desire to tell her more. To unload his pent-up angst about how he and Emilie had never got on. How they had become estranged until their parents had died. Then the slow attempt of redemption to pull them back together. That had been cut short by her death at the hands of a killer.

A killer that may have once been a close friend.

He desperately wanted to unload it all on Wendy. He felt comfortable with her. Trusted her. And it had been far too long since he could talk to anybody like he could with her. Luckily, the rational part of his brain was screaming at him to shut up. It was a story guaranteed to slaughter the mood. He certainly shouldn't finish it by telling her about his tumour.

He steered the conversation onto her job. She was a classroom assistant, and clearly overqualified. She dipped in and out of stories about how some teachers had become robots, desperate to get through the day just so they could go home. Their passion for teaching children had long since dried up. Wendy felt demoralised and trapped. On one hand, the job was grinding her enthusiasm. She felt she'd left it too late in her life to train as a teacher. She wanted to leave and explore another career – but if she did, then she'd be leaving the kids to a lacklustre education. She had to break her personal cycle, but lacked the courage to do so.

"I'd thought about working in a library, but I'm not sure

there are many left. Or a bookshop. But then I realised I wouldn't make enough money to even live here. And this place is rented, so any hope for a house of my own is just wishful thinking at this stage in my life."

She filled their glasses up again, and the conversation drifted to travel. She wanted to see the world, but had only been as far as Europe a few times. Garrick felt the same, and other than a few trips to France and Spain, he hadn't seen the world either. His sister had inherited the adventure gene, not him.

The room was warm, but not unpleasant. Wendy wore a blue dress that he thought looked fantastic on her slightly curvy figure. She curled close to him with her black tight clad knees on the couch. She smelled wonderful, too. Garrick didn't have the sophistication to break it down to anything other than *pleasantly musky*. He was feeling a little aroused, but with the low lighting coming from a pair of lamps, and several battery-powered candles on the mantle, the atmosphere was having a soporific effect on him, which wasn't helped by the wine. He wasn't a drinker, but seeing how he wasn't driving, he threw caution to the wind.

Wendy served the food: good old pasta and meatballs with garlic bread. Whatever the sauce was, it lit up Garrick's taste buds. He was afraid his compliments sounded over the top for a meal Wendy admitted was basic. Mortified, she confessed that it was a Charlie Bigham's Meatballs Al Forno from Sainsbury's, and that she wasn't a very good cook.

"Thank God for that!" Garrick laughed. "I'd hate the idea you had some super culinary skills I could never match."

"Ready meals for life!" she laughed, and they clinked forks together to seal the deal.

When they'd finished, with the promise of New York

cheesecake for dessert later, she put a hand on his knee and looked him straight in the eye. The simple motion expelled any fatigue Garrick had been feeling, and the desire to kiss her overcame him.

"I know you have been looking forward to this as much as I have," she said in a low voice, her fingers pressing deeper into his thigh and turning him on. "So we're going to do it. There's no turning back."

Then, slowly and tortuously, she raised a Broadhaven DVD box set between their faces.

"I cannot wait," said Garrick in a tone that made it clear he'd rather have his eyeballs gouged out.

Wendy tittered as she put the first disk in the DVD player. "It makes me feel as if I'm helping you with your work. And you might notice I haven't asked you any questions about the actors."

"That reminds me." Garrick went into the hall to retrieve a gift from his jacket pocket. He returned and handed her a crew cap. Fanta had pulled through and snaffled the cap. She'd even got a signed photograph of Will Sadler for him, but considering where Will would soon be heading, he didn't think it was an appropriate gift to give his girlfriend.

As he sat back next to her, she was whooping with joy as she put the cap on and kissed his cheek. Garrick wasn't listening. It surprised him that he'd once again referred to her as his girlfriend. The term made things suddenly seem more serious, yet made him feel a decade younger. And he had to admit she looked sexy in a baseball cap, with her long blonde hair poking from the back in a ponytail. Her wide smile highlighted the dimples he'd found adorable on her *HeartFelt* profile picture, and her blue eyes sparkled in the low light.

"How do I look?" she struck a heroic pose.

Beautiful, thought Garrick. Instead, his inner shy schoolboy sputtered, "Nice. It suits you."

You dickhead, Garrick fumed to himself. The fact they were sitting here at all was barely believable after an abysmal first date. Something they still had never had the courage to address. Luckily, she had been desperate enough to contact him again.

But they had put the inevitable off for long enough, and she put the pilot episode of Broadhaven on. He had never seen the show before, but he instantly recognised the theme tune. It had become embedded in British pop culture over the last few years. The familiar sight of Laddingford Manor appeared, and he was impressed by how a talented cinematographer could turn the familiar aging edifice into something mysterious and romantic. The story unfolded with the beautiful young Lady Victoria being told by her parents that the family had lost their fortune and it was vital that she should marry so they didn't lose the estate.

Garrick was no expert, but he found the dialogue stilted and unrealistic. Everybody in the world of Broadhaven was far too good-looking, from the stable lad to the lord of the manor.

Wendy shifted position and lay with her head on his shoulder, nestling up to him. He put his arm around her and felt himself sink into a comfortable slump. To his amazement, he was actually enjoying the show. Until twenty minutes in, Will Sadler made a dramatic entrance as he galloped a horse alongside a wayward carriage and leapt onboard to wrest the reins from the hands of the driver who had, rather improbably, suffered a heart attack. With inches to spare before they plummeted off a cliff, the young hero brought the carriage under control, only to discover he had saved the beautiful Lady Victoria. It was love at first sight. It was a shame for her that ten minutes earlier, her family had matched her up with another dashing stud who, ironically, would turn out to be a creep.

"Is he like that in real life?" Wendy asked during a scene of repressed sexual tension between Will and his leading lady. In true Victorian temperance, he couldn't even bring himself to touch her hand.

"No," said Garrick firmly. "He's *nothing* like that."

He looked down at Wendy to find her blue eyes looking adoringly at him. It felt as if gravity was pulling his head towards her, and in seconds they were passionately kissing. Her hand softly ran up his thigh, and he felt an excitement he hadn't experienced for years. He combed a lock of hair from across her eyes and gazed longingly at her.

"Your pants are vibrating," she said.

For a second Garrick thought she was flirting, before realising his phone was vibrating in his pocket. He cursed for not turning it off as he'd promised himself. He pulled it out, determined to ignore it–

But before he could toss it aside, he saw the text message that arrived.

Gina Brown had died.

He was now dealing with a double homicide.

Triple, if he counted the passion that had just been killed stone dead.

19

Garrick spent all morning pacing in front of the evidence wall like a panther ready to strike. With news of Gina Brown's death, the media circled the story once again. Rumours that the accidents were really murders appeared online, and Molly Meyers once again began leaving messages on Garrick's phone.

As they were so far behind schedule and only able to film smaller scenes, Marissa Carlisle was forced to bite the bullet and pay everybody overtime to shoot on Sunday. The team, except for Harry Lord, who Garrick had forced to have the day off to recuperate from his old injuries, was at the manor.

Over the weekend, digital forensics had come back with more information about Karen's voice message. It hadn't been recorded on Gina's phone; it had been sent to her using the phone's wireless AirDrop feature, a system only available on iPhones, which Karen and Gina both had. It also meant that Gina would have to be within thirty feet of whoever sent it. They couldn't rule out that Karen had recorded it on her phone and deleted the original. Why she would do that, Garrick couldn't be sure.

All the evidence weighed heavily towards Will being a serial sex offender. But no matter how much he loathed the man, Garrick knew murder was a whole different league. The taste of blackmail was all over the case, but those lines came in from all angles. Simon Wheeler wanting revenge on Will and Marissa. Freya Granger was a spurned actress. Any of the crew who'd discovered Will's secret...

There was always pressure to close any investigation, and Garrick had experienced his fair-share made worse by media interest. This should be no different, but when Drury called him, he sensed a political dimension to the case.

"Morning, ma'am."

"Like the rest of the country, I learned about Gina Brown's death on the news this morning."

Garrick could never tell if she was stating facts or issuing a reprimand. He hedged his answer.

"I was gathering the facts for the report, rather than rely on hearsay."

"And do the facts point to a speedy conviction?"

Garrick's hesitation betrayed his doubt. "I'm in the station as we speak. Where are you, ma'am?"

He knew the moment the words were out that he sounded sarcastic.

"I'm playing golf with Scott Edwards." Garrick didn't need it spelled out that Edwards was Kent Police's Crime Commissioner. An elected position responsible for overseeing the force and reporting up the governmental chain. Drury had often said that staying on the Commissioner's good side was one of the most critical aspects of her job. It was important enough for her to give up a precious Sunday, and probably deliberately lose at a game she excelled in.

"I'm sure you have everything in hand," she said with no conviction. "The Commissioner was telling me what a fan of the show he is, and how it is a symbol of Britishness."

"I'll get him some autographs then."

Drury's tone dropped to sub-zero. "You do that. And ensure things are tightly wrapped up too. I look forward to hearing about your progress."

She hung up. Garrick rubbed his temples. Why was it politicians only started rattling cages when it involved pubs, sports, or their favourite television shows? He supposed that victims, criminals, food banks, and poverty were not as glamourous.

He sat on the edge of a desk and stared at the wall, running each scenario in his mind as if it were a short film. With each suspect, he tried to shoehorn the murders in. Had they been complicit or accidental victims in a larger tale of deceit?

He lost himself in thought for the best part of an hour, which was a welcome distraction after the embarrassing evening with Wendy. With the mood killed, they'd finished the rest of the wine as he grumpily disclosed aspects of the case to her. By the end, he felt physically and emotionally exhausted so called a taxi to take him home. He mumbled profuse apologies, and Wendy assured him everything was fine; it was the nature of his job, and they had plenty of time ahead of them.

With his thoughts so off-track, he almost missed the gentle ping of an arriving email. It was a report on the soil sample he had retrieved from the pedals of Will Sadler's hire car. He'd expected little, so was surprised when there was a curious match. They contained traces of orange sand and a couple of fresh tarmac pieces that matched repairs to potholes near the east gate of Laddingford Manor. Exactly in the direction Gina's killer had fled. There was a caveat that the sand and tarmac were pretty generic and found at most roadworks across Kent. But the coincidence was there.

Coincidence... Garrick hated the word more each time he heard it.

Who took the car from the hotel? Will was the obvious suspect, but he had to remind himself that Marissa, as the producer, had ultimately been the one to hire the vehicle, and the way he'd left the keys on the table suggested that security wasn't Will's priority. Could Simon have taken them?

The more he thought about it, the more he strayed away from Will being a possible killer. Then another thought struck him. They had focused on the crew, but was it possible that somebody at the *hotel* was blackmailing Will? Somebody who knew his secret? Dillinger? Smith? Or even Mia?

He felt as if he was grappling for a thread that had been there all along, but just as he tried to focus on it, his phone rang. It was Chib. He was needed on-set immediately.

Nicholas Meyer was apparently in his late fifties, but his weather-beaten face and wiry grey beard added a decade. Every time he talked; his huge hands scratched his chin with thick, dirt-encrusted fingernails. His rural accent proudly indicated his gene pool had started and ended within a ten-mile radius. In his filthy dungarees and wellington boots, Garrick and Chib found it difficult to keep up as he led them along a winding trail that stretched beyond the folly. Garrick was puffing for breath, but Nicholas had talked almost non-stop since Chib had introduced him.

"Me great-grand was a Man of Kent," he said proudly,

dividing the county between east and west. "Worked here before Sir James took on the title. I been lucky to be kept on for what it's worth."

DS Okon had finally tracked down the estate's ground-keeper, who had been on holiday at a campsite in darkest Exeter. As he tended not to be required when film crews were around, he took whatever opportunities he could. He was due back tomorrow, but had been keen to show Chib around.

"Is he a good boss to work for?" gasped Garrick from the back of the pack.

Nicholas snorted and spat to the side of the trail. "He's always late payin'. And every time there're folks renting the grounds, he's always causing a *rockery*."

"You mean an argument?" asked Garrick, trying to unpick the slang.

"Aye, that's what I said. And that girl of his is the rummest of them. A total *nabbler*."

Chib glanced back at Garrick and shrugged.

"She got a right strop on when Sir asked me to prepare for a shootin' season. I came up here, and she went *roil* on me for poking 'round."

"Why? What did you find?"

They reached a small glade about ten feet in diameter. A fallen moss-covered log bridged a narrow stream. With the morning sunlight streaming through branches that were crowned with buds, it looked like a page from a fairy tale.

"Very nice," said Chib. "Did she come here a lot?"

"For that, aye." Nicholas pointed to the clearing.

Chib and Garrick exchanged a look, but they couldn't see what he was driving at. Nicholas issued a loud sigh and moved over to the longer plants.

"This 'ere!"

As his eyes adjusted to the growing foliage, Garrick recognised the distinctive serrated leaves.

"Cannabis?"

"Aye, grows around here."

Chib crouched to look. "I thought it needed specialist lamps and heat?"

Nicholas laughed. "Not the feral stuff. Usually comes out in May, but it's been a warm April. It's all 'round here. And this, too." He moved closer to the log and indicated a slender white fungus growing on it.

"Magic mushrooms," Garrick confirmed. "She grows these?"

Nicholas shook his head. "Nah. She ain't got a green finger on her. But she likes to keep 'em growing, and I know she uses 'em. She gave be a right *bannick* when I threatened to clear 'em for the game drive."

Chib put her hand inside a plastic evidence bag she had in her pocket. She gripped one mushroom and pulled the bag inside out, sealing the fungus inside and preventing contact with her skin.

"I'll get this to the toxicology lab. See if they can match it. What do you think, sir? To me, I think we're there."

Garrick felt Freya Granger's link to the murders themselves was still too patchy to make an arrest, but he couldn't deny the evidence was stacking up.

He puffed his cheeks. "The question is, do we bring her in, or rattle the cage to see what else falls out?"

They found Freya Granger in the video village, a small area away from the action where monitors from the various cameras could be viewed by non-essential crew. She was with the director in what seemed to be a heated conversation. Other members of the crew kept their distance. On the monitors Will was having his costume adjusted by Liliana Davies, while he chatted to another good-looking cove who he vaguely recalled from the cast list.

"That's Alexander Reynolds. He's been in the last two seasons and was brought in today. He wasn't scheduled for another week."

His dark skin and charming looks had given the show an exotic flavour since he arrived.

"He's the one rumoured to be taking over if they bump Will's character."

"You don't see many black fellas in these period dramas," said Garrick with his usual bluntness.

"We existed back then," came Chib's sharp reply.

"I didn't mean it like that, and you know it. I meant colour-blind casting. It's a good thing."

"And I'm saying black people existed in society back then. Before everything was whitewashed. They found evidence of black sailors in Henry VIII's navy."

Garrick decided he was on safer ground by staying silent. He kept his eyes on the monitor, watching as Liliana knelt to adjust the baggy legs of Will's trousers. Was it his imagination, or did she look mortified? Will brushed the top of her head and she sharply pulled away. He laughed, and Liliana scooted off-camera. Garrick made a mental note to check her statements.

Simon suddenly noticed the detectives, broke off the conversation with Freya, then marched towards the set. Freya motioned to leave, but Garrick intercepted her.

"I hope we interrupted nothing important?"

Freya took a seat at the monitors and shook her head. "Just the usual."

Garrick joined her while Chib stayed behind them.

"What's the usual these days? Seeing how you are not actually part of the film?"

"I make contributions," she said airily.

"Such as?"

"Such as helping my father renegotiate the contract so they can continue using the estate. Our home has become the symbol of the show."

"It is only television." She looked at him as though he were insane. "What I mean is, couldn't they do something with computer graphics? Or maybe have an earthquake shake the house to its foundations so it needed to be rebuilt?"

"Are you an amateur screenwriter, Mister Garrick?"

"It might spice the show up. A few natural disasters here and there. What I'm getting at is the possibility they don't need you as much as you think. It must be just as easy to reinvent a location as it is to write-off a major character."

Her alarm revealed she knew about Will's potential fate. Garrick pressed his advantage.

"And are you contributing on Will's behest too?" The look she cast him was filled with venom. Garrick indicated Will on the screen. "I'm impressed he can keep faking his enthusiasm, knowing what's coming. You are aware of his history with the director?"

"Of course I know." She was indignant, a sign that she hated to be out of the loop. It was perhaps the hubris that Garrick needed to poke to get a confession.

"I'm sure he's looking forward to the last scene of the film."

Freya gave a mirthless chuckle. "It won't happen. They

need him more than he needs them. It's just a threat, and his agent is falling for it."

"But you're still trying to persuade Simon to keep him in."

"Is that what you think?" She sniggered. "He is a director with several other projects lined up. Ones that I would be suited for."

A missing piece clicked in place for Garrick. "So you're trying to get in with Simon's good graces? That must be difficult since he knows Will is a friend of yours. Didn't he have Karen Dalton lined up for his next film?"

"I don't know," she muttered, her eyes fixed on the monitors.

"Yes, he did. And I'm sure it's a role you might suddenly be perfect for now."

"I was perfect for it, anyway."

Garrick laced his fingers together over his chest and circled his thumbs together as he casually set out his thoughts.

"Then it's quite fortunate for you she's out of the picture. No pun intended."

"It's sad what happened to her…"

"Oh, of course it is. Her death is most unfortunate. A terrible thing. Unforeseen." Out of the corner of his eye, he saw her glance at him. "But it happened. And coupled with that is something she found out. Something about Will…"

Freya remained silent, but her fist clenched as she tensed.

"Of course you know about it. What with you two being so close."

"He's famous. People like to knock the successful down. It's all driven by jealousy."

"It must be difficult for you. Stories of what could be described as predatory behaviour from the man you love."

Freya stiffened in her seat. Her cheeks tightened as she reined in her natural instinct to lash out.

"Especially when it isn't returned, and he gets engaged to people like Kelly Rodriguez. Although it shows his nice side that he tried to get you a break on stage. It's a pity it didn't work out. I imagine it's a kick in the teeth to be replaced by Karen Dalton and made all the worse when she rolls up on this film." He shook his head sadly. He was now lined up for the *coup de grâce*, although the Swiss cheese holes in his theory gave him a moment's hesitation before he plunged on. "And then to find she is being used as a mouthpiece by his alleged victims to blackmail him..." He gave a sympathetic sigh. "I suppose it's only natural to protect somebody you care for. Somebody you assume must be innocent. So what better sweet revenge than to get Karen Dalton thrown off the movie." He snapped his fingers and leaned forward as if the idea had just occurred to him. "Slip her a psychedelic drug so her performance is so awful she would have to be fired. If only there was a lovely little glade somewhere on the estate where magic mushrooms grew. Then it would be so easy. But what if it didn't go to plan? What if it was *then* you discovered she had evidence about Will's sexual assaults? There she is on some wild trip, lying in a river she'd stumbled into. All it would take is a little pressure, and the problem is solved."

As he said it, he felt sure the assumption Will and Karen had planned a quick shag was completely wrong. He only had Will's word for that. What if she wanted to talk to him alone, to tell him what the blackmailers had on him?

Garrick had expected Freya to yell her innocence and retaliate with a tirade of facetious remarks. Instead, she was pale and slack-jawed.

"Freya Granger, I'm arresting you for the murder of Karen Dalton."

He almost added Gina Brown's name, but stopped short. The investigation had been working on the assumption there was a killer.

What if there were *two*?

20

There was something disarming about Freya's quiet dignity as she left in a police car with DS Okon. The growing *bastard of press* at the gate had erupted as they vied for a photograph. Garrick had no wish to speak to the persistent Molly Meyers, but in an effort to keep her on-side, he sent a text message stating that Freya Granger had been taken in for questioning. He knew the resourceful Molly would figure out that she'd actually been arrested, but he wasn't going to do the whole job for her.

Sir James's reaction had been more predictable. He immediately began the hunt for the most expensive solicitor he could afford. Sean Wilkes had followed them to the station and would assist Chib in her interview. Garrick stayed back with Fanta to watch the reaction around the set. Both Marissa and Simon were suitably shocked. He watched over the monitors when, between takes, Marissa told Will what had happened. He was nonplussed and ready to continue his scene.

The more Garrick thought about the timeline, the more

convinced he was that there was another guilty partner around him. Freya fit the narrative so far, but it didn't explain Gina Brown's murder, or who had travelled from the hotel that morning. That whittled the list to three names. But even those names didn't completely satisfy him.

He and Fanta headed to craft services for a drink. He poured water from an urn to make his own green tea, while Fanta waited for the staff to make her a vanilla soy latte.

"Hanging around here is giving you ideas above your station," Garrick sighed.

"Just enjoying how the other half lives, sir. How did the autograph and cap go down with your... *friend*?"

Garrick ignored her implication. "Much appreciated, Fanta. Thank you. Do you still think Will Sadler is a shining star?"

She took her proffered drink and scowled as they walked to an empty table. "I hope somebody comes forward and gets him arrested. They don't want to talk about it, but it's obvious nobody enjoys being around him. I'm sure he's hit on every girl on the crew and slept with a chunk of them." She caught Garrick's look as they sat. "What? Some women will still sleep with him. It's the ones who don't want to who are afraid."

"Who interviewed the wardrobe department?"

"I did. They let me try on some costumes..." her smile faltered, and she trailed off under Garrick's hard stare. "It was research, of course."

"Of course. Did any of them seem particularly nervous?"

Fanta looked through the notes on her phone. "Liliana Tyler. She's Will's dresser. I got the feeling she's more than aware of the rumours but isn't saying a word."

"I saw her earlier. She flinched when Will touched her. If

nobody has the courage to speak out, they've got to be encouraged. I think Gina was trying to do that, but worried if she did, she might get fired, or even have her career destroyed. I'm sure her death sent a strong signal to everybody to keep their mouths shut."

"Do you think it's Will?" Fanta said in surprise.

Garrick pulled a face. "It's obvious... which is why I don't like it."

"If we're looking for somebody to spill the beans about Will, you think Liliana might?"

"She may be perfect for a little cajoling, now that Freya's been arrested."

"So, if not Will, then...?"

Garrick swirled his tea thoughtfully. "There are two avenues to explore here. One, somebody is trying to blackmail him by threatening to reveal what they know. Two, somebody is trying to protect him from being exposed and has resorted to murder to do it."

"Wait, I thought we'd just arrested Freya for that?"

"Her spiking Karen's food, I can believe. Drowning her, I can believe. But something about Gina's death doesn't feel right. I see Freya as artillery."

"Now you've totally lost me," said Fanta, as she stirred two sleeves of sugar into the mass of frothed milk in her cup.

"She attacks from afar. Getting up-close and personal to confront Gina doesn't fit her MO. And there is the issue of who left the hotel the morning of Gina's attack? The probability points to that person being Gina's attacker. The sand traces on the pedal, the size nine footprints, the timing, the direction the attacker took off. If we flip our assumptions around and focus on who gains to *protect* Will, where does that put us?"

"It rules Simon Wheeler out completely. Will obviously stands to gain from protecting himself..."

"Which leaves Marissa. Keeping Will safe means she can finish her film on time and on schedule."

"Not anymore."

"No, but now she's playing damage limitation. And she is forced to kill his character off if his agent doesn't play nice. She wins and loses whichever way we look at it."

Fanta dropped to a whisper as she looked over his shoulder. "Speak of the devil."

Marissa entered the tent and walked their way.

"Why don't you get down to wardrobe and become everybody's friend? You'll enjoy that."

Fanta quickly departed as Marissa sat with him.

"Well done, Detective. I have to say, I had my suspicions that family was corrupt. Will had always said she was a bit weird."

"I thought they were friends?"

"Used to be. She started badgering him to get her roles on things. When he didn't, she got abusive. She's done it to me, too. She's got a real narcissistic side to her." Marissa propped her elbows on the table, put her head in her hands, and massaged her scalp. "I can't tell you how glad I am this shitstorm is over. We're going to run two weeks over schedule, which is going to cost a fortune."

"And you have lost two lives," Garrick said sharply. "Not everything can be valued using money."

Marissa was offended. "Of course not. But as I told you, I have an army who are depending on me. When we wrap, trust me, I'll grieve. I've already talked to the studio about paying for both funeral costs. It's not much, but it's something."

"Are you still going to kill Will? His character, I mean."

"The plan is to shoot both endings and see how his contract negotiations shape out."

"That's quite an aggressive negotiating tactic."

"This is an aggressive business. To succeed, you must plan. I was dead against it. The studio forced my hand."

Garrick peered at her over his cup of tea. "It makes me wonder if this is entirely related to his contract."

"What else could it be?"

"You must be aware of allegations of sexual misconduct?"

Marissa sat upright, taking a defensive stance.

"If I had a pound for every allegation I hear in this industry, I wouldn't have to work ever again."

"You know Will. You've slept with him after all. There must be something in them. And if there is, I imagine it would sink Broadhaven without a trace."

"I take every complaint seriously. I encourage all my team to come forward if there is *anything* inappropriate from *anybody*." Her voice was like steel.

"And nobody has come forward?"

"Not to me. And if they did, I have made it clear that I have, and the studio has, a zero-tolerance policy."

"That's good to hear. If I may, I'd like to throw out a scenario. What if somebody came to you with the threat of exposing an incident or two?" He held up his hand to stop her from talking. "Ones you were not aware of, of course."

"I would want proof."

"And let us say they were trying to blackmail you to keep it from the press?"

"Blackmail?"

"It's purely hypothetical."

"Then hypothetically I would come to you." She forced a

smile and stood up, signalling the end of the conversation. "I need to get back to set. Once again, thank you for arresting the right person."

Garrick watched her go. He was suddenly reassessing the entire case. And he didn't like where the trail was leading him.

arrick hitched a ride home from DC Fanta Liu in her unwashed Volkswagen Golf and found him up to his ankles in advertising flyers and discarded wrappers in the footwell. A couple of parking tickets poked out of the detritus, too. The cluster of air fresheners that hung from the mirror were so old their fragrances had long faded.

He'd received the notification that an RAC engineer would arrive within the hour to look at his Land Rover. It was a priority, as he was feeling restricted by having to rely on others to ferry him around. Drury had laughed him off the phone when he'd asked if there was a car in the pool that he could borrow. Before Fanta could update him about her conversation with Liliana, Wendy called. She was bubbly and enthusiastic, despite the previous aborted evening, and wanted to know if Garrick was free for a drink later. She could even pick him up.

Garrick felt rotten for turning her down. With a suspect now arrested, he had plenty of work that needed to be done within a limited timeframe, assuming his car could be repaired. He was painfully aware that Fanta was listening in on the conversation, so kept his side of it clipped and monotone. He hoped Wendy understood why. When he ended the call, Fanta said nothing, but he could see it was taking all her willpower to remain silent.

"You were going to tell me about Liliana," he prompted.

"Everybody heard about Freya's arrest, and nobody is surprised. A couple of people talked about how close she was to Will, but as usual, everybody was tight-lipped with details. Every time I tried to get Liliana on her own, that Chloe Aubertel just would not leave. She treats her department like an army barracks. She might have won an Academy Award, but it turns out she can still be a monster. Everybody says she had a temper. I think a lot of the people under her are awed and scared at the same time."

"Did Liliana open up?"

"She's quite a jumpy person and didn't directly deny if Will had tried anything with her, but if he's as nasty as everybody is making out, I wouldn't be surprised. She's very pretty and looks vulnerable. Just his type. She also let it slip that she'd seen Freya going in Will's trailer the morning we found the phone."

"Really? Freya said she never went in."

"Apparently she looked agitated. She could have been looking for Karen's phone."

"Or planting it in his trailer."

"Why would she do that?"

"The more I think about it, the more I think Will isn't linked to the murders."

"Now he's suddenly a nice guy?"

"Being a scum bag doesn't mean he's guilty

of *every* crime."

"You mean, two wrongs don't make a third wrong."

"In the history of sayings, that will never catch on. But that's my gist."

He didn't want to say anything more at this stage. He had a theory. It was nebulous, and he didn't quite believe it, but as a seasoned investigator, he knew that even a dead end could help break other previous misconceptions.

Fanta scowled and honked her horn aggressively as a driver tried to pull out in front of her. "I don't think we're going to get much more out of people now Freya has been arrested. They think the killer's gone, and it's business as usual."

"Even if the usual is living in silence and fear?"

"I think they're riding it out for the pay cheque. Once the job is over, they can breathe easy on the next one because he won't be there. I also don't think anybody is going to shed a tear when they find out Will's being written out."

"Nobody suspects that?"

Fanta firmly shook her head.

"He's too big a star for them to think it possible."

Garrick's arrival home perfectly coincided with the arrival of the RAC mechanic, who diagnosed the problem within the first two minutes.

"First of all, your battery's dead."

"It's a brand new one. I bought it from you fellas."

"Maybe your alternator's shot and not charging it. Still, it shouldn't be flat like that. The second problem is you ran out of fuel."

"I had half a tank left."

The mechanic was used to dealing with public stupidity, so amiably skirted around his customer's incompetence. As the battery was only a month old, he replaced it with a new one. Now powered up, Garrick could see the fuel needle was resting against the pin. The tank was indeed empty.

Garrick rode in the RAC van on a quick diversion to the local garage to fill a jerry can, then returned and emptied the diesel into the tank. It took a minute to coax the engine into firing, but it did eventually stutter to life and ticked over with an irregular stutter. The mechanic performed a little more alchemy under the bonnet and soon had it steadily idling.

"I reckon you've got a gasket problem. The timing's slipping, and there's some corrosion on the mounting brackets."

"But it's fixable?"

"It'd be cheaper to scrap." The mechanic spent thirty minutes diligently checking the fuel tank and lines. "There's no fuel leaking, but the system was bone dry. That's why it didn't start up straight away. Your fuel pump could be knackered, too. You must've coasted home on fumes. Literally got here on the last drop of diesel."

Garrick swore he had plenty left last time he looked and wondered if some local chav had syphoned it off in the night. He hoped so. The alternative was that he was suffering serious lapses in memory.

It was six thirty, so he still had time to get to the hotel before the crew wrapped at 9 pm. Stopping only to brim the tank, he headed to the Footman's Hotel and felt a lump of regret that he wasn't meeting Wendy instead.

Dillinger was still on duty, and Garrick questioned if the man ever left. He seemed the type to sleep in his office. He showed him a picture of Freya.

"Have you seen her before?"

Dillinger's nose wrinkled in undisguised loathing. "One of Mr Sadler's acquaintances. She has been here several times. On the last occasion, Miss Carlisle asked me to prevent her from entering if she ever turned up again."

"Why is that?"

The manager raised a pompous eyebrow, and Garrick thought he was about to incite guff over client confidentiality. Then he bobbed his head imperiously.

"Ms Carlisle had arranged a private dinner with the members of the crew staying here, and Miss Rodriguez."

"Was this when Karen Dalton arrived?"

"Indeed, it was the last evening poor Miss Dalton was with us." He indicated Freya's picture. "She barged her way in just as the entrée was being served. I wasn't present then, but I understand she was furious at not being invited. She had a very vocal altercation with Mr Sadler, which was when I arrived after the waiter alerted me. She was quite vulgar towards Miss Dalton and claimed she shouldn't be there. It was Mr Wheeler who took the young lady outside to calm her down."

"Do you know what was said?"

Dillinger shook his head. "Mrs Smith said she heard raised voices, but he returned to the dining room after no more than three minutes. That is when Ms Carlisle took me aside and told me not to allow her to enter again."

Garrick retrieved his phone. "Is Mrs Smith still on duty?"

Dillinger glanced at his watch. "For another eighty-four minutes."

"I'll talk to her." Dillinger shuffled in his seat. "*Alone*, that is. And tell me, the key cards for each room, is there only one copy?"

"Cards are issued per guest. Being electronic, a previous guest's card will no longer work once they checkout."

"Can the staff access any room?"

"No. I, or the night manager, have one that opens any door. Mrs Smith has another. Housekeeping only has keys while on duty, and they change every day. Of course, the reception can make up a new key should one be lost. It's all recorded on the system."

With his thoughts colliding with a mixture of improbable combinations, Garrick walked through the hotel until he found Mrs Smith. They sat in her cramped office that was little more than a glorified broom closet.

"Tell me about the altercation with Freya Granger during dinner last week."

"Would that be Mr Sadler's acquaintance we had to bar?"

"The very same. Your boss seems to think you overheard her and the director shouting in the car park."

"Well, I heard her, at least. Mr Wheeler is much more circumspect."

"Naturally, I'm keen to know what they said."

"There was plenty of effing and jeffing from the young lady. I could only hear her side of the argument, and then not with clarity. She believed Mr Wheeler owed her something but felt stabbed in the back."

"Stabbed in the back?"

"That was the phrase she used. I think I heard 'betrayed', but I can't swear to it. But it was very clear that something had gone awry between them."

It was clearly something nobody neither of them thought he should know about. If they were so adamant about keeping secrets, then it was time to shake things up. If Marissa thought she was free and clear to continue her film, then she was in for a shock tomorrow when she and Simon found themselves in the station for a long, formal statement.

"Is Mia on duty tonight?"

"I gave her a few days off. The wee poor thing is still quite shaken." Her orchestrated stern demeanour folded, and she rubbed her eyes. "I've tried to encourage her to talk to you, but she's so afraid. Going sent home is a fate worse than keeping silent."

"And please keep trying. What happened between her and Will may be key to everything. That said, please don't take what I'm about to say the wrong way. I have to cover all bases. This is now a multiple murder enquiry."

"I understand. You're going to ask me again if I believe her, aren't you?" Garrick nodded apologetically. "Nothing has changed my mind. If she was lying, then she deserves to have a starring role in that film. That man has broken the Mia I knew."

"Understood." Frustration burned Garrick. He had no reason to doubt Mia, but unless he could formally speak with her, then there was little he could do right now. "Did she have access to your key card at any point?"

"Certainly not!"

"How many key cards did Mr Sadler have?"

"We issue guests two as standard. Of course, they can ask for more."

"Can you find out how many have been issued for his room?"

It took a few moments for Smith's computer to respond to her query. Like the hotel, the IT systems were quaint and period.

"Three."

"Three?"

"They were issued at the same time. Now I recall why. Two for Mr Sadler as standard, and a third for the assistant with him."

"What assistant?"

"The young lady from the production company. You showed me her picture last time."

Garrick's hand was trembling as he took his mobile out of his pocket. He selected a picture of Gina.

"Her?"

"Aye. Pleasant she is. She'd arrived ahead of him to check the room was in shape, and she brought the hire car along for him. She was always in and out collecting things, dropping off props or whatnot. Fruit baskets. I must say, these stars may earn a lot of money, but they get so much for free it makes you wonder if they ever spend a penny."

"Just to confirm, she had a key?"

Smith nodded. Garrick made a mental roll call of Gina's personal possessions. There had been no reference to a hotel key card. That would have instantly been flagged. But she possessed one, and she had complete access to the hotel and staff.

"Did you ever recall her speaking with Mia?"

Mrs Smith raised her eyebrows in despair and laughed. "You flatter me by thinking I can remember every tiny detail like that. I wish. But it is possible. After all, she was coming and going all hours, whether or not Mr Sadler was here."

Garrick pointed at the computer. "Does that register every time a key is used?"

"Yes. Access is time stamped. We're not entirely old-fashioned, Detective Garrick."

"And can you distinguish which of the three cards was used?"

"Every time a key is issued, it has a unique identifying number."

"I will need a copy of that list. And I'll need Mia's

address."

Somebody needed to talk to her. And that somebody would not be him.

Driving home, Garrick considered calling Wendy to suggest dashing for last orders. Then he had second thoughts that were laced with doubt. Every time he saw her, he'd either come from a chaotic day and was exhausted, or work interrupted the evening. She deserved better. She deserved him to be more alert, for one. Next time he would try to make an effort, ditch his phone, and focus all his energy on his girlfriend.

That word still sounded odd to his ears.

His instincts were right. By the time he arrived home, Garrick was utterly exhausted and wouldn't have lasted five minutes in a noisy bar. Mrs Smith had printed out a spreadsheet of every time Will's room had been accessed. He chuckled, thinking of the look on DC Harry Lord's face when he tasked him to match it with Will and Gina's movement. Garrick placed the plastic wallet containing the printout on the table next to the front door. He crowned it with the letter from his consultant. He would read it and contact her first thing in the morning.

Then he'd summon the courage and tell Wendy all about his condition, his sister, and his whole broken life.

The incident with his car had excessively worried him. He could handle the occasional hallucination. Leaving the front door ajar was a lapse in judgement, but it could happen to anybody. Perhaps a squirt of WD40 on the lock might solve that problem. But his lapses in memory were a concern. He found comfort in Dr Harman's last words, but still wished she'd call him back, if only to help him focus on opening up to Wendy. He added a call to the therapist on his list.

Perhaps it was because letting the fuel in his car dip to nothing was such a mundane thing to forget that it hit home the hardest. He'd heard stories of Alzheimer's being diagnosed with the smallest of hints. Forgetting a name, burning toast, misplaced keys. He couldn't recall a time he'd ran a car dry. Even when he was broke and still living in Liverpool, he'd never ran out of fuel. It was something so simple, so intuitive, that it was a concern. Like leaving the house without trousers.

Despite agonising over the different strands of the case, combined with the worries of his own mental health, David Garrick was sound asleep within seconds of going to bed.

He awoke feeling fresher and more alert than he'd felt all year. A quick glance at his watch suggested he'd had nine hours of sleep. Again, unheard of. He wolfed down breakfast, avoiding any news channel that might threaten to sour his day, and examined the fossil Wendy had found. He was sure it was a tooth, and he felt the desire to strip away the rock matrix and polish it up. It was a pleasant feeling to *want* to do his hobby for a change. Perhaps it was the sense that the last few clues were falling into place, but whatever it was, he was feeling optimistic for the first time in a long time.

He took the plastic folder containing the printout from the table beside the door, put the consultant's letter in his inside jacket pocket, and briskly marched out of the house with thoughts of buying himself a new Barbour to replace the bloodstained one still in evidence.

"What the hell...?" he blurted.

Some bastard had parked right across his driveway, blocking him in. He circled around the gleaming white Range Rover, noticing it had this year's plates. It was a beauty of a vehicle, and it dwarfed his beige Land Rover in the same way Will Sadler's dazzlingly good looks intimidated most men around him. The door was locked.

"Hello?" he shouted, hoping the owner would come running. When that didn't work, he rocked the car to set off the alarm. That didn't work, either. Reluctantly he pumped the horn of his Land Rover, which only summoned one neighbour who didn't know whose car it was.

Garrick was pissed off that some imbecile had disrupted his morning the second he'd left the house. Just to spite whoever blocked him in, he called the office and spoke to DC Harry Lord, who had just arrived. Lord made a few calls and, forty minutes later, a police flatbed tow truck arrived and hoisted the errant vehicle onto the back of it.

Garrick thanked the driver and told him to take it to the police pound. The driver gave him a puzzled look.

"Are you sure?"

"Or throw it in the Channel. Just get rid of the thing and let the owner worry about it."

"You are the owner."

"No. I live here. It was blocking my drive. Unfortunately, that piece of crap is my car." He pointed to his beige monstrosity.

"No. I checked. This is registered to David Garrick at this address. And you're him, aren't you?"

Garrick had to pinch himself to check he wasn't still dreaming.

"What're you talking about?"

The driver showed him the computer screen in his cab. It was connected to the DVLA's vehicle register. It clearly showed David Garrick had been the registered owner for the last two months.

22

"It could be a bizarre clerical error," Fanta said as Garrick drove his old Land Rover rather too aggressively in her opinion. "It was mis-registered, then delivered to your home."

"In the dead of night. A brand-new car. Without the keys."

"Maybe a gift from the studio for solving the case?" She tapered off when Garrick shot her a withering look. "If you don't want it, well, you've been in my Golf..."

Garrick expelled a long breath and tilted his head to the left, then to the right. He heard a satisfying click as he eased the tension. A glance at his speedo and he tapped the brakes to slow them to legal limits. Fanta visibly relaxed next to him.

The incident had put him on edge. Somebody was playing mind games designed to wear him down. However, his only culprit was dead: John Howard. Still, any motive to do such a thing was obscure. The purchase of the vehicle demonstrated several months of planning, so it was easy for him to believe the car, like the letter before it, was a series of psychological games pre-planned before John Howard's death.

Games he was playing against a dead man.

To what aim, he couldn't imagine.

Before picking DC Fanta Liu up from the station, he'd called DCI Kane to tell him what happened and to voice his assertion that John Howard was reaching out to him from the grave, figuratively, if not literally. For him, it left no doubt that Howard was responsible for the death of his sister. He tried to recall any time he'd offended Howard; anything he could've done to trigger a psychotic grudge, but he drew a blank. Kane had assured him that his team would look into it.

That didn't reassure Garrick. He was feeling sick, vulnerable, and left wondering what else lay in store for him. He was finding it difficult to focus on his own case. After dropping the key access records on Harry Lord's desk and avoiding questions about the mysterious vehicle, he made a swift exit with Fanta as they headed out to speak to Mia.

Mia Alvarez lived in a flat share in Gillingham, between the train station and the football grounds. It wasn't the nicest of areas, Harry Lord had cautioned. He'd worn shoe leather in the area during his days as a PC. It was where he'd been stabbed for the first time, he added with a trace of macabre pride.

Mia didn't want to talk in front of her housemates, so they arranged to meet in a cafe on the high street. Fanta wrinkled her nose at the back-to-back rows of betting shops, 99p thrift stores, a slot machine casino, and fast-food outlets that felt the need to prefix their names with the word *'quality'*, as if desperate to remind their customers.

"Don't be such a snob, Fanta," said Garrick as they walked

to the rendezvous. "Places like this are the lifeblood of society."

"This society is DOA if you ask me," she muttered as they passed a gang of scowling teens sat on a bench smoking and drinking lager from a cheap four-pack, even though it was only lunchtime. The cafe itself looked like the sort of place greasy spoons went to die. Mia waited for them at a corner table. She barely lifted her head in acknowledgement as they sat down.

"Thanks for agreeing to talk to us, Mia," Garrick said. She gave the smallest of nods. "Just to say again, you're in no trouble at all. None. This is my colleague, DC Fanta Liu. She's not an old white relic like me, so if you feel uncomfortable talking to me, tell me to bugger off and Fanta will talk your ear off instead."

That got a slightly better reaction. He noticed she hadn't even bought herself a drink.

"What would you like to drink? Coke? Tea?" She nodded for the latter. Garrick studied her further and wondered what kind of slave wage Dillinger paid her. He was sure the luxury hotel didn't pay luxury salaries and recalled Mrs Smith's comments about being fortunate that guests were big tippers. "And lunch is on me." He passed her the small, laminated menu.

"You're a big spender," said Fanta with a tight smile, as Mia pointed to a chicken and chips dinner.

"I said *her* lunch was on me." He left them to it and ordered a double-sized portion and teas for the three of them. The food was already preheated; no expense spared or spent in this establishment. When he returned, Fanta and Mia were talking as if they were old friends. It was worth him playing the role of waiter, thought Garrick. His DC had an uncanny ability to get people to open up. She had a great career ahead of her, and he was already regretting the day when somebody would poach her off his team.

"I've always wanted to go to the Philippines," said Fanta in a dreamy voice. "The beaches there are mind blowing. White sand!" she exclaimed in awe. "Mia was just telling me how much she'd like to go back and visit her parents."

"I hope you get the chance soon."

"It is expensive," Mia said sadly. "And living here is expensive."

Fanta rolled her eyes. "Tell me about it."

Mia shovelled her way through the hot meal as if she hadn't eaten for days. Garrick didn't want to interrupt her enjoyment with questions, so he let Fanta prattle on about a Filipino friend who worked on cruise ships, and how she'd be travelling the world to exotic locations if she wasn't sitting in this greasy spoon café in Gillingham. Whether she meant it, it got an appreciative smile from Mia – and it was an oddly enjoyable distraction from Garrick's own woes. Finally, he judged it was time to press ahead with his questions. He showed Mia a picture of Gina Brown. Mia nodded before he'd even asked the question.

"You've seen her before?"

"Of course. At the hotel. She came with a lot of things for Mr Sadler."

"You can drop the pleasantries, Will or Sadler, or bastard, if you prefer. We know who you're talking about."

That got the briefest smile. Her gaze fixed on the phone. "She always says hello. She's nice. Always bringing things for him all the time."

"In the evening?" asked Fanta. Garrick leaned back in his chair, giving her subtle licence to lead the questions.

"Sometime late, yes."

"How did she seem around him? Happy? Tense? Worried?"

Mia thought about it for a moment. The bubbly personality that had surfaced moments ago now retreated behind shame and insecurity.

"Not happy."

"Did you ever see Will touch her or say anything that made her feel uncomfortable or threatened?"

"One night I hear shouting from his room. When she was in there. I was supposed to deliver a bottle to him. It went quiet, so I left it outside. I was too afraid to go in. Later, I saw her run out and leave. She was crying she looked... her shirt had been ripped."

"Do you think he raped her?"

Mia nodded. "After that, she was never smiling. I grew afraid as he had tried to touch me, too."

"This was before he assaulted you?"

"Three days later he did."

Fanta reached out and squeezed Mia's hand. A small gesture, but the gratitude that flooded across Mia's face was unmistakable.

"Every time I saw her, she was scared. Then one day we passed in the corridor, and she asked me if he'd assaulted me." She hung her head in shame. "I think she saw it all over me." She gestured to her face.

"It's nothing to feel ashamed about, Mia," Fanta assured her. "He's the one who should feel bad."

Mia noisily slurped her tea, then used a paper napkin from the metal dispenser on the table to blow her nose.

"She asked if I would help get back at him. I said yes."

"Did she say how?"

Mia shook her head. "She talked a lot to Miss Dalton. I think she told her what had happened. So, when she died..."

"You became afraid?"

Mia's hands were shaking. She inhaled deeply to calm herself. "And then Gina was killed." She quietly sobbed. Fanta squeezed her hand tightly and didn't let go.

"I imagine it terrified you. Thought you were next?"

"He scares me," she whispered.

Garrick could see the strands of the investigation coming together around an inevitable conclusion... it just wasn't the one he had expected. He swiped through the photographs until he found Freya's image.

"What about her?"

"She was his friend."

Garrick frowned. "Was?"

"When Kelly Rodriguez arrived, they argued like cats fighting."

"You mean Freya and Kelly?"

Mia nodded. "They hated each other. Will told her to stay away and not come to the hotel ever again. He said he was tired of helping her. She would never act, he said. She was upset." Mia shrugged and had nothing more to say.

"But she came back, didn't she?" Garrick pressed. "She interrupted a dinner she wasn't invited to and was thrown out. Did you see that?"

"All the staff saw that. Mr Wheeler escorted her outside."

"I don't suppose you have any idea what they were talking about?"

Mia toyed with the napkin she'd blown her nose on. She twisted it so hard it broke in two.

"I listened. I thought it would help Gina." She picked up

the phone and studied Freya's face. "She was angry because he'd promised to get her in the film."

"Simon had promised her a part?"

"He said it was now impossible, but he would put her in his next one if they stuck to the plan."

Garrick's senses tingled. "What plan?"

"I am not sure. Something about blackmail to keep the end a secret."

Garrick and Fanta hotfooted it back to his car.

"I knew I could taste blackmail!" he said.

"I don't get it. We know Simon Wheeler hated Will and wanted to ruin his career, but why would he blackmail Marissa?"

"Maybe it was Freya's idea, and he was going along with it? Don't forget, Simon hated them both. So screwing money out of her and ruining him is a perfect revenge."

"But how is that connected to the murders?"

Garrick thought that through. "Freya spiked Karen Dalton's drink or food during the break in order to ruin her performance. She was jealous she'd got the role, the very girl who'd supplanted her in the theatre. Her hope is that Karen gets fired, and in her head, Simon gives her the role. It goes wrong. Karen wanders down to the folly, not to sleep with Will, but to confront him about the allegations of sexual misconduct Gina told him about. Maybe he got that voice message from her. That's why he agreed to meet."

"He hadn't yet tried anything on with Karen."

"Exactly, and now, as the leading lady, she was in a position to really do him serious harm."

"So *he* killed her?"

Garrick hesitated. "I still think Freya did. I think she followed Karen down to the folly, saw her stumble in the river, and took her chance, fuelled by hate and jealousy. You spoke to the students at Cambridge. Maybe she didn't intend to kill her, but that's what happened."

"Then Will finds her... but he's drugged, too. Why?"

"Spite? We've just heard how he'd turned against Freya in front of his fiancée. After all the years they'd been friends, that must've hurt. You've seen the catering. It's easy enough to spike some snacks that have been left out."

"They could've eaten the same donuts."

"For example. Yes." He suddenly remembered something. "People saw them having a heated talk before she left. Then Simon took him aside. Freya was there. If toxicology can work out how much psilocybin was in Karen's system, then maybe we can back-time events and work out when she ingested it."

"Which could point straight to that moment they were together!" Fanta exclaimed. "Brilliant." Then she frowned once again. "Blackmail though? Simon isn't exactly poor; he's a director in demand."

"But Freya is broke."

"Her father is..." they said at the same time and swapped a look, suddenly wondering if they'd overlooked Sir James.

Fanta considered that. "And Gina Brown?"

As they waited at a traffic crossing, Garrick clicked his tongue thoughtfully. He couldn't avoid the feeling that they were pushing some square pegs into round holes. Without a direct confession or some damming proof, all they had was circumstantial evidence and Mia's testimony. To her credit, Fanta had got Mia to agree to testify. She promised as much anonymity as they could and protection from Will. She assured her that once the charges had been formally made, he'd be behind bars and unable to hurt her. The traffic crossing beeped, and they marched across.

"Let's make a new timeline," Garrick suggested. "I think we are dealing with two crimes that intersect on Will."

"I'm all ears, sir."

"He's a sexual predator, using his position to sleep with as many girls as he can. He's probably done the same to more of the crew, but they're too afraid to come forward, like Mia. Gina is the one to fight back. She's trying to get others to come forward and then they'll hit him together. Just that we haven't connected Gina and Karen working together in the theatre doesn't mean they didn't cross paths in auditions, social circles, whatever. There could still be some history there. Karen comes onto the film, so she warns her about Will. Concerned, Karen wants to talk to him, but away from the others."

They reached his Land Rover in the train station's car park. He unlocked the doors, but they made no motion to enter. Fanta wasn't convinced.

"What is it, Liu? You're going to tell me, after all my experienced years of climbing the ladder to become a detective chief inspector, that I'm wrong."

Fanta was aghast. "No, sir! I would never tell you that to your face." Before he could pick her up on her phrasing, she powered on. "I keep going back to the fact nobody has anything to gain from the film not being complete. If Simon and Freya were blackmailing Marissa for money, they wouldn't want it stopped. Simon wants Will to be killed off in a multimillion-dollar franchise. Why would he stop that? And Karen Dalton spilling the dirt on Will? No matter how disgusted she is, if he goes down before the film's released, then it won't be the career springboard she dreamt it would be. If I were her, I would *warn* Will that people knew and hope it'd stop his behaviour. Once the movie's out, maybe she wouldn't have held back. But she's in a difficult position. Would she sacrifice *everything* because of him?"

That chimed with Garrick. So did something else.

"One problem with this job is that we naturally assume the deceased are innocent. That they led wholesome lives. How many times have you heard on the news a family member lamenting what a sweet boy Billy was, and how it wasn't his fault he stabbed his mate to death before another gang member killed him. They always paint the dead in a positive light. That's human behaviour." He gazed into space until Fanta prompted him to continue.

"I'm not saying Karen Dalton was guilty of anything you or I wouldn't do. Selfishness is not a crime. What if Gina warned her about Will? What if Karen was disgusted and went along with it... until she realised it would destroy her own career? She thinks she can convince Will to stop, so she tries. But before that, she also realises the pressure Gina has placed her under. Like you said, she's between a rock and a hard place. So that phone message was intended for *Gina*, not Will. A threat to make her back off so that Karen's moment in the spotlight isn't snatched away."

Fanta considered that, then nodded sadly. "It sucks, but in some ways, I don't blame her."

"Now Gina's plan is derailed without a key ally onboard. With Mia, she's still ready to bring the production crashing down. She can't go to Simon because he wants to bring Will down in his own way and wants to finish the film. Marissa would probably fire her. But then Karen is murdered, and Gina is suddenly frightened. She thinks it could be Will, Freya, any of his allies."

"So she calls you."

"My guess is that Freya got wind of this. Perhaps she was afraid that Gina knew what she'd done."

"So now she had to kill Gina before she could talk?"

Garrick pointed at her. "Exactly."

"But the footprints at the scene. Size nine. They match Will."

"They'll match a lot of the crew. It's a pretty common size. But something about that bothers me. The report said the prints were unbalanced."

"Like somebody with a limp," Fanta said. "Like Sir James."

"Or made to look like him. Will is an actor. What if the killer was drunk? If they had to summon up the courage to kill her? Will's a drinker and on medication..." Garrick shook his head to stop getting side-tracked. "I was going to suggest the killer was wearing a size or two over in order to throw the investigation off the scent. I'm pretty certain Freya's feet are smaller."

"Clever. Okay. I think I buy that. The only thing we're lacking is evidence or a confession. But other than that..."

Garrick opened the driver's door and sat inside.

"Do you know what your problem is, DC Liu? You always ruin a good theory with your obsessive need for hard facts."

23

The plan had been to bring Simon Wheeler into the station to make a formal statement. However, considering Mia's revelations, Garrick saw more value in talking to him on the set, where he'd be more likely to open up.

The team had all been in the incident room, putting together a solid line of questioning designed to make Freya admit her guilt. Garrick and Fanta filled them in on Mia's statement and tasked DCs Lord and Wilkes to comb through the statements and evidence to see what fit with the new narrative. DC Liu and DS Okon sharpened the timeline and reworked the line of enquiry they needed to take with Freya.

Drury popped in to offer lukewarm congratulations on Freya's arrest. She also warned them Sir James had brought in legal counsel from London. An old family friend apparently, who had the reputation of a rottweiler. If there were any cracks in their case, then he was the sort who'd have her walking free in a jiffy. And that would be terrible.

Garrick had expected her to mention the morning's

bizarre car incident, but she didn't raise the subject. Perhaps he was feeling a little too paranoid, but he sensed there was an iciness in her demeanour. She'd known Garrick for many years and had backed him up when he'd been in the tightest of corners, so he was pretty certain he hadn't heard the last of the incident, either.

Harry Lord held up one of the printed key card logging sheets. He'd diligently gone through it with highlighter pens, a different colour for each card. He pointed to a single green streak.

"That, sir, is the key used to access Will Sadler's room the night before somebody lifted the car keys off his table and drove down to the set just before Gina Brown was killed." He indicated an orange line underneath. "This is Will leaving. And then, a few minutes later," he pointed to another green line, "the same card is used to access his room, presumably to return the keys. All the un-highlighted lines are house-keeping."

"Whose card was used?"

"It was Gina's."

"Obviously it wasn't her," said Garrick. "She was attacked before Will had left his room. Somebody else has her key."

"But it doesn't give any clue who that is."

"It wasn't amongst Gina's personal effects. So they may still have it."

The evidence was not quite a dead end, but it still led them nowhere. Despite everything, he drove to the location with a heavy dose of bullishness.

A receptionist with a singsong voice answered the phone on the fourth ring. Once Garrick had introduced himself, she bubbled with delight.

"I'm afraid Dr Harman has taken some time off."

"Ah, that explains why she didn't get back to me."

"Oh? If you'd left a message, I would've responded."

His car's Bluetooth connection crackled, almost drowning out her last words.

"I left a message..." he began, but then felt the same icy fingers that had gripped him when he'd forgotten Wendy's surname.

"I didn't get it, I'm afraid. Her schedule is rather full when she gets back. So we're looking at least three weeks from now." Garrick paused for so long she thought they'd been cut off. "Hello?"

"Sorry. I'm still here. Okay, let me get back to you. Thanks."

Three weeks from now, God knows what state his mental faculties would be in. A call to Dr Rajasekar's office secured him an appointment in two days' time. He felt a wave of relief just from making the call. It made him question how much he was bottling up inside.

He'd told Wendy almost nothing about his sister. And when it came to the growth lurking under his scalp, he hadn't even been honest with himself, never mind her. Even if it was benign, even if it was not growing or shrinking, the stress of it combined with his job must be having an adverse effect on his health. And that would be his own fault. Perhaps it was time for a real break. A holiday at least.

Wendy had been patient and open with him, yet he had fostered a veil of secrecy and a policy of avoidance. He could hear Dr Harman telling him it was a defensive mechanism preventing him from getting closer to Wendy, yet his heart was demanding the complete opposite. He considered calling her, but it was after lunchtime, so she'd be in a lesson.

Perhaps it was the deaths of the two women, but he felt

the desire to stop living such a cloistered life. He knew that was a direct reaction to the John Howard situation. A friend, a killer, and now it seems a traitor. Had he targeted Garrick from the moment they'd met? Groomed him, intending to focus his perverse desire to kill the ultimate target: a police detective?

Now he thought about it, Garrick was perplexed why John had killed his final victim. Garrick already had two suspects in custody, and John Howard could have easily walked away and hidden in some far-flung country with no extradition treaty. Garrick hoped the case would've collapsed. The thought he could've sent innocent men, or at least men innocent of murder, to prison rankled him.

But that final victim had always felt as if Howard was taunting the investigation. Taunting Garrick. Seeing how far he could push him until... what? He was broken? Or until more people died? Garrick valued systematic logic and was aware of the irony in expecting it from a sociopath. But Howard was smart and calculating.

Had his sister been the victim in a plan to torment him? Or had her death fermented the idea in John Howard's sick mind? If he'd killed Emilie, then he'd planned not only the murder, but the consequences afterwards. Mind games, from the envelope to the car. Even the silent telephone calls to his house must be premeditated. An automatic service dialling him up at certain times, perhaps? Sending him messages designed to confuse and wear him down. The last sick game of a dead man. A game with no apparent motive.

Garrick wanted answers from DCI Oliver Kane. Just as soon as he'd tied up this case, he'd make John Howard his next priority.

The questions kept distracting him as he arrived at

Laddingford Manor and parked his car. The place was bursting with activity. Two coaches had deposited over a hundred extras. Queues of them lined up at catering, men and woman dressed in lavish period costumes and all beaming with excitement and the novelty of the job. He bumped into Marissa Carlisle as she stepped from a production trailer. She'd aged due to lack of sleep. The once indomitable spirit Garrick had admired had been pummelled out of her.

She groaned when she saw him. "No offence, detective, but this is not a good day to be seeing you."

"The very nature of my job means that it's never a good day to see me. Story of my life, really."

"If you're pitching your life story as a movie, go away and write the script before I reject it."

"You're shooting the marquee scene, I take it?"

"Your people said they had cleared it as a crime scene. You took my light and props in as evidence, so I had to hire more, and I can't keep putting it off."

She began walking. Garrick followed.

"Without your leading lady?"

"Haven't you read the script? She's not in this scene. And no, her contract still isn't closed, but it should be by the end of the day. Then we can finally push through scenes."

"Has it cost a lot?"

"The overages are hellish. I suppose I have to thank you for not completely shutting us down, otherwise the bond company would've nailed me to the wall."

"I imagine there is a lot of money passing through here."

Marissa gestured. "Look around. Everything you see costs me money. That trailer. That guy," she nodded at a passing assistant who was talking on a radio. "And his radio and the coffee he's drinking."

"I see. So it would be easy to misplace a chunk of cash in all this if, for example, somebody was trying to blackmail you?"

Marissa stopped in her tracks. She was too exhausted to conceal her astonishment.

"What've you been told?"

The tremor in her voice alarmed Garrick more than how tired she looked. She was a broken woman, and he felt a pang of sympathy. She switched her balance from one foot to the other as she looked around to make sure nobody was within earshot.

"It's not a crime to pay a blackmailer. It's only a crime to be one. Why didn't you tell me?"

"How would that have helped? I tell you, then you start asking questions. The asshole who's fleecing me finds out, and they drop the news to the press, anyway."

"The news about writing Will out of the series?"

"I know it probably doesn't seem like much to you, but it's a key selling point for the movie. We're expecting to gross north of a hundred million dollars on a bad day. And it all hinges on a shocking ending. I wanted you to focus on the deaths of my crew. That is obviously more important than paying some bastard to stay quiet."

"How much did you pay?"

"Two hundred thousand."

Garrick gave out a low whistle. "Pounds or dollars?"

"Pounds. With this exchange rate, they're not stupid."

"You must have your suspicions who's behind it?"

Marissa nervously rocked on her heels and waited for a pair of women from wardrobe to pass-by, rolling a clothing rail packed with plastic-covered costumes.

"Sir James is top of my list."

"A little close to home, isn't he? Pardon the pun."

"It was a shit pun, detective. But he's been trying to fleece me for years." She licked her lips and lowered her voice. "I made the drop off as we'd arranged, and then Gina was killed. That really freaked me out." Garrick cocked his head, prompting her to explain. "It happened at the same time."

"Whoa, hold on. You paid the ransom at the same time Gina was attacked?"

She nodded and bit her thumbnail. "I dropped the cash here that very morning."

"Where exactly?"

"Outside the old east gatehouse."

Exactly the direction Gina's attacker fled. A chunk of the puzzle fell into place.

"You took the car keys from Will's room."

"I couldn't really use my driver or a taxi. I wanted some anonymity."

"Does Will know you took the car?"

She sneered. "He's either drunk or knocked out on sleeping pills. I don't think he even realises we add an extra hour on his call sheet so he's not late. I could walk in there shouting and he wouldn't wake up."

"Using Gina Brown's key?"

Marissa straightened, suddenly defensive as she stepped onto dangerous ground. "They're all the production's keys, Detective. It may have been assigned to her, but I can give it to whoever I want. I still have it," she admitted guiltily.

Garrick glanced at the trailers and the crew darting back and forth. All paid for by the producer. The killer had attacked Gina and run to the gate to pick up the cash. Could it still be here?

"What did you transport the money in?"

"A black Adidas sports bag a runner picked up for me."

"Did Gina know you had her key?"

Marissa nodded. "She was looking for an excuse not to go to the hotel."

"Do you know why?"

"A falling out with Will," she murmured.

"Was she aware of the blackmail?"

"No. Nobody was. I kept that between myself and the studio."

"Nobody else knew? You're sure about that?"

"Positive."

Garrick marched up towards the manor to find Simon Wheeler. He eyed the enormous house as he passed. With dozens of rooms, the old building no doubt held many dark secrets. Combined with the sprawling estate, there were many places a ransom could be stashed - if it was still here. He called Harry Lord and asked him to get a search warrant ASAP. With Freya in custody, and the high-profile nature of the case, he was sure Drury would pull enough strings to action it within the day.

He found the director with a small second unit camera team shooting a conversation between Will and a young woman he recognised as a regular minor character from the series. A maid, Edith, but he wasn't sure if that was her actual name or her character's. During one of Fanta's monologues, she had told him about second units, and how the production used them to film scenes concurrently to save time.

He noticed Liliana standing to the side next to a costume rail. Her arms were folded, and she uneasily glanced between

Garrick and Will. When he caught her eye, she looked sharply away. Fanta hadn't been able to glean much from her, but he was certain she was another victim. There was nothing to be gained by pressing the matter right now, but he wondered just how many people would surface once the truth became public.

"Cut!" snapped Simon. He noticed Garrick and glanced at his watch. "Reset in five." He crossed to him without a hint of a smile. "Come to say goodbye, Detective?"

"Crossing the t's and dotting the i's. I need to ask you about Freya Granger."

"I thought you might. Well, I've got nothing to hide. Lock her away for life, I say. She's a psychopath."

They walked across the manicured lawn to distance themselves from the unit. Garrick glanced back and saw that Will was staring at them while Liliana was nervously fussing with his costume.

"She was constantly nagging me to get her on the film. Not as an extra, that would have been easy enough, but a featured role."

"And you helped her?"

"God, no. I said I would. But she can't act. She has no talent, and Marissa can't stand her, either."

"But you told her she could be in your next film."

"I told her that to shut her up." He nodded towards the house. "This is her home, so we have to put up with her. Once we wrap, I'm never going to see her again, so I can promise her the moon for a quiet life." Garrick's disapproving look made him smile. "You still haven't worked it out yet? Making movies is all about politics. Nobody said it was nice."

"Is Freya aware of that?"

"I think she is. She was pressing for a contract before the end of this shoot, which will never happen, of course."

"Is this why she interrupted your dinner with Will and Karen?"

"Ah, that. Yes. She's one of those pricks who thinks they're privileged enough to have whatever they want without having to work for it."

"She must've been desperate."

"Desperate enough to kill Karen?" He shrugged. "Like I said, she's a psycho. I make it a rule not to believe anything she says. I'll give you the same advice."

"Interesting. Because she talked about blackmail..."

It wasn't strictly true, but Garrick observed his reaction. He didn't flinch, but nodded. He'd had plenty of time to prepare his side of the story.

"Ah, that old chestnut. If I was going to give her the benefit of the doubt, then I'd blame her father."

They stopped in front of the house the very moment the sun broke through the white clouds and bathed it in sunshine. Despite the obvious wear and tear, it was a handsome building.

"He wanted the location fee increased. The studio said no. James's problem was while he could threaten to refuse future filming here," he gestured to the house, "it has become so iconic nobody else wants to use it. His bookings have dried up. The studio is aware of that. They've got him over a barrel."

"So blackmailing the production was his alternative. And you knew about it?"

"I knew Marissa was being blackmailed about the ending being leaked to the press. I always suspected Sir James. Marissa suspects everybody. Even me." He wagged a finger. "But it was nothing to do with me. I had no part in it at all."

"I suppose, considering your relationship with Marissa, why would you stand in their way? The only problem now is two crimes are colliding together. Gina Brown gets associated with the extortion racket the moment Marissa took her key to access Will's room to take his car. And Gina is already snarled up dealing with Will's behaviour."

"Ah..." Simon shifted uneasily. "That."

"Yes. That."

"There is no love lost between Will and me, and frankly, I believe everything I hear about him."

"But you've done nothing about it."

"I told Marissa. Which is my duty. Gina came to me after he assaulted her. I told her to tell Marissa."

"It sounds like you're passing the buck."

Simon pointed to the floor. "On set, the director is God. Off set, we're just another employee. I did my legal duty and helped her report it to Marissa. We sat in there," he flicked a glance at the house, "and Marissa and I listened to what had happened." He rubbed his fingers across his mouth, recalling the conversation. "I even said she should go to the police."

"Even if it meant Will being arrested and the film being shut down?"

Simon shrugged. "I'd get paid anyway, and I'd still have the satisfaction of seeing his career die in flames. Marissa is the one who convinced her not to tell the police. It was all very passive-aggressive, but she said without evidence his lawyers would destroy her. She made Gina feel guilty about shutting the production down and putting everybody out of work. She even hinted that it would make Gina unemployable in the future."

"Who else has come to you about Will?"

"Nobody. But let's face it, there isn't a member of our crew who doesn't know how I feel about him. Christ, the poor things have to put up with us squabbling every day on set. It doesn't lend itself to the most pleasant of working conditions." He became thoughtful. "That said, I know there are others. You get a sense of these things. If I'm going to be impartial, I'd point out there are some women who welcome the attention. I know that's not a very 'PC' thing to say, but there it is. Screwing a movie star is just another notch on their belt, as much as it is for him. Of course, if I go on record saying that, then I'm the one who'd be crucified as an enabler."

"So, Gina was threatened into silence and everybody else was too afraid to come forward. What do you think happened next? Why did she have to die?"

Simon gave a long look at his watch in a clear signal the interview was over. "I don't know. But I think there was more than one person who was happy to see Gina dead."

24

Sir Edward Kaplan's Saville Row suit probably cost more than Garrick earned in two months. Freya's lawyer wore an expression of such privileged smugness that his cheeks had folded into place like a withered prune. The sixty-year-old's flowing black hair didn't show a single follicle of grey, and Garrick had to stop his eyes from automatically moving upwards as he wondered just how many people the obvious hair transplant had come from.

Freya was pale and refused to make eye contact. If she could have curled any further into the plastic chair, she would've become part of it. The annoying hum from the interview room's air conditioner wasn't helping anybody. Since leaving Laddingford Manor, Garrick's migraine had suddenly assaulted him. The co-codamol he'd taken from his house had provided only minimal relief. It had since been inflamed by the notion there may be two killers.

"We have a search warrant, Freya. And officers are combing through the estate." To his surprise, that hadn't been bluster. Drury had pushed through the request with unparalleled efficiency, aided by those with a political interest in the case. He could only marvel at what politicians were capable of when they expressed interest. "You can save us a lot of time by telling us where the money is."

"My client has already given her statement on that issue." Kaplan made a note on the laptop open in front of him. "And I once again state for the record that you have arrested my client on nothing more than an ill-founded hunch."

Garrick normally enjoyed taking legal representatives on face-to-face. He knew they were only doing their job, but some, like Kaplan, considered it a personal crusade. Today, Garrick was in no mood for games, so he blanked the lawyer. Chib sat next to him. Sensing the peculiar mood from her boss, she said nothing. Until Garrick had marched into the room ten minutes ago, she and Fanta had been cross-examining Freya with little success. Garrick had curtly dismissed Fanta and taken over the interview without even the most cursory of introductions to the lawyer.

"Marissa Carlisle dropped off two-hundred grand at the east gatehouse, just as you'd arranged. And you collected it."

Freya stared at the clattering air conditioning vent above his head.

"And we have statements from people who overheard your argument with Simon Wheeler outside the hotel the night before you murdered Karen Dalton."

Freya snapped to face him. "I didn't kill her!"

It was the only response she'd given during the entire interview.

Unperturbed, Garrick pressed on. "I am confused why you're willing to take the fall for your partner in crime. They may get away scot-free while you grow old in prison."

Freya shrank further back in her chair as she glared at him. Kaplan gave a gentle chuckle.

"Please provide your supporting evidence for these vacuous claims. Or is it all eyewitness testimony from people who have a grudge against my client?"

"You mean Marissa Carlisle, who she was blackmailing? The one who wouldn't allow her a part in the film? The same producer Sir James was trying to renegotiate his contract with, but getting nowhere?"

"I don't see how Sir James fits into this," Kaplan said tartly.

For the first time, Garrick set his eyes on him.

"Then you are very blind. Forcing his daughter to carry out the exchange? Quite cowardly, really."

"I must protest!"

Garrick shrugged. He didn't give a shit. He massaged the bridge of his nose to ease the tension as he turned back to Freya.

"After paying off Emma Rowan in Cambridge, he'd always felt you were a burden, didn't he?"

"Accusations–"

"Mr Kaplan, you're the lawyer that facilitated the pay off. The one who drafted the NDA that Sir James forced her to sign." Garrick gave him a crocodilian smile. "Now, doesn't that put you both in a dilemma? You can refute that happened, or you can sue Emma for breaching the NDA, which is an admission of your guilt, too. *Mmm*, curious. I look forward to seeing how that pans out." He leaned forward to target Freya. "You became fixated on Emma. You couldn't let her go. Love, attraction, whatever it was, it led you to attack her. But you can't help yourself, can you? You've always been obsessed with Will Sadler."

"Speculation!" Kaplan interjected, slapping his palm on the table.

Garrick ignored him. "You fantasised about a life with a Hollywood star, but it was clear his interest in you was purely platonic. And that must've really hurt. Not only because of the callous way he rejected your feelings, but also because you knew he was sleeping around with so many other women. So, what was wrong with you?"

"This line of questioning is wholly inappropriate!" Kaplan snapped.

Garrick shot him a look. "Then I better warn you, it's going to go from a PG rating to an 18 very quickly."

Freya's eyes were wide and glassy as she fought to control her emotions. It wasn't evidence enough for a court, but Garrick knew he was on the right track.

"That's when you decided to quit university and become an actress. Why not? You're attractive, connected, driven. You've got what it takes. You have everything. Except the talent. Will knows this, but he still pulls strings for you. Your first outing for *Mood Music* doesn't go down well. Then for *The Sins of Agatha* you get fired. Worse, you're replaced by Karen Dalton. She wasn't just front of house staff at the Troubadour. You've encountered each other on the London fringe circuit too. Both you and Gina Brown, in fact."

He pulled a sheet of paper from Chib's folder and slid it across the table. Wilkes had finally drawn up a comprehensive map of the actors' various interactions.

"Joe Public, like me, thinks actors are just in films, TV shows, or on stage. We forget about radio, music videos, commercials. In fact, it seems you and Karen coincidentally auditioned for the same two music videos and six commercials. One of which she got for a payday loan advert. She even worked with Gina on it. Small world. Everybody was getting something except you. Then Will gets engaged, and that sent you over the edge. The only thing you have left to cling on to is Simon Wheeler in the hope he'll give you a job in his next feature."

Tears streamed down Freya's cheeks as she stared at the list of auditions in front of her.

"I spiked Karen's food at the snack bar so that she'd screw up her scenes."

Kaplan raised a hand. "Freya!"

Freya propped herself on her elbows and ignored him. She seemed relieved to get things off her chest. "That's all I did. It's not poisonous. It could never kill her. I didn't know she was going to wander off. I saw Will had eaten some too, not much, but after what he did to me, I didn't care."

"The problem is Will takes a prescription drug to control his bipolar disorder. Did you know that?" Freya shook her head. "Lamotrigine. He had an adverse reaction between that and the mushrooms. You'd almost doubled his dose. It knocked him out."

"She would've been tripping in front of the camera. I thought it was funny. It couldn't kill her... so when I found out she was dead... I was scared."

"You stopped visiting the set as much." Freya nodded. "Stopped seeing Will. But you still went to his trailer to speak to him."

She leaned back and took a moment to line up her thoughts.

"Gina told me what Will had done to her."

"You didn't believe her?"

Freya pulled a face. "I'd seen the way she looked at him. She led him on."

"Plenty women would contest your view."

"She said there were at least ten others who wanted to report him. She asked if he'd ever attacked me. I thought she was nuts. She'd even turned Karen against him before they'd met on set."

"Had he assaulted her?"

"Not as far as I knew. Gina and Karen seemed to know each other like you said. She wanted to warn her and thought if she'd get her on side..."

"It would strengthen her argument. And you confronted Will about this?"

Freya nodded. "He said it was all bullshit, of course."

"And you believed him?"

She sighed. "I didn't believe it up until that point. But I've known him for years. I know when he's lying. I know him better than anybody else." Garrick glanced at Chib; she'd noticed the slight manic rise in tone. "I knew he was lying to me."

"When was this?"

"The day before they all had dinner." She put her head in her hands and stared at the table. "It was that afternoon I caught him in his trailer screwing a girl from wardrobe. He didn't see me. I ran."

Silence filled the room. Garrick took satisfaction in seeing Kaplan's smug grin had dried up.

Chib broke the silence. "That must have been heart-breaking."

Freya nodded. "That's why I went to the hotel that night to confront him. I was drunk. And I hadn't expected them to all be there. I told him I'd seen him screwing the girl. Said he was a slimy bastard. Simon took me outside and told me to calm down."

"He told you to stick to your plan to blackmail the production. To take the money and run?" said Garrick softly.

He had been hoping for an inadvertent acknowledgement, but Freya said nothing. She may be upset, but she was in control.

"I think that dinner caused everything. Kelly and Will weren't getting on, and now she had confirmation he was sleeping around. She ended it. Karen realised everything she'd been warned about was true. That would ruin her big star break if it got out. That's why I think she wanted to talk to Will at the folly. And it destroyed what was left of our friendship. It destroyed everything."

Garrick sat back in his chair and ran a finger in a small circle over this throbbing temple. Freya would never blunder into a confession, and as much as he hated to admit it, Kaplan was correct. They still lacked hard evidence, yet he felt more convinced than ever that she hadn't acted alone.

"How did Marissa Carlisle react when you burst into the dinner?"

"I don't know. I wasn't paying attention."

"Gina Brown had gone to her with accusations over Will's behaviour. She wanted to keep a lid on everything."

Freya spat out a single barking laugh. "Of course she did. She only cares about that show. Not people. She would do *anything* to keep the truth buried."

25

DCI Garrick didn't trust himself to drive, so Chib drove them to the set in her Nissan Leaf. The near-silent electric car was a blessing for Garrick's headache, and he spent most of the journey with his eyes closed. They had ended the interview when DC Sean Wilkes had messaged them to say they'd found something at the manor. The interview had only firmed up his belief that Gina Brown's death resulted from two separate crimes crossing one another. During the drive, he finally ventured his hypothesis.

"What if Marissa Carlisle killed Gina to silence her?" with his eyes closed, he plotted out the timeline in his head. "She dropped the ransom off. Remember, she didn't know who was blackmailing her. The Grangers may have been our obvious choice, but she had other people to contend with. A lot of women were upset that she was effectively covering for Will. Then she finds out Gina was talking to me so had to stop her or the entire production would come crashing down there and then. Her attack felt impulsive rather than anything premeditated, and with

Karen Dalton already dead, she could pass it off as the same killer."

"Two killers. Different motives."

"Mmm." It was obviously possible, but statistically...

"We have evidence that places Marissa at the house during the correct window. And she has admitted to being there. Even so, it's a lot of conjecture."

"I'm aware of that, Chib. What happened to the old days when a miscreant shouted it was a fair cop and admitted everything?"

"I don't know. Perhaps people just became smarter. Besides, it doesn't quite answer everything."

"The phone."

"The phone," she agreed. "What was it doing in Will's trailer? I know you're still not invested in him as a killer, but he had just as much to lose as Marissa. More so. And it feels more compelling that he would've killed Karen, especially if he was stoned."

"Karen was warning him, not accusing him. Even if she was doing it to lookout for herself, why wouldn't he see her as an ally?"

"Perhaps he didn't know what she was going to say? Especially after Freya's outburst the night before. And that would explain how he had Karen's phone and why it was in his trailer. Gina, knowing it was missing, was ringing it to find it, hoping that there would be something on it to use against Will."

A calmness smothered the estate, as almost everybody was at the marquee set. Chib parked close to the house, which had three police minibuses outside ferrying officers from across the county to conduct the search.

DC Sean Wilkes greeted them at the door with a

triumphant smile. He'd been coordinating the operation, and after just over an hour, they had hit pay dirt.

"I wouldn't ordinarily trump my own efforts, sir," he said as he led them through the grand entrance hall towards the family's private quarters at the rear. "But I think this has been the quickest search in history."

"Congratulations," said Garrick. "I'm sure your quarry tried to outfox you at every turn."

"Unless they were terrible at hiding things," said Chib with a knowing smile.

Wilkes's face fell. "It wasn't *that* badly hidden. And I got a confession from old man Granger, too."

Sir James and Lady Helen morosely sat at the kitchen table. Garrick asked the two uniformed officers accompanying them to wait outside. On the table between them was a crumpled, grubby black Adidas sports bag.

Garrick took a seat opposite them and gave the empty bag a cursory inspection.

"You must be very hard up to pull a stunt like this," he finally said.

Sir James sighed. "First, my daughter was only doing what I asked her to do. She had no other role in this. My wife knows nothing. This is entirely my doing."

"Enlighten me."

"Desperation, Detective. When you have so much to lose, you feel the pain so much sharper when you hit the floor."

"Ah, the old argument that the rich suffer the hardest. I've always found it a difficult one to digest."

"This estate is in debt. I'm facing bankruptcy." Lady Helen blew into a tissue. The news was fresh to her. "The location fees barely take us into the black and the house is now so sewn into Broadhaven fiction, we're at the bottom of every-body's location wish list."

"So blackmail was your only solution?"

"Yes, when it became clear that I couldn't win the renegotiation. And I couldn't afford to lose the production, either." He sighed heavily. "It was Freya who discovered the alternative ending they'd planned. Will was understandably furious. That's when I had the idea. There are always disgruntled crew. I thought it would be easy to pin it on one of them."

"Where's the money?"

"In a safe deposit box in London. I took it there that very day."

Garrick recalled Sir James leaving for business that afternoon.

"We found the bag in a spare room used to store junk," said Wilkes.

"When Freya picked it up, we placed the cash in briefcases. She was going to dispose of the bag, but when we heard about Gina, she was frightened and not thinking straight."

"I imagine the incident really shook her up," Garrick said as neutrally as he could.

Sir James raised both hands. "I can assure you she was here the entire time, except when she left to collect the money at the gate. She watched Marissa drive off at speed, and she returned to the house."

"You seem to forget I was there," Garrick said. "There were footprints that led from the crime scene, past the house, to the gate."

"But do they return to the house?" Lady Helen said suddenly. She must have seen a flicker of doubt cross Garrick's face, because she gave a thin smile. "I watch a lot of

American crime shows, and it's just the sort of question Jessica Fletcher would ask. My daughter is not a killer. I'll be the first to admit she has temper issues. I think she is most definitely on the spectrum. Autism wasn't something that seemed to exist when she was younger. But even a blind mother can see her behaviour is not exactly normal, but to do those terrible things is beyond her."

Sir James spoke up. "I have sat at this very table and had Marissa threaten to kill me if I put her precious franchise in jeopardy. Don't be fooled by what she says regarding the studios. Broadhaven has made her very rich. She makes money every time it's shown anywhere in the world. The money she paid me, I would wager, came out of her own pocket. She wouldn't risk the studio knowing about her incompetence."

Garrick studied Sir James carefully. He hadn't raised the claims about Will, which would have been an easy deflection. He realised it must still be a well-guarded secret amongst the crew.

"I'm afraid your daughter's case is still ongoing. However, this," he flicked the bag on the table. "Appears to be resolved. It will come as no surprise that we'll have to arrest you."

Garrick let DC Wilkes make the arrest. The evidence had been poorly hidden and quickly found, but he could hardly punish the lad for that, and the arrest would look good on his file. The seconded uniformed officers continued searching the house, hoping they'd turn something up on Freya, but Garrick suspected the blackmail matter was now closed.

Lady Helen's comments regarding the footprints had struck a chord. While Freya had all the motives for killing Karen Dalton, he was now certain she had nothing to do with Gina Brown. The direction of the prints suggested Marissa was the culprit. She had the motive, and they could place her at the crime scene. Wearing a pair of oversized boots taken from the wardrobe department to hide her own smaller feet was the sort of thing she would think of. And Freya had seen her drive away, so all he had to do was confirm the time with her. If it wasn't Marissa, then the killer would have literally run past Freya as she was picking up the money...

Which left Will Sadler. The correct foot size, and he was an actor. Presumably he could fake throwing his weight around to put the police off the scent. But he had no way to make it to the hotel and back if Marissa had his car.

So that circled him back to the obvious suspect. He just needed proof.

Sir James made no fuss as Wilkes led him to the police car parked outside the entrance hall. There was no need to cuff him. And since he had lost everything, Garrick thought he should keep some of his dignity.

As he and Chib watched the car snake down the driveway, Marissa joined them.

"I heard he took my money," she said with barely contained satisfaction.

"Some news travels fast," Garrick replied moodily.

"Well, thank you, Detective. I take it I'll be getting it all back?"

"It'll be taken in for evidence. But yes. You'll get your money back, eventually."

Marissa shook her head sadly. "What a family. We've worked together for the last four years, and this is what it boils down to? Murder and blackmail. It's sickening."

"I'm curious where it puts you if he loses all of this when he becomes bankrupt."

"It'll be easier to deal with the receivers than with him."

She smiled with relief. "Now I've just got my errant star to deal with, and I may just be able to save this movie."

"I think you know how that's going to turn out, don't you? There are women ready to speak out against him." He enjoyed watching the colour drain from her face. "It didn't end with Gina Brown. And when the truth behind her death becomes public, I think many more people will speak out. It won't be a case of which ending do you show. It will be a case of writing off this entire film. How much did you say the budget was? Thirty-five million quid that the studio will never make back."

Marissa's fists clenched and her shoulders tightened.

"I have seen no proof of these claims. Just stories of young girls who got in a tizzy because a handsome Hollywood heartthrob wouldn't give them the time of day. Without proof, there is no case to answer."

"They don't need proof," Chib said. "These days voices are easily heard, and the mob moves into action. You've heard about cancel culture, haven't you? Rightly or wrongly the mob bays and suddenly Will Sadler's integrity and career is flushed away, all without a criminal trial."

"Why does this sound like a threat?"

Garrick hesitated. He had nothing on her. He could keep clutching at theories, or he could push her into making a mistake.

"Karen Dalton died at the hands of a jealous woman. But not the same person who killed Gina. Gina was killed because she called me to blow Will Sadler out of the water. Who knows, maybe she thought Will had killed Karen to silence her? As luck would have it, you were here dropping off the ransom. What better cover than to kill Gina and pin it on your blackmailer. With luck, the police would arrest the blackmailer and think they'd caught the killer too, while you walk away, win awards, and live the high life because of your precious show."

"Me?" she laughed contemptuously. "Really?"

Garrick nodded. "You have everything to lose. You've the perfect cover story that brought you down here in Will's car and got you back to the hotel to clean up, all before your driver arrived. And you had access to boots from the wardrobe department, Gina's key card, and Will's vehicle. If nobody was arrested for the murder, then you win because every other woman out there who was thinking about reporting him would now be living in fear. You even chose the same sized boots as him because you knew he had a rock-solid alibi, but everybody else would wonder, just a little, did he really do it? It would be fear enough to keep silent."

She snorted derisively. "And if you arrested Freya for both murders, then what's preventing all these miserable cows from destroying my movie, anyway? How do I benefit?"

Garrick hadn't thought that far ahead. Marissa seized on his hesitation.

"You're full of shit, Detective. And I deal with people like that day-in, day-out. You don't have a shred of evidence because there is none. Do you know who else has access to the boots from the wardrobe department? *Everybody* in the wardrobe department! All the actors' personal effects are in their safes. Hell, the crew uses them. Me, Simon, Gina – everybody! You better be careful about the accusations you toss around."

Without another word, she stormed to the marquee set. Chib raised her eyebrows and gave a low whistle.

"Talk about highly strung."

"I did just accuse her of murder."

"Yes. I thought that was... bold, sir."

Garrick rubbed his head before realising he was massaging the spot where his tumour lay. He'd built a career on being circumspect and diligent. Could his condition be making him reckless?

As he watched her disappear amongst the trailers, he had a sudden flash of inspiration.

"Do you have the list of people who'd signed in with security before Gina's assault?"

He started slowly walking towards the trailers as Chib took time to go through the messages on her phone. "I don't have them."

Garrick called Harry Lord and repeated the question. Harry took time searching through the details on HOLMES. Garrick covered his phone as he spoke to Chib.

"Do you remember Fanta saying who the first and last people to leave the set are?"

"The wardrobe department..."

"Exactly. And Freya walked in on Will having sex with one of them."

"But she didn't say that was an assault."

"No. Somebody was willing to... do Will." He was interrupted when Harry came back with a list of names. "*Uh-huh.* How many of them were in the wardrobe department? Oh. Wait, were there any who hadn't checked-in?"

Garrick's eyes went wide when he received his answer.

26

Everybody jumped when Garrick opened the door with just a little too much force. He stepped into the wide wardrobe trailer. One wall had mirrors and a long bench filled with pins, clips, and just about everything required to fix, patch, and repair bespoke movie costumes. There was enough space for three chairs. Duncan Reynolds stood in front of a mirror as Chloe Aubertel pinned his costume.

Will sat in a chair, bare-chested, as Liliana Davies held his shirt, which was covered in what looked like wine. She jumped at the noise and stared at Garrick like a startled deer.

"Liliana Davies, we need to ask you some questions." He gestured to Chib, who was staring at Will's perfect six-pack. She looked away, embarrassed.

"I need her at the moment, Inspector," Chloe said in her strong French accent and through lips clenching pins.

"This won't wait. And Will, you stay too."

Will gave Duncan and Chloe a pleading look. Chloe put the pins onto the counter and wafted her hand theatrically.

"Come, Duncan, we are being tossed out of my trailer!"

She flounced out with Duncan in tow. Will made no motion to cover himself. Liliana clung to his dirty shirt like a life preserver. She edged behind the actor, using him as a shield.

"I have some direct questions for the both of you."

Will shrugged. "Fire away."

"How long have you two been sleeping together?"

Will shook his head. Liliana shot a filthy look at Garrick.

"Detective," Will said with a chuckle. "Liliana and I have our thing. But it's *our* thing, if you get my meaning."

"Freya saw you both in your trailer the day before Gina was murdered."

Will's look darkened. "Well, Freya should keep her nose out of other people's affairs. She's turned into somebody I don't know. She won't leave me alone. I told her to stay away."

Garrick moved closer, so he could better address Liliana directly.

"Liliana, why don't you tell me your opinion, rather than me get it from Golden Boy here?"

Will spluttered, unused to being spoken to like that.

"Will and I are in love," she whispered.

Will leapt from his seat and held up a hand. "Wait a second. No, we're not. This is just a shag. An on-set perk."

From Liliana's expression, she clearly didn't agree.

Will turned to Garrick. "A lot of women want to sleep with me."

He had the audacity to wink at Chib. Garrick thought the frosty looked Chib returned could shrivel his genitals off at fifty paces. He held up his finger an inch from Will's nose.

"Sit down. And shut the fuck up." Garrick's voice was barely above a whisper, and he was having trouble resisting the urge not to punch Will squarely in the face. "She might not know what type of creep you are, but I do." He turned back to Liliana, who looked confused. She moved to a rack of costumes densely packed on a rail. "You love him, don't you?"

"You said you were leaving Kelly because of me."

Will was bubbling with anger, but lacked the courage to act on it.

"We'd finished anyway," he muttered. "I don't know why I'm here."

He made to push past Garrick – but Garrick thrust a palm against Will's chest to stop him.

"Stay right where you are, mate." Garrick's voice dripped with menace. "Like I said, Freya saw you two the day before Gina's death. It was the day I found Karen's phone in your trailer."

"I told you she had never been in my trailer!"

"And I believe you. Because Liliana put it there, didn't you?"

Will looked at her in confusion. "What? Why would you have it?"

"There's a safe in here, right? I bet your phone's in there. As was Karen's. Except Liliana had taken it out after Karen died. All Karen's personal effects had been handed over before she could return it. So, assuming your leading lady had been in your trailer at some point, she dropped it there for somebody else to find."

Liliana remained motionless; her head turned away.

"Why would you do that?" Will asked.

When Liliana didn't answer, Garrick did.

"Because she was erasing anything on it that may incriminate you. Including a voice message that she'd sent to Gina Brown. Gina was trying to warn Karen about you, only Karen was more afraid of scuppering her own career. So she tried to warn you instead. Liliana was protecting you because she knew there were several women ready to nail you to the mast."

"Is that right? You were looking out for me?" He sounded so pleased that Garrick wanted to punch him there and then. Liliana turned and gave a small nod. She was frozen, clinging to the hanging costumes.

"I thought we were in love."

"That's why you followed Karen down to the folly, isn't it? You knew she was meeting Will, and because of his reputation, you thought they were going for sex."

Garrick watched Liliana's expression as the truth dawned.

"So when Karen fell into the water because she was tripping - because her food, and yours," he glared at Will, "had been spiked by Freya – she had reasons of her own to get Karen fired." He focused back on Liliana. "But for you, it was a chance to get rid of the competition. You'd fallen hook, line, and sinker for this bozo." He jerked a thumb at Will. "And Karen was so exquisitely beautiful. I mean, that's why she got the role, aside from the fact she was also a terrific actor. How could you compete against that? There she was, face down in the water. All you had to do was grab her hair and push..."

Will was appalled; he took a step back. "Lil?"

She refused to look at him. Garrick pressed ahead. His theory was stringing itself together with little pre-planning. He was just allowing himself to swing from clue-to-clue and was as surprised it was stitching together so well.

"Gina proved to be more difficult, didn't she? She'd already canvassed the women on the crew to stand up against Will."

Will opened his mouth to speak – but Garrick raised another warning finger.

"Your life's over, Mister Rapey. One of your victims has already testified to what you did to her."

Dumbfounded, Will staggered backwards into his seat. Then he sobbed. Not because of the lives that had been lost around him, but over the death of his career. Garrick ignored him. He was on a roll with Liliana.

"You knew what Gina was about to do, so you had to do something to protect Will. Too late, you learned she was planning to tell me everything about him. But what could you do? Wardrobe are the first in, last out, right? If you were on-set when she was killed, then you'd be a suspect. So it was better that you weren't here. So you sneaked in. And that's where you really cocked up. You were the only one from your department *not to* have signed in. You came in and out another way. A short walk around the perimeter road, and through the main gates, signing in conveniently *after* the attack. The *only* one in your department not to be here already."

Will's sniffling was becoming a distraction. Garrick pressed on.

"The problem was the ground was wet from morning dew. You could see Gina's footprints leading to the marquee. You knew she was in there. So you came back here, took a pair of boots that obviously wouldn't match you. Then you went back and killed her before I got there. I bet she thought you'd turned up to agree to help. After all, it was an open secret Will was sleeping with somebody from this department. Did she know it was you?"

Liliana was so quiet and motionless, Garrick wondered if she hadn't somehow passed out while clinging to the clothes.

"You didn't have time to kill her because I turned up and you ran. You knew the east gatehouse was the easiest way in and out. So that's what you used. Only you weren't the only one to use it. Talk about bad timing. You almost ran into Freya and Marissa, making their exchange. What a narrow escape. Now, with nobody threatening to speak out against him, Will was safe. He was all yours. Once the movie is wrapped, you'd fly off into the sunset and live happily ever after."

Will took a tissue from the counter and blew his nose. In minutes he'd transformed from a leading man into a vulnerable, weak nerd. Garrick had to admit the man had range.

"You're a bloody psychopath!" Will sprang from the chair and snatched his hoodie top hanging from a peg. "You stay away from me!" He marched towards the door.

That provoked Liliana. She whipped around and looked at him with open hostility.

"You said we'd be together!"

"I tell everybody that! That's all you dumb bitches want to hear! It's just a game! It means nothing!"

Tears rolled down Liliana's cheeks. "It means *everything* to me!"

Will shook his head. "But you mean nothing to me."

If Garrick thought Will had acting range, then Liliana's transformation was award worthy. The upset, soft, doe-eyed girl, who was too petite to pose a threat, suddenly melted away. The betrayal in her wide brown eyes was visceral, but it didn't spread to the rest of her face. Her expression was neutral, as if she were observing events rather than experiencing them. A typical sociopath veneer; one that was confirmed seconds later when she withdrew her hands from the clothing rail.

She was clutching a shotgun.

Garrick recognised the silverwork on the stock as one of Sir James's hunting rifles that should sit in the fourth space in the display cabinet. She must've taken it even before Karen was killed. How long had murder been on her agenda? She aimed it at Will.

Garrick acted on pure instinct. Had he thought about it for a second, then his actions would've been very different. He booted Will hard in the side. The actor toppled against the wall as the shot rang out.

Garrick felt warm blood fleck his face.

He heard Chib shout his name as she tackled him to the floor as a second shot came. His head struck the side of the bench, and everything faded to black.

He woke lying on his back, with the ceiling swirling above him. He rolled over, his hand slipping in blood on the floor. The first thing he saw was Will clutching at his side, blood seeping from between his fingertips. He was pale, his lips tinged blue as he fought for shallow breaths.

As the world steadied itself, he couldn't see Liliana, but saw Chib lying on the floor with her back to him.

"Shit! No! Chib?" She rolled over, looking dazed but alive. "Are you hurt?"

"No..." but she was stunned. She spotted Will and was suddenly on her knees by his side. "Pass me that!" She pointed at a costume.

Garrick staggered to his feet and yanked one of Will's riding jackets from the rail and tossed it to her. As Chib began using the coat to stem the wound, Garrick handed her a first aid kit from under the bench.

"Call an ambulance," she said.

Garrick staggered to the door. He looked out in time to

see Liliana running through the avenue of trailers as curious crew began gathering towards the noise. He saw the shocked faces of Marissa and Chloe staring at him, and realised he'd been splashed with Will's blood.

"Call an ambulance," he growled. "Gunshot wound. Hurry." He ducked his head back into the trailer. There was little he could do to help Will. "She's making a run for it."

"Go. I've got this," Chib said without looking up.

Still feeling woozy, and with his head throbbing from butting the bench, DCI David Garrick gave chase.

27

His first few steps from the trailer almost had him sprawling face first into the gravel. He shouldered into a production assistant, which helped keep his balance. He was groggy and unbalanced as he sprinted in pursuit of Liliana. Everybody who'd appeared to investigate the gunshots swiftly parted as he barrelled through them towards the car park.

Garrick couldn't see if she still had the shotgun, and with both barrels spent he was hoping she didn't have the time or ammunition to reload, but he couldn't take any chances on a woman who was clearly disturbed and placed no value on life.

His arms windmilled wildly as his distorted balance threw him sideways, forcing him to slow down just to stay upright. His head throbbed, and he felt nauseous. The need to get fit rattled through his mind as he panted for breath. Reaching the end of the trailers, he stepped into the packed car park. He couldn't see any sign of Liliana.

He slowed to a walking pace as he watched for any movement between the vehicles. He coiled, ready to dart for cover if she started firing. The sound of an engine made him start. He whirled around to see a black Jaguar XF turn into the lot. It was a vehicle used to chauffeur the stars around. The driver jammed the brakes – and the car skidded a couple of yards, stopping inches short of hitting Garrick - who slumped across the bonnet. The driver leapt out with a barrage of apologies.

Then the buzz of an electric vehicle, like an irritating mosquito, made Garrick spin as a blue Peugeot e-208 burst from its parking bay. Liliana was at the wheel. She skidded the car across the gravel – blasting up a wall of stones that forced Garrick and the Driver to protect their faces. He felt pebbles painfully lashed the backs of his exposed hands. Three pebbles struck the Jaguar's windscreen with such force they chipped the glass.

The Peugeot sped up - with more gravel fanning in its wake.

"I need your car!" Garrick yelled as he shoved past the driver and sank into the driving seat. It was in a much lower driving position than his elevated Land Rover, but he was already pulling away. Momentum slammed the door closed and pushed him back. It was a much more powerful vehicle than he was used to.

Ahead, the Peugeot hurtled towards the wooden barrier across the gate. The security guard sat on a stool, reading a newspaper, when the growl of Garrick's Jaguar made him look up. By that time it was too late to do anything, as the Peugeot was already upon him. It smashed the barrier into splinters.

A reporter, alerted by the noise, made his unfortunate appearance from behind the wall. With a camera raised to snap any vehicle emerging, he hadn't expected the near-silent Peugeot. The fender's passenger side caught him in the leg – and he was flung over the bonnet. He smashed against the windshield, his shoulder cracking the glass into an elaborate spider's web. He bounced over the roof and slumped into the grass on the other side of the entrance.

Garrick was travelling too fast to stop in time. He blared his horn as he sped through the gate – just as the reporter's heavy digital SLR camera came down and punctured his windscreen at thirty-five miles per hour. He just had time to dodge his head aside as the camera rebounded off his headrest with enough force to angle it sharply back. The SLR bounded around the back before coming to a rest in the rear footwell.

Garrick almost lost control of the Jag as it skidded on the tarmac, but the vehicle's all-wheel drive saved him as it gripped the surface of the road. Without easing up on the accelerator, he twisted the wheel hard right to follow the Peugeot.

The Jaguar may have had the greater power, but the nippy Peugeot's electric engine responded instantly as Liliana pulled away. Garrick's hand went for the gear stick, and his foot uselessly pressed the floor where the clutch should be. It was an automatic. He ignored the unusual feeling as he gripped the wheel in both hands and inched the accelerator down.

The pain in his head was blinding now, and his left eye twitched closed. His vision trembled as a migraine loomed. He had effectively stolen the car, *police acquisition* being something that only happened in the movies, and he was breaking every rule by engaging in a high-speed chase. But with an armed and dangerous suspect he didn't dare think what mayhem she could bring about if she got loose.

Horns blared as an oncoming postal van narrowly avoided a collision with the Peugeot. Liliana's car erratically bobbed left and right across the road, and he wondered what she was doing. Lees Road was *just* large enough for two narrow lanes of traffic and a single footpath. Trees crowded in from both sides, offering glimpses of fields beyond. The occasional orange flash of bricks denoted a lone house as they sped past.

Liliana suddenly slammed on her brakes, forcing Garrick to do the same. He felt the car slip across the road despite its sophisticated ABS. Then the Peugeot jinked into the opposite lane and overtook a black Micra with learner plates. Liliana must have been feet away from a collision. He had to stop her.

His hand once again automatically went for the phantom gearstick as he pulled into the opposite lane to overtake. Almost instantly, Liliana swerved in front of the Micra, and Garrick heard the wail of a deep horn. A white delivery van was speeding towards him. With nowhere to go, and his heart in his throat, he jerked the wheel to the left and crushed the brakes so he could pull back in behind the Micra.

The van passed so close it snapped his wing mirror off. Ahead, he saw Liliana press her advantage and speed up while the Micra's terrified learner slowed down, forcing Garrick to do the same.

"Come on!" yelled Garrick.

There was a bend coming up, but he had a narrow window in which to overtake. He didn't hesitate. He stomped the accelerator to the floor. It took a second for the engine to respond and deliver maximum power. He overtook the Micra just as Liliana disappeared around the right-hand bend ahead. Garrick drifted back into his lane in time to avoid a car coming head-on - the driver oblivious to the near miss.

With the rev counter redlining on the digital dial, the Jaguar ate the distance between him and Liliana. Again, she was weaving across the road. He couldn't continue the chase until either one ran out of fuel. He had to be proactive.

On the next straight, as a field opened out on his left, Garrick delicately bumped into the back of the Peugeot. It didn't feel like a dramatic impact, but a glance at his speedometer showed they were doing sixty-six miles per hour.

The impact jolted him forward, and he realised he wasn't wearing his seatbelt. There was a crunch of metal and fiberglass. Shards of crumpled plastic from her bumper clattered across his bonnet. A few pieces made it through the hole in the windshield and one caught his cheek, drawing blood. Then the Jaguar lurched as it crunched over something more substantial. In his rear-view mirror, he saw the remains of the Peugeot's rear bumper spinning across the road.

He looked back ahead in time to see why Liliana had been drifting erratically. She had been reloading the shotgun in the cramped car. She held it upside-down in her left hand, vaguely pointing it in his direction.

The shot obliterated her rear window, the remains of his windshield, and a portion of the roof over the passenger seat. Safety glass pelted him like hailstones. He felt a stinging sensation from his left ear and neck and knew he'd been cut.

He was saved from the second shot as the recoil jerked the shotgun from her hand and it fell onto the backseat.

Immediately, he heard another bang – and a football sized hole appeared in the panel above the driver's side rear wheel arch. He saw fragments of rubber fly as the tyre was shredded.

The Peugeot lurched as the rear wheel rim now sprayed sparks over the Jag. The car slewed to the side, threatening to flip over as it approached a give way. It was only Liliana's remarkable skills that kept her on the road – but barely with control. Her car slid sideways – slamming into a DPD delivery van that had been waiting to make the turn. The impact saved Liliana from careening into the field beyond – and she pulled away to the left.

Garrick stomped the brakes and skidded to follow her. The Jaguar's computerised suspension ensured he made the turn without hitting the van.

The electric vehicle was unstoppable. Anything with a standard engine would now be a smoking heap, whereas the electric Peugeot sprang spritely forward. Ahead, the road narrowed, and a set of traffic lights were on red to halt traffic from passing over a single-lane humpback bridge.

Liliana jumped the lights. Garrick had little choice but to follow. The bridge gracefully arced over the River Medway. Only when they were both on it could they see a grocery truck hurtling towards them from the other side. Smoke rose from its wheels as the driver jammed on the brakes.

Compensating for the missing wheel, Liliana's car ricocheted off the left wall, crumpling the fender – then it cut across the path of the truck and into a triangular lay-by built into the right-hand side of the bridge. She was moving so fast the stonework crumbled, and the Peugeot nosedived off the bridge and splashed into the turgid brown water below.

Garrick pushed both feet on the brake. He could smell

burning rubber as the Jaguar stopped an inch from colliding with the truck. He could hear the driver yelling from his cab as he sprinted to the gap in the wall. He was still feeling dizzy as he propped himself on the edge. The roof of the car was visible as it rapidly sank, surrounded by a curtain of bubbles as water poured in through the rear window frame. As far as he could tell, Liliana was still inside.

"Shit!" he snarled, pulling his jacket off and slinging it behind him. He sucked in a deep breath and, knowing he'd lose his bottle if he thought about it, Garrick jumped off the bridge.

His feet broke the water with a force he felt along his spine, but the stinging cold overwhelmed the pain. Garrick submerged into a cold world of brown debris. In the murk, he couldn't see beyond his hand. He struggled to the surface and sucked in another breath before swimming hard towards the Peugeot. He wasn't a strong swimmer, but he was good enough to quickly close the gap, aided by the powerful current created by the weir on the other side of the bridge, one hundred and fifty feet upstream.

The current almost pushed him past the car. He had to grab the lip of the roof through the broken rear window to anchor himself before the current could sweep him away. His eyes stung as he forced them open in the water. He could just see Liliana slumped behind the wheel, pinned by her airbag and seatbelt.

Breaking the surface to snatch a final breath, Garrick pivoted vertically down and swam through the vehicle's missing windshield. The car had flooded almost instantly and was now steadily descending. She wasn't moving; her hands were raised in the water as if surrendering. He couldn't tell if she was alive or dead. Air bubbles occasionally drifted from her lips and nose.

Garrick wedged himself in the car, the roof keeping him in place as they slowly sank. He clawed at the airbag, but his fingernails couldn't break the fabric to deflate it. Debris from the car swirled, turning visibility into soup, and further stinging his eyes. He hooked his fingers under her seatbelt at the shoulder and followed it down to the lock. A quick press on the release button disengaged it, but the belt didn't retract. He had to pull it free.

He tried not to think about his burning lungs as he hooked his hand under her left armpit and pulled. She moved – then her foot snagged on something in the footwell. The car suddenly shook around him – they'd struck the bottom of the river. He was feeling lightheaded, but couldn't give up now.

Bracing his feet against the edge of the windscreen, he heaved as hard as he could. There was a dull crack as Liliana's ankle snapped – but she suddenly slipped free. Hooking one arm under her shoulders, he kicked for the surface.

Emerging from the filthy water, he inhaled a deep breath and cradled Liliana's head as he backstroked to shore. Five people who'd stopped on the bridge were already clambering across a field to reach them. Garrick crawled up the muddy riverbank and rolled Liliana over, noticing that her right foot was twisted at an unnatural angle. Water dribbled from her mouth. Positioning Liliana on her back, he began chest compressions.

"Give her mouth-to-mouth!" somebody yelled.

Garrick spoke between keeping count of his compressions. "No. She drowned. You don't do that." He increased the force of his compressions. "Come on!"

Liliana suddenly spluttered. Water and stomach contents spewed from her mouth as she fought for air. Garrick watched as she coughed and gagged, spewing up more liquid. He slumped heavily onto his arse and finally caught his breath as others moved in to comfort the murderer.

28

"It was important that you came to me several weeks ago," said Dr Rajasekar in a soft voice that didn't fit the stern look she fixed Garrick with.

"I know," he mumbled, feeling like a schoolchild, "but work was—"

"Work is irrelevant if you're dead, David. I can only help you if you cooperate."

Garrick nodded, but didn't say a word. She softened slightly as she called up the details of his last MRI scan. Garrick glanced out of the tall windows that offered a view over Tunbridge Wells' Lower Common and the ever-busy A26, which was jammed solid with people doing the morning school run. He'd never enjoyed coming to his consultant's practice, but once through the door, he was swaddled by a blanket of calm.

"As we discussed last time, I hope you've at least been keeping your physical exertions to a minimum?" She didn't look at him as she clicked her way through the computer system.

"As easy as possible."

When the ambulance had arrived at Yalding Lees and taken Liliana, Garrick had waited for a second vehicle to take him to A&E to have the network of tiny lacerations caused by flying broken glass cleaned up; stitches put in his cheek; his stomach pumped after ingesting an unhealthy amount of the River Medway; and a tetanus shot administered to stave off any infection. The jump from the bridge had sprained his ankle, and he was still limping several days later.

Rajasekar regarded the network of tiny injuries as she'd watched him limp into her office.

"Perhaps try a little harder in the future." She glanced at the information on her screen. "Right, so the last MRI scan showed a slight abnormality in the tumour's size. We are talking fractional. Less than a millimetre. There are several factors that could cause this, so we needed to perform a regular check. It's no use doing this haphazardly. The bad news is I want you to have an MRI twice a week. If it has grown, then we need to discuss a major operation. Do you understand?"

Garrick nodded. She was making perfect sense, yet somehow he was reacting in the third person, as if she was delivering bad news to somebody else.

"If it is stable or shrinking, then we will finally take a biopsy, which will not be pleasant either. Even with less than a millimetre growth, it could be applying substantial pressure on your brain. Have you experienced any more hallucinations? Memory lapses? Confusion?"

He couldn't be one hundred per cent sure, so took the coward's way out.

"I'm feeling pretty good, all things considered."

"What about loss of appetite? Dizziness? Feelings of nausea?"

He pretended to think about it. "Not that I can recall..."

He swore the look she gave him cut through his veil of lies. "So I don't need to increase your medication?"

"A few more sleeping pills would be welcome, but I put that down to the stress of work."

"Your blood pressure is elevated, so I suggest you talk to your GP about bringing that down. When we get inside your head, we'll need that under control." She issued a long sigh and sat back in her chair. "Rest assured, David, you're in the best possible hands. It's not pleasant, but what you're going through can easily be beaten. A little dedication from you, a little discomfort along the way, there's no reason you can't eventually put this behind you. The important thing is to stay positive."

As if swayed by the power of suggestion, he left Rajasekar feeling more upbeat than he had in a long time. He promised himself to see Rajasekar's treatment through until the end and decided not to call Dr Harman's office back to schedule that appointment. He was done with therapy. It was useful, and he couldn't kid himself that it was pleasant to spend time with her, but no matter how attractive he'd found her, his thoughts resolutely turned to Wendy. Her large blue eyes. The dimples when she laughed. Her quirky humour. She was everything that had been missing from his life for far too long.

After dealing with brutal cases and lives taken before their time, he had to embrace the moments he was alive. Enjoy them. Cherish them. He'd take Wendy out at the weekend for an Indian meal, and tell her everything about his sister, about his condition, and about the fact he'd like her not to run for the hills after learning how damaged he was.

He had the horrible feeling that he was falling for her.

Back at the station, there was the usual downhill slog of dealing with the aftermath of a traumatic arrest and preparing for the protracted judicial trial ahead. Luckily, Chib had been unhurt in the shooting. After ballistics had looked over the crime scene, it became obvious her quick reactions had saved his life. He took her aside in the station's canteen and offered a simple thanks. What else could be said?

"You'd do the same," she said dismissively.

She had made Garrick buy her a coffee, which made him feel so cheap it mortified him. He put in an official request to Drury for DS Okon's bravery to be recognised. She had also stayed with Will Sadler until the ambulance arrived. The right side of his waist had been caught in the first blast, and Garrick's impulsive actions had saved the young man's life. It was nothing more than a flesh wound, but it had bled profusely and needed stitches. While still in hospital, Chib arrested Will Sadler for raping Mia Alvarez.

At the time, Garrick was still in A&E, yet knew the arrest had been made because his phone suddenly lit up with calls, texts, and emails from reporter Molly Meyers. As he'd been vague last time, and appreciating the value of having a reporter on his side, he told her everything he could. Off the record, he warned her to brace for many more accusations to appear. Breaking news of the A-lister's crimes was going to bolster her career.

The following morning, thirty-two victims of Will's harassment had come forward to the police. Garrick handed the case over to the specialist rape and sexual abuse team, who had the delicate skill sets needed to investigate. He wondered how Mia was, but as she was no longer directly relevant to his case, he had no reason to check up on her. He just hoped she was feeling a strong sense of moral victory in bringing her serial abuser to justice.

The Broadhaven production was shutdown the following morning. Although not directly responsible, Marissa Carlisle was now being targeted as an enabler because of her silence. Garrick suspected that her career was also abruptly cancelled.

With no case against Freya Granger, other than being an accessory to her father's blackmail, she was released and returned home. But how long it would be her home for was now a matter of bankruptcy proceedings against Sir James.

Liliana Davies was recovering well in hospital and was being kept under twenty-four-hour guard. Not only was she a flight risk, even with a broken ankle, Garrick wouldn't put it past her to be a suicide risk, and a danger to others. DCs Wilkes, Lord and Liu had excelled in analysing the triggers that had turned Liliana into a killer.

Her life had been tragic from a very early age. Abused by her English father, she'd been taken into care. Her Spanish mother wanted little to do with her, and when her father died of cancer, she never had contact with her mother again. Despite her crushing personal life, she was a meticulous student and, against all odds, achieved outstanding grades. She flourished creatively, and by the age of eighteen had her sights set on fashion design.

Fanta had contacted her past teachers to build a profile. They all believed she had a promising career in the fashion industry. Her lucky break had been in college when she landed a job on a film as a wardrobe assistant. She quit her A-levels, took it, and never looked back. She had worked with Chloe Aubertel on three other features, and the award-winning designer had taken Liliana under her wing.

Unfortunately, history had left deep psychological wounds. She sought abusive relationships while unable to cling onto friendships that could have saved her. Being in the orbit of somebody like Will Sadler had been intoxicating. The attractive, vulnerable woman was exactly his type of prey, and she needed his twisted protection.

In his first official interview, Will insisted that everything they had done was consensual. She seemed to like it more when he was vile to her, and he got a kick out of that, too. He'd noticed she'd become defensive over him, but he'd taken that as a good sign rather than the disturbed machinations of a woman who was in love and thought she owned him.

That was the assessment the forensic psychologist had arrived at in her very first meeting at the hospital. Liliana Davies was not a victim. She was a predator who lulled men into a false sense of security. In Liliana's mind, Will Sadler was the perfect prey. By defending him, she owned him, cared for him, looked out for him. Even after shooting him, she was convinced he'd come back to her after learning the lesson that if she can't have him, nobody else could.

There was plenty more going on deep within the labyrinth of her mind. Karen Dalton had been an easy first victim, killed out of jealousy. That had made it easier for her to murder Gina Brown. There was no moral reason that would prevent her from killing again.

Garrick was starting to have his fill of sociopaths.

The final piece of bad news from the case came when he was told that his beloved Barbour jacket would remain in evidence until sentencing, not that he thought the blood would wash out. He tried not to talk about details of cases to Wendy. It was important to keep a clear distinction between his worlds, but he still lamented about his jacket when he called her at lunchtime. With so much donkey work to trawl through, the team had to stay in the incident room until late. As a reward, Drury had bought them dinner courtesy of Deliveroo, and the office now smelled wonderful. Over a chicken korma, Garrick received an email showing the brand-new Barbour jacket Wendy had just bought him on the internet, along with the message: *happy early birthday! When is that anyway??*

As invasive as ever, Fanta peered over his shoulder and saw the message.

"Is that from *your* friend I met?" she smirked.

Garrick gave her a stern look. "My *girlfriend*, DC Liu. As if it's any of your business."

Fanta couldn't resist an impressed smile as she hurried back to her desk. She waggled her eyebrows knowingly at Sean Wilkes. Garrick pretended not to notice. He was just relieved the two of them appeared to be getting on now that Fanta had cleansed herself of the crush she'd had on Will Sadler.

Drury wanted an update for the following morning, so the team didn't head home until after ten. Garrick sat in his Land Rover, silently swearing as it refused to turn over. He had heard nothing more from DCI Kane about the brand-new vehicle that had been dumped on his doorstep, or any further leads into the connections between his sister's death and John Howard.

As the engine fired to life on the fourth attempt, he decided it was time to have a clear and polite talked with the

Met Detective. He wanted in on the John Howard case, even if it meant taking time away from the Kent Force. If he was the victim of some sadistic game, then he wouldn't sit idly back.

It was time to act. It was time to play.

Even with his newfound sense of optimism, Garrick felt a flutter of relief when he arrived home to find nothing amiss. No strange car in the driveway. No front door open to the elements. It began to rain, so he hurried inside. Groping for the light switch, he was suddenly brought up short by paint dripping down the staircase.

A thin rivulet of red cascaded from the very top step.

He glanced around. Nothing had been disturbed.

This couldn't be something he'd accidentally done and forgotten about. The trail was too fresh...

He slowly ascended the staircase, keeping to the edge to avoid the creaky steps. He didn't have paint. Why did he think it was paint?

He quickened his pace.

Of course, it wasn't paint. He knew it wasn't.

It was blood.

Lots of blood.

He sprinted up the last few steps and stopped on the landing.

There was a body blocking his path. It had been hacked apart so gratuitously that it was almost unrecognisable.

Almost.

He could tell who it was.

His legs buckled, and he slid down the wall as a wail of grief escaped his lips. Then he noticed the message scrawled on the wall in blood:

Miss me?

ALSO BY M.G. COLE

info@mgcole.com

or say hello on Twitter: @mgcolebooks

SLAUGHTER OF INNOCENTS

DCI Garrick 1

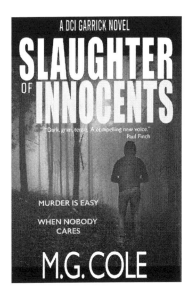

MURDER IS SKIN DEEP

DCI Garrick 2

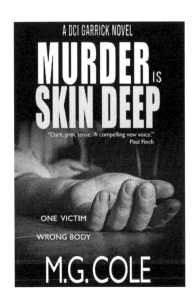

DEAD MAN'S GAME

DCI Garrick 4

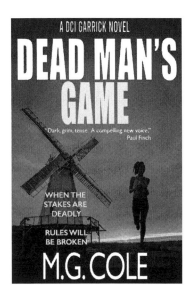

CLEANSING FIRES

DCI Garrick 5

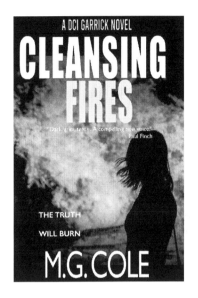

THE DEAD DON'T PAY

DCI Garrick 6 - COMING SOON!

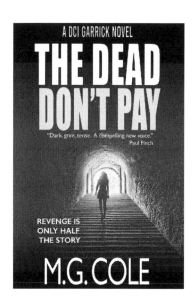

A DCI GARRICK NOVEL

THE DEAD
DON'T PAY

"Dark, grim, tense. A compelling new voice."
Paul Finch

REVENGE IS
ONLY HALF
THE STORY

M.G. COLE

Printed in Great Britain
by Amazon

16822389R00155